Heiress Without A Cause

A MUSES OF MAYFAIR NOVEL

Sara Ramsey

ISBN: 978-1-938312-00-7

For my parents, who gave me the courage to explore the world, a safe haven to return to, and the love that makes every day sparkle.

CHAPTER ONE

London - 6 April 1812

She stood outside her aunt's ballroom and breathed as deeply as her stays allowed. She had walked into innumerable ballrooms in the past decade, but she still felt that old excitement — that moment of speculation, wondering if tonight would miraculously distinguish itself from all the other nights that stretched behind and before her in a dull grey line. Her life had all the color of a debutante's closet. Since she would never wear the rich colors of a matron (or, better, a widow), that grey line was unlikely to change.

Chilton, her aunt's butler, ushered her through the great double doors to the ballroom. "Lady Madeleine Vaillant," he announced to the horde mingling below.

None of them turned.

They wouldn't, after all. She lived with her aunt and had been a fixture at Salford House since her parents died eighteen years earlier. Still, the contrast between tonight, at this proper ball, and the previous night, in a very different milieu, was sharp enough to hurt.

Here, in a white muslin ball gown, with her brown hair tucked into a spinster's cap, no one spared her a first glance, let alone a second.

Last night, wearing breeches and a wild, unkempt wig, everyone cheered at her feet.

She kept a vague half-smile on her face as she descended the steps into the ballroom. Aunt Augusta had trained her well, and she never displayed her disappointment when each night became just like every other. There were a few guests ahead of her on the landing, waiting to greet her aunt and her cousin Alexander Staunton, the earl of Salford. The delay ensured that her mask was firmly in place before Aunt Augusta saw her.

"Are you feeling well, dear?" her aunt asked when she finally reached them.

"Well enough, Aunt Augusta," Madeleine said, making her voice sound the tiniest bit tired. She had feigned illness for the past two weeks and planned a final relapse the following night, but she couldn't miss her aunt's opening ball of the season. She should have come down almost an hour earlier, but she used her illness as an excuse to cut the night short.

Augusta frowned. "You should retire early. No one will miss you, I'm sure."

She knew her aunt didn't mean for the words to cut like a blade, but she still winced.

Then she sternly told herself to stop being dramatic. It was just one night, like any other night. Her aunt and cousins loved her, even if the ton didn't. And her inconspicuous nature gave her the freedom to behave as she had the past two weeks — she should be grateful that she could take such a risk.

So she smiled and said in her sunniest voice, "I'm sure a ball is just what I need to recover. I feel better than I have in an age."

"Don't dress it up too much, cousin," Alex said. "When have these affairs ever improved our health?"

He grinned, a fellow prisoner to Aunt Augusta's expectations. He escaped more frequently than Madeleine, since he often chose his club over the events of the marriage mart. But if he hadn't inherited the earldom when his father died, he probably would have left London entirely.

She grinned back. "There is always a first time. Perhaps Aunt Augusta's ball will magically cure us all."

Her aunt sighed. "Do try to behave, both of you. Not that I usually have to request good behavior from you, Madeleine, but your illness seems to have addled your senses."

"Why do you say that?" Madeleine asked.

"You can't fool me forever, dear. According to the doctors, there is nothing physically wrong with you. You just seem preoccupied — like my sister before she married her French marquis."

Augusta pressed her lips shut after she spoke, the severe gesture marring a face that was still beautiful even in her early fifties. With her fading blonde hair and sharp blue eyes, she was an older version of her daughter Amelia, but her age had made her more circumspect. It was an unusual slip — she rarely mentioned Madeleine's mother.

Madeleine didn't respond. More guests arrived and she seized the opportunity to flee, with a stricken look from Augusta and another sympathetic smile from Alex. As much as she loved the adventure she had created for herself, and as much as she would cherish the precious memory of these past two weeks, she still hated lying to Alex and Augusta. At least Sebastian, Alex's younger brother, was on his Bermuda plantation this year. She couldn't have kept her secret from the cousin who understood her desire for rebellion.

But even he wouldn't support her decision to risk everything and act on a public stage. And since she was too careful to be caught, no one beyond Amelia needed to know.

She took a seat at the edge of the ballroom. The chairs were new, upholstered in green velvet to match the lush new drapes. Aunt Augusta's redecoration made the ballroom feel like a fairy forest, filled with the bright sounds of the hidden orchestra and illuminated by hundreds of candles in the chandeliers. Madeleine was just grateful that Augusta had replaced the chairs along the walls; the last batch had hit her just wrong, making her feet fall asleep at every ball.

As she settled in, her friend Prudence emerged from the crush. The woman sank into the chair beside Madeleine as though the effort of escaping the crowd had left her mortally wounded.

"Do you think Aunt Augusta bought these chairs because she knows we shall always sit in them?" Madeleine asked, too familiar with her friend to waste breath on greetings.

Prudence ignored her question. "Madeleine, you will *never guess* who is standing in your aunt's foyer."

Madeleine laughed. Prudence Etchingham was the academic bluestocking in their little circle, but she had a sense of adventure that she kept well hidden from her formidable mother. "Napoleon?"

"Even better."

Madeleine would have liked for it to be Napoleon, if only so she could join the queue of people who wished to skewer him. Aunt Augusta would like it too — Napoleon's death in her receiving line could only enhance her position as one of the top hostesses in the ton.

But killing Napoleon wouldn't revive her parents or buy back her life in France. Before she could press Prudence about who was in the foyer, a disturbance at the top of ballroom steps caught her attention. It wasn't a disturbance, precisely — more like an unexpected silence, which spread in a slow wave across the ballroom as people turned to the entrance.

Chilton cleared his throat with unusual vigor. "Her grace the duchess of Harwich. His grace the duke of Rothwell."

The butler's announcement, designed to carry out over the room, dropped like a cannonball into the crowd below. Heads snapped up from their conversations, dancers missed their steps, and Madeleine heard the shattering of at least one champagne glass. They hadn't noticed Madeleine, but they couldn't ignore the latest arrival.

Rothwell had finally returned to London to claim his title. He had last been seen nearly a decade earlier, when everyone knew him as Ferguson — a third son with no prospects and a scandalous reputation. Now, inheriting a dukedom in circumstances that the ton had speculated about for over a month, he was a sensation.

"I thought he went mad," Madeleine whispered.

Prudence shook her head. "I heard it was the French pox that kept him out of London, but he looked healthy enough when I saw him in the foyer."

"He could look quite healthy and still be mad, Prue. His brothers were always pleasant enough. But why did he choose to make his first appearance at Aunt Augusta's ball?" Madeleine asked, watching him bow over her aunt's hand. "I heard he arrived in town days ago. And Aunt Augusta is powerful, but not powerful enough to wait for."

"Perhaps he had to wait for the moon to turn so that he could appear sane," Prudence said with a giggle.

Madeleine stifled a snort. Even at this distance, Rothwell's dark auburn hair gleamed in the light of the massive chandeliers. Sophronia, the duchess of Harwich and his father's sister, stood beside him, more ramrod straight than usual. She looked ready to battle anyone who might have an opinion about her nephew — not that anyone would dare to cross one of the highest-ranking women in Britain.

"Rothwell hardly seems cut up over his father's death, does he?" Prudence observed.

She was right. The new duke wore a tightly fitted dark blue jacket and buff breeches, without even a black armband to indicate mourning. Madeleine had heard that he skipped the funeral, and his attire suggested that he intended to forget his father entirely.

Lady Amelia Staunton, Aunt Augusta's only daughter, joined them then, taking the chair on Madeleine's left. "Isn't this a shock! I would dearly love to ask him for the real story of the old duke's demise, if only I thought he would share it."

Prudence laughed. "You would care more about the story than anything."

"Better a story than some dry treatise on ancient Babylon," Amelia said. It was their usual argument. Prudence wrote academic papers — under a male name — that were well received by other scholars, but Amelia secretly wrote novels. If Madeleine could pursue her artistic passions as easily as they did, perhaps she wouldn't feel so restless.

She tried to redirect them to the topic — or rather, the man — at hand. "You can't ask him what happened to his father, Amelia. The *Times* said it was a carriage accident, and we must leave it at that."

"Of course the *Times* would say that if they were paid enough. I like the rumors better."

"Your Gothic sensibility has addled you, dear," Prudence said primly. Then she grinned. "Of course, patricide in powerful families is a common historical theme."

Amelia smiled victoriously. Madeleine rolled her eyes before turning back to watch the new duke. He finished with Aunt Augusta and strode down the steps like he owned them, already so in command of his title that he took others' deference for granted. A half-smile played on his lips, as though he expected such toad-eating and was amused by it.

If that were all Madeleine saw, she would have hated him on sight. Arrogance was not a trait she found attractive. He had gone into exile in Scotland a year before her debut, but she had heard enough to know that even as a third son, he was never humble. Still, the amusement lurking on his face intrigued her. It was almost like he was playing a role — and laughing at those who could not see through his deception.

She knew how that felt.

The old urge to dance flared up again. This time, it was the partner she desired more than the movement. She bit down on her desire before it fully formed. The most notorious rake, now duke, in London would never notice the spinster she appeared to be.

Near the base of the steps, where he could still survey the room, he turned to his aunt. She made a gesture toward the back of the room — more precisely, toward Madeleine's circle. Rothwell raised his quizzing glass to examine them, the amused look never leaving his face. Then he set off again, lost in the crowd.

Unless Sophronia warned him away from their corner, there was little doubt that he would soon appear in front of them.

"Prepare yourself, Amelia. You may get to ask your question

when he dances with you," Prudence said.

Neither Amelia nor Madeleine disagreed with Prudence's assessment of the duke's intentions. Of the three of them, only Amelia still attracted suitors. Madeleine could have landed a husband if she wasn't so shy in her first years and bored in the later ones — while her dark hair and green eyes were unfashionable, her uncle Edward had given her a dowry equal to Amelia's, and it was large enough to cover any number of flaws. Prudence had light brown hair and serious brown eyes, but worse, she had no dowry and no hope of attaining one.

But Amelia, with her blonde hair, blue eyes, silver tongue, willowy figure, and substantial fortune, was always in demand. She had also developed a reputation as "the Unconquered," which led each year's crop of bachelors to worship at her altar in hopes of being the one to win her.

Amelia didn't like the attention. She would rather be at the family estate in Lancashire, writing novels. But she didn't deny her popularity either. It was easier for all of them to evade suspicion if they appeared in the ton as they should, and so Amelia attended these parties as though she lived for them. There were times — like when she wanted to dance — that Madeleine almost hated her for her popularity, even though she would never admit it.

Unfortunately, this was one of those times. Madeleine steeled herself for the moment when she would watch Rothwell lead Amelia away. She tried to relax, to remember that she was in the midst of a different adventure — to tell herself he was just an arrogant rake and forget that she had spied something else lurking beneath his façade. She might never dance with Rothwell, but withering away from boredom did not have to be her fate.

The crowd thinned in front of them. Rothwell emerged like a predator stalking out of the forest. His clothing civilized him, and he still looked amused, but there was a primal intensity in his eyes that Madeleine had not seen when he entered the ballroom. He seemed to be on a mission, determined to make quick work of whatever he had come to accomplish.

Sophronia stepped forward and conducted the necessary introductions. Rothwell bowed to all of them — a spare, elegant move that had not suffered from his rustication.

Then Sophronia made a heart-stopping gesture toward Madeleine. "She's the one you need, Rothwell. Do get on with it."

His deep blue eyes hadn't left her since they were introduced, but until Sophronia's comment, Madeleine had pretended otherwise. She finally stopped staring at his cravat and dragged her gaze up to his face.

That insufferable smile was back. "Will you do me the honor of this dance, Lady Madeleine?"

He was already reaching for her, not waiting to hear her acceptance. The waltz reached for her too, and she longed to twirl around the dance floor...

...but not with someone who took her obedience for granted. She was *tired* of being a dull, well-behaved spinster. She had vowed that this season would be different — and so far, it was, even if Amelia and Prudence were the only ones who knew of her rebellion.

So despite her desire to dance, and the deeper desire to know the secrets hiding behind his smile, she looked coolly at his hand before meeting his gaze with a direct one of her own. "I do not dance with rakes, your grace."

He stared at her, stunned, and dropped his hand to his side.

Some part of her screamed, demanded her to take back the insult and beg for a dance. It was a lie anyway — or rather, she would happily dance with rakes if they ever thought to ask her.

She waited for him to become a glowering version of a man scorned — but a genuine smile replaced his affected grin.

"You are correct, Aunt Sophronia. Lady Madeleine will do well enough."

Sophronia humphed. "I did not bring my nephew over here so he could ruin you, young lady. But he has a proposition for you that I strongly desire you to accept."

The dowager duchess was one of Madeleine's favorite older matrons, even though she was a known battle-axe. Madeleine unbent just enough to look at Rothwell again. "What proposition would you like me to consider, your grace?"

"Please, call me Ferguson," he said. "Are you sure you would not like to discuss this while dancing? I shan't bite, I assure you."

Prudence nudged her. The duchess fixed her with a glare. Only Amelia left her alone, too shocked to know what to recommend.

Madeleine sighed and took his hand, letting him lead her to the floor. The guests they passed examined them with undisguised curiosity. With her hand firmly in Rothwell's grasp, she was attracting more notice in these five minutes than she had in the last five years.

She wanted to curse, but she held her tongue. Her secret activities over the past two weeks depended on maintaining her usual anonymity. The duke's unexpected notice of her would not help her cause.

He pulled her into the waltz and they settled into the rhythm of the dance. The caricatures of him that were so popular a decade earlier often mentioned his "hellfire" hair, but it was darker than she had expected, almost brown, with just enough warmth in it to look like a dying ember. With her hand resting lightly on his shoulder, she could feel the firm muscle beneath his jacket — as though he was used to manual labor, not endless games of whist. And her right hand, clasped by his left, was sensitive enough that she could feel his calluses even through her glove. She knew a few men whose pursuit of the hunt left them well muscled, but she had never met a duke who had the body of a... laborer? Warrior?

Whatever he was, he was too elemental for a ballroom, despite his perfectly tailored clothes.

He turned his attention to her with a brilliant smile that was equal parts alluring and dangerous. It was a smile designed to melt, to seduce, to turn a woman's legs to jelly.

Even though she knew his flattery for what it was, it still worked.

"So will you call me Ferguson, or shall I languish in despair without your favor?"

"I've no doubt you will find any number of women who will call you Ferguson."

He expertly navigated her around a slower couple. She began to feel that intoxicating, breathless wonder that only happened when dancing with a perfect match. "And is that a comment on the morals of your fellow debutantes, or an aspersion on my character?"

She laughed despite herself. "Both, your grace."

He smiled again, but this time it looked natural — almost like he was enjoying himself with her. "I confess that I've little use for propriety, Lady Madeleine. Perhaps I can call you Lady Mad? You could drive me mad if I gave you the chance."

It was the same harmless flirtation that couples participated in all over the ballrooms of the ton. But it rarely happened to her.

So it was with just the slightest hint of suspicion that she said, "I trust you will think otherwise when you have been out in society for a few weeks."

The duke rolled his eyes. "I could have been in London for years, but I chose to remain in Scotland. Do you think I am unaware of London's dubious charms?"

From the path he cut the last time he was in town, she suspected he knew all of London's charms quite well. The reminder of the rake he was — and the duke he had become — pulled her out of their banter. "What is it you want from me, your grace?"

"Sophronia said you wouldn't suffer fools. It is why she recommended that I approach you with my delicate request."

He couldn't want to marry her, but she couldn't think of anything else a man might ask a proper young woman, particularly not in public. She nodded at him to continue, holding her breath...

"Would you be willing to chaperone my sisters?"

She missed a step. A marriage proposal might have actually been preferable, even from a man she had never met.

He steadied her without losing the tempo of the waltz. "My twin sisters are already one and twenty, and they should have come out years ago. Unfortunately, our family tends to lose someone every season, and they've been in mourning for ages. Sophronia said they could benefit from someone younger than her to shepherd them, and Ellie..."

He broke off abruptly. Ellie was his sister, the widowed marchioness of Folkestone — and her reputation was not what one would desire in a chaperone.

"Why me, though? Surely you have other connections."

"Yes, but none I can stand above an hour. Too much moralizing.

And you've surely heard the rumors — according to Sophronia, half the ton thinks we're mad."

She colored slightly, but he didn't notice her guilty look. "You, on the other hand — my aunt says you've a perfect reputation and impeccable intuition, which would do much to help the twins debut successfully despite the family's current reputation. But she also said you have felt poorly for the past few weeks, so if you prefer not to chaperone my sisters, I understand."

The duchess's concern was misplaced. If she knew why Madeleine was "sick," she would cut her without a second thought.

Then Madeleine realized the full implication of what she was being asked to do. She suddenly, quite unexpectedly, felt like crying. If the dowager duchess of Harwich, one of the foremost etiquette experts in the ton, thought Madeleine could chaperone two unmarried girls, it meant Madeleine was so firmly on the shelf that no one expected her to ever come off it.

Even though it was true, it still hurt.

She wanted to say no, if only to deny the implication that she was unmarriageable. But if her less than perfect behavior ever came to light, she would need powerful allies to see her through the storm. There was no stronger ally than Sophronia — and if Madeleine chaperoned the duke's sisters, he would have a vested interest in making sure her reputation stayed secure.

"Very well," she said. "I would be honored to chaperone your sisters."

Their waltz ended shortly thereafter. She was desperate to leave the man who thought her only value was as a chaperone, but she still felt a pang of regret. Rothwell was an excellent partner, even if he was a rake. She tried to remind herself that he had learned those steps and that heart-melting smile with a whole regiment of other ladies before her, but that didn't make him any less entertaining.

When he left her with the other spinsters, she sank into her chair. She looked around, half unseeing, resisting the desire to bury her face in her hands. Everything in the room, from the wallpaper to the door handles, had been added in the last few months. She wiped her hands on her skirt, even though she couldn't do anything about the clammy feeling under her gloves. Her dress, her cap, her slippers, even her undergarments were all new. But she felt like something old and broken accidentally left in the remade room, waiting for a chambermaid to notice and sweep her away.

Twenty-eight shouldn't have felt old, but now she knew for certain that it was.

How perfectly depressing. At least she had one final night of adventure ahead of her, even though no one could ever know about her daring. One last night to enjoy who she might have been — before she resumed the life she had neither chosen nor found a way to escape.

CHAPTER TWO

The following night, as he walked through Seven Dials with a few of his old acquaintances, Ferguson stepped around a suspicious amber puddle seeping into the cracks between the cobblestones. London was still recognizable after a decade away. There were more townhouses springing up in Mayfair, better lighting on the main thoroughfares, and other supposed improvements.

But it was still a cesspool.

And the upper classes of British society drained into it every season, just as they had for centuries. It did not matter how long one stayed away — inevitably, a man of his class would be sucked back into its depths.

A duke might be expected to confine his entertainments to the fashionable clubs of Mayfair, but Ferguson couldn't stand another moment there. Seven Dials could be dangerous, particularly at night, but the overflow of crowds from nearby Covent Garden mitigated the risk. During his quick, carefully planned career as a rake ten years earlier, he had seen everything London offered, from the boudoirs of the most exclusive Cyprians to the lowest gaming dens in the rookeries of St. Giles — Seven Dials could not shock him.

Ferguson needed to visit London at least once — it was his

duty to make sure his sisters were settled. But there was nothing else to keep him here. He was occasionally bored in Scotland, but his career as a rake had burned bridges he didn't care to rebuild. Once his sisters found husbands, he would return to Scotland and forget his father's title.

At least Lady Madeleine had agreed to chaperone them. There was a moment after he asked her when she looked like she was going to bolt — but she acquiesced in the end.

It was too bad she was a virgin. She wasn't his usual type — medium height, brown hair, a passable figure wrapped in muslin rather than silk. She had smallish breasts, perfectly suited to her narrow waist, but nothing like the bounty of his past mistresses.

But then, he hadn't liked many of the women he dallied with then, using them to shock the ton rather than please himself. He thought he might like Madeleine, if only because she had a sense of humor hidden somewhere under that spinster's cap. And there was something about her vivid green eyes that hinted at wildness — true desire, not the calculated wiles of a hardened jade.

Even though he couldn't risk compromising one such as her, she had invaded his dreams the night before — and there, she was anything but innocent.

"I say, Ferguson, you might have chosen a better venue than this," Lord Marsham said as his heel sank into a muddy pile of indeterminate origin.

"After Scotland, any entertainment is welcome, my friend," Ferguson replied, voice dripping with carefully maintained ennui.

The other two men with them chuckled. He didn't remember their names, nor did he care to, but he knew their faces from a decade ago despite the toll taken by their drinking. None of his past acquaintances knew he had sought out his exile, and he didn't intend to enlighten them. Not that enlightenment was possible for these men. They were hardened gamblers and inveterate rakes, speeding through life with one hand on the whip and the other hand on the bottle.

But it was either spend time with them or sit alone at Rothwell House. His more respectable peers might not accept him unless it was clear he had changed his ways, and he refused to grovel for their company. So he returned to the fastest circles — they would accept anyone with the blunt necessary to meet their stakes. He could survive a month with them, especially since the solitude of Scotland waited for him at the end of it.

"Come along, gentlemen. If the address is correct, we're almost there."

Their destination was Legrand's Theatre, part of a tract of property his duchy owned in central London. One of his estate managers suggested that he inspect the theatre; the *Hamlet* staged there, and particularly the actress who starred in it, had an excellent reputation with the lower classes and might enable them to raise the rents. Ferguson didn't care about the funds, but he needed to escape the house. The twins had taken their meals in their room ever since he arrived, and Ellie did not respond to his notes. If he stayed alone in Rothwell House a moment longer, he would go just as mad as everyone expected him to.

As soon as they entered the theatre, a woman hurried over to them, her jet-beaded bodice gleaming in the chandelier-lit foyer. Her nose quivered like she smelled freshly minted coins. She had the air of a former courtesan — all uncompromising determination beneath a soft, inviting façade. She appeared to be in her mid-thirties, with clear brown eyes and the grace of a dancer. "How can I assist you, my lords?"

"May we speak to Mr. Legrand?" Ferguson asked.

The woman's eyes turned wary. "Monsieur Legrand is no longer with us," she said. Her accent was odd, vaguely French but mostly something unidentifiable. "But I am his wife and can assist you as you need."

Ferguson didn't know that the theatre operator was a woman, and he suspected his estate manager didn't either. But the stream of people moving toward the interior doors, an odd mix of servants, merchants, and professionals, indicated that an intermission was ending. So instead of pursuing the matter of her management — and his ownership of the property — he inquired about tickets.

After the second intermission, there should have been many empty seats as theatregoers went off to other amusements. But according to Madame Legrand, the lead actress was such a success that she kept everyone until the end. The best they could do was stools near the stage.

"Madame Guerrier already rivals the best actresses of our time," she said as she accepted their money. "You are just in time, too. She is about kill Claudius."

"She is playing Hamlet himself? Not Ophelia?" Ferguson asked.

Madame Legrand nodded, leading them inside. "Strange, I know. But when you see her, you will wonder how the role could ever be played by another. Even the great Mrs. Siddons's performances as Hamlet are cast into the shade by her."

That was high praise indeed — Mrs. Siddons was the greatest actress of her generation. His companions snickered. None of them believed that the next star of the stage would be found in Seven Dials.

Madame Legrand ushered them to a door near the foot of the stage. The orchestra, which was not blessed with good instruments or the talent to play them, was mercifully falling silent. As with many other small venues, they played music under most of the play to skirt around the legal monopoly held by the few theatres allowed to stage serious drama. After a whispered order from Madame Legrand, a footman picked up four small stools from a darkened corner and carried them a few feet away from the door, setting them in front of a merchant and his irritated wife.

As they settled into their seats, Ferguson realized he had never heard a theatre so silent. Even Marsham and his cronies stopped their jokes, shamed into it by a sharp rebuke from the harpy behind them. Most theatres were merely an excuse for people to congregate, with the audience ignoring the actors on stage — but here, every head in the house turned in the direction of the "man" who entered from the wings.

The actress wore clothing more suited to the previous century, with a well-powdered wig, an elaborate coat, breeches, and high-heeled shoes. Her face was partially obscured by the wig — the disheveled hair of Hamlet in his maddest hour — and the frothy cravat high up under her chin, but there was a definite feminine tilt to her nose. He guessed that they were in for a tedious hour. Her figure was trim and neat, but she lacked the stature to be convincing as a man.

But then the actress opened her mouth and he understood why the audience was enthralled. The last act was familiar to him; Hamlet's lines about the skull of "poor Yorick" would turn to melodrama in the hands of a lesser actor. Yet even though she was small, her voice was rich, warm, and imbued with precisely the right amount of tragedy for the moment.

Her French accent was also more convincing than Madame Legrand's. It was a voice made for whispering naughty desires in the dark, and yet somehow suited to Hamlet's unraveling sanity.

He stared at her as her voice washed over him — then stared more intently as he realized that he was seeing a woman far more clearly than even the fastest society ladies, in their low-cut bodices and dampened chemises, could ever be viewed.

She wore padded shoulders to pass for a man, but the flare of her hips and the soft curve of her buttocks in the scandalously tight breeches betrayed her. He looked down, to the slender calves outlined in ivory hose, then to the perfectly trim ankles giving way to diminutive feet within the bejeweled heels. Her damned cravat unfortunately concealed her bosom, but the hint of its swell was there. Even in Hamlet's madness — especially in his madness — she was a vision.

Lord Marsham exhaled. "Isn't she a sight?"

Ferguson did not say anything — could not say anything. He was too distracted by the sudden, furious rush of blood to his cock. It had been months since his last encounter, years since he had taken a proper mistress. He had sacrificed the physical pleasures of London, knowing that building a life free of his father was worth the cost — but this was the kind of woman who could make a man forget everything but her.

They all sat enraptured, even though they knew what would happen — Ophelia's funeral, the duel with Laertes, Hamlet killing his traitorous uncle Claudius before succumbing to Laertes's poisoned sword. As she fell to the stage, her death speech ringing out over the crowd, not a single person spoke. Ferguson heard women sobbing behind him, and even Marsham coughed.

When the curtain fell, the audience erupted into ecstatic applause. Ferguson joined them despite himself. Madame Guerrier truly was a talent to be admired. He did not intend to stay in London long enough to need a mistress, but if he did take one, he wanted one just like her. She was composed but wild — the same qualities that drew him to Lady Madeleine — and it was safer to seduce an actress than a spinster. If she was as beautiful in a dress as she was in a pair of breeches, having her in his bed might make his stay in London bearable.

She returned to take her bows, embracing the applause like parched soil soaking up rain. He willed her to look in his direction, but her gaze flickered over the crowd like she was trying to blink away tears, and she never met his eyes. She finally left before the applause died, with one last, longing glance at the audience. There was something sad about her, something at odds with the attitude one expected from a star performer.

His companions stood, no longer complaining about his choice of venue but still eager to seek out the nearest gaming table. He hung back as they picked up their walking sticks, surprised by the strength of his desire but unwilling to fight it. "Go along without me, friends. I trust you can find a fourth at the club."

Marsham laughed. "Have an eye for the French chit, eh?"

Ferguson gave the cocky, conquering grin they expected. They clapped him on the back and wished him luck with the chase. He watched them go, glad to be rid of them. Only an evening in their company made him wonder how he could survive the time it would take to marry off the twins.

Unless his sisters deigned to talk to him, he would be relegated to seeking out drinking companions like Marsham — or, he could embrace his new title and watch as people began currying his favor. He remembered when his father had inherited the dukedom years ago; the change was quick and irreversible.

Alternatively, he could take a mistress — a soft, willing woman who excited him without fawning over him. He didn't just want sex, though. He wanted a companion.

And something about the way Madame Guerrier said farewell to the stage told him she could be what he needed — either on his arm or in his bed.

CHAPTER THREE

Madeleine strode to the front of the stage at the end of the play, maintaining Hamlet's mad, wounded air to the end. As she bowed, she reveled in the thunderous applause and hoots of appreciation from the crowd beyond the lights. The theatre was a glorious cacophony of sound, and she let it pour into her, filling the empty spaces she usually tried so hard to ignore.

Aunt Augusta would be outraged to see her before such an audience — but the bigger outrage was that this was her last performance. She knew she should make her exit, but she lingered in adoration of the crowd. Their roars, the uncouth stamping of feet, even the smell of hundreds of warm bodies undisguised by expensive perfumes — it was all so intoxicating. She finally knew why so many lower class girls gave in to the lure of the stage.

She waved a final time. The stage crew shot her dark glances from the wings; they needed to reset the props for the pantomime following the play. She sauntered offstage, never breaking character — until she found her maid waiting for her behind the curtain.

"Josephine!" Madeleine said as she embraced the woman and twirled her around in a circle. "Have you ever heard such an audience?"

Josephine sniffed and patted Madeleine on the head. She was in her fifties, the same age as Aunt Augusta, but her dark hair was almost entirely grey and her once-slim figure was now round — a travesty she blamed on the Stauntons' English cook. She and her husband Pierre had spirited Madeleine out of France at the age of nine, delivering her to Augusta while her parents went to Paris to die. While Josephine did not approve of her charge's first act of rebellion in over twenty years, she did not stop her. "If these two weeks have ended your passion for theatricals, I think it a very good thing."

Madeleine pulled her out of the way as a man wheeled out a Gypsy cart for the next set. "I promised you only two weeks, and now I will never speak of theatricals again. I will go back to being a dull spinster, and you can burn these breeches as you would like to."

She said it lightly, but from the sharp look Josephine gave her, Madeleine suspected she did not sound cheerful enough. Two weeks of freedom had whetted her appetite, not sated it.

And now that her life included chaperoning other girls as they made brilliant matches and left her sitting on the shelf, she would like it even less.

But an agreement was an agreement. With the season starting in earnest, it would be harder to maintain the illusion of illness that gave her these precious two weeks. Her career had to end now, whether she was ready to give it up or not.

She walked behind the stage, past the old painted scenes of forests and castles, to the small, closet-sized room where she stored her clothes. "Stay here, mademoiselle," Josephine said. "I will ask the door guard to find a cab."

Josephine's husband was now one of the Stauntons' coachmen and usually brought them to the theatre. But he was driving Aunt

Augusta tonight, leaving Josephine and Madeleine to navigate alone. It felt foolhardy, but it had to be safer than taking another driver into their confidences.

As she waited, she ran a hand over the slightly tarnished mirror leaning drunkenly against the bare wooden wall. With her wig and men's clothes, she barely recognized herself — or perhaps it was the light of triumph in her eyes that she didn't recognize.

It didn't matter, though. While she was hard to recognize and therefore unlikely to be caught, particularly in Seven Dials, Aunt Augusta or Alex would someday catch her if she kept sneaking out. She turned away from the mirror. She was ready to go home, if only so she could mourn privately. But when Josephine returned, Madame Legrand swept into the room behind her.

"Madame Guerrier, darling, you were marvelous!" Madame exclaimed in the contrived French accent that always made Josephine roll her eyes. No one had ever seen Monsieur Legrand, and Madame was definitely not French, but Madeleine admired the woman for starting a theatre alone. Madame opened her arms wide as though to capture Madeleine — and the patrons she brought to the theatre — within her embrace. "All of London is transported!"

Madeleine extended her hand to Madame Legrand. "Many thanks, Madame. What play shall you stage next?"

Madame looked outside the closet, then shut the door and dropped her voice to a whisper. "Lady Madeleine, please. I know you could only risk staging this play for two weeks. But is there anything I can offer to keep you? My theatre is full for every performance, and with such little time to spread word of your talent. Tonight there was even a party of gentlemen in the audience — think of how well we would do if the gentry came to see you!"

After making their agreement, Madame never used Madeleine's real name — but it was the news she imparted, not the usage of her name, that made Madeleine's stomach rebel. "Who were they?"

"They did not introduce themselves, but I could never forget the red-haired gent. He was a fixture in Covent Garden when I was a dancer there. He's the one what just inherited the dukedom."

"Ferguson? Or rather, Rothwell?" Madeleine asked, closing her eyes against the blow.

"Aye, Rothwell," Madame exclaimed, slipping into the Yorkshire accent she worked so hard to hide. "He was enthralled. As soon as he saw you enter, he only had eyes for you."

"My God," Madeleine whispered. "I am ruined."

"Ruined? No, this is excellent news. We will make a fortune!"

Madeleine had trusted Madame Legrand for five years. Despite her misgivings, Augusta let Madeleine stage holiday theatricals at Whitworth, the Stauntons' country estate in Lancashire. Madame was still a dancer when Madeleine hired her to produce the first performance, since it was customary to let professionals run the show while the amateur houseguests giggled their way through their assigned parts.

The last Yuletide theatrical had been particularly unbearable. Augusta's friends were too well starched to participate, and Alex and Sebastian would only play along for so long before escaping to the billiards room. Madeleine wanted to act on a real stage, with real actors and a real audience. Madame had somehow saved enough to open her own theatre the previous year, and she was the only one Madeleine could trust with such a mad request.

Madeleine tried to reason with her. "We cannot continue. If I am caught..."

"But your talent! You cannot walk away — I have never seen a debut like this. Besides, I've seen you many times as Lady Madeleine. I vow no one would recognize you as Hamlet."

Madeleine could hear the roar of the crowd in her ears again, the sound filling her to the brim. She *did* have talent, she knew she did — but she also had a reputation, and expectations, and responsibilities.

She had stolen two weeks from her real life. But real life always came back.

"I can't," she said, her voice matching her misery.

Madame pursed her lips. In the awkward silence, Madeleine heard the distant laughter of the audience watching the pantomime. She wanted to go home, crawl into bed, and stay there the rest of her life, reliving the memories of tonight and letting her possible ruin wash over her.

The chance that Ferguson — she had dreamed of him with that name the night before, even if she would die before admitting it — recognized her under her wig and breeches was enough to make her feel ill. How could he not recognize her, despite her disguise?

Madame interrupted her thoughts. In a brisk voice, she said, "I am truly sorry, but I have to think of my theatre. You simply must extend your performance."

"It is impossible," Madeleine said, firmer now, like Madame was a chambermaid banging the tinderbox too early in the morning. "I am not some desperate country girl. Why would I continue now that I have almost been caught?"

"You may not be starving, but I think you would do anything for your reputation. The gossip column of the *Gazette* would pay richly for my story."

Madeleine's backbone crumbled. "Why would you do that to me?"

"I really do not want to force you, my lady," she said, with such sympathy that Madeleine almost believed her.

Then her face hardened. Madeleine saw the steel that enabled her to rise from penniless opera dancer to successful theatre owner. "You saw the clientele before your debut. Your talent could accomplish in a month what it would take me years to build. We can make a new agreement — just another month, I promise. If you play four nights a week, I will let you go at the end of it and never breathe a word of your identity to anyone."

"How can I know you won't betray me again?"

"My word is good, Lady Madeleine," Madame said, sounding almost affronted. "I won't keep you forever, and I know it is a risk for you. But a sold-out month would be enough for me to lease a bigger venue next season."

Madeleine couldn't breathe. It might have been the bindings around her breasts that still kept her compressed. More likely, it was the thought of Ferguson cutting her in front of the entire ton that made her pulse flutter and her vision swim.

"I could buy you a new theatre. Salford will write you a cheque if it saves me from ruin." She didn't want to tell Alex about her acting, but he would surely help her to end it.

Madame Legrand shook her head. "It is not just the funds. You saw the audiences this past week. The theatre's reputation rises daily. What good would a new building do if I can't keep the audience after you leave? Staging your play for another month lets me improve the next offering. If you quit now, we are not ready to replace you and the audience will trickle away."

Her words struck home, right in the center of the place that secretly wanted to continue. Madeleine looked at Josephine, but the maid looked away. Josephine loved her, but she was still a servant. Only Madeleine could decide. She rubbed her temples, thought through her choices — and realized she had already made her choice.

"Very well," she said. "But if Ferguson recognized me, your blackmail won't bring me back. I will be ruined before the night is out."

Madame smiled. "He will not recognize you. When you take off those breeches and become your prim society miss, he will never guess you could be such a delight onstage. And if he does recognize you, use your skills to convince him that he is mistaken."

Madeleine said nothing, stepping past Madame Legrand and making her way to the stage exit. She would think about her predicament later. At present, it was more important to sneak back to Salford House before anyone noticed her absence.

If she was lucky, she wouldn't see Ferguson again for several days — long enough for him to forget Madame Guerrier.

But if luck was on her side, it had a diabolical sense of humor. She stepped out of the theatre, sought out the waiting cab — and stumbled straight into Ferguson's arms.

CHAPTER FOUR

He had looked notorious the night before, striding through the ballroom with his devil-may-care smile.

Tonight, dressed in stark black and holding her against him, he looked *powerful* and notorious. His icy blue eyes saw straight through her makeup and his sculpted jaw clenched as he looked her over.

But where a gentleman would have apologized profusely to a lady of her birth and set her on her feet, he kept his grip on her arms. "Madame Guerrier, it was an honor to see you perform."

His silky voice stole her breath away. He hadn't recognized her — unless he was toying with her. "*Merci*, your grace," she said, keeping her voice low and heightening the French accent she used at the theatre.

He arched a single brow. "I did not know we were acquainted. Surely I would remember being introduced to one such as you."

It was a fatal slip. If she was the actress she claimed to be, she would never have seen him before. "Of course not, your grace. Madame Legrand said a red-haired duke was in attendance. I merely guessed you to be the duke."

He still looked at her with those disturbingly perceptive eyes. "I do hope I haven't inconvenienced you, but I must ask you a question of a rather... delicate nature. Shall I accompany you to your carriage?"

This was the second time in twenty-four hours that he wanted to ask her a question, but she had no illusions this time. He knew who she was. She was certain he knew — the way he looked at her, as though assessing a target; how his hands gripped her, as though she might run. She would be ruined, and by a man whose own reputation was hardly spotless. The only question was whether he would ruin her with a clean cut direct — or demand something to buy his silence. The shiver that went through her on that thought didn't feel much like fear, but she refused to consider what it might be instead.

She dug deep, ready to brazen it out. "You may not escort me to my carriage. My mother does not permit me to associate with strange men." She nodded in the direction of Josephine, who closed her mouth and attempted to look dignified.

"Your mother?" Ferguson asked. He was understandably skeptical, since Josephine was nearly six inches shorter than Madeleine and dressed in plain, serviceable grey. "And what of Monsieur Guerrier?"

"Sadly, he left me alone in the world," she said, sniffing as though the memory of her nonexistent husband still caused her pain.

"A pity, I am sure," he said, a predatory smile playing on his lips.

She swatted his arm and tried again to pull away. "It was a tragedy. Now if you will excuse me, I really must be home before the hour grows any later."

He smoothly turned her, taking her arm as though they were a couple on promenade. She could feel the taut muscles trapping her against him — and was reminded that this was not a weak lordling,

but a man used to having his way. "My dear Madame Guerrier...
what is your Christian name?"

The question caught her off guard. "Marguerite," she said,
maintaining her fake identity despite the slamming of her heart
against her ribs.

"Marguerite," he said, the word rolling over his tongue as
though he could seduce her just with the sound of it. "Marguerite,
I can hardly hope you will give me the answer I want to hear — but
tell me, have you taken a protector?"

She stopped in her tracks. Of all the questions she thought he
might ask her — why she was in disguise, how she could act in such
a place, what she would do to stop him from ruining her — she
didn't expect this. "How can you ask such a thing?"

"This is surely not the first time a man has asked you?"

She waved a hand in the air, pretending she had been offered
for many times before. "The ton would expect you to do better than
an unknown actress from Seven Dials."

He laughed. "All mistresses start somewhere, darling. But I
must confess I have little use for the ton, nor it for me."

He said it lightly, but Madeleine caught a glimpse of the lost
boy beneath his polished masculinity. He almost sounded lonely.

Rather how she often felt herself.

So even though she should have run shrieking from him, that
flash of sympathy made her soften the blow. "It is too soon to speak
of such things, your grace."

"I have not taken a mistress in years, nor have I ever offered
for one without having a single conversation. But you are too lovely
and too talented to miss. It is not just likely that you will become
someone's mistress — it is inevitable."

She narrowed her eyes at him. "If you think so little of my virtue, then I must bid you good evening."

"Your virtue is something you wish to protect?"

"It is," Madeleine said. If there was a tremor in her voice, it was from indignation at the way his hand forced her chin up to look into his face, not from the pleasure she got from his touch.

He held her there for an endless minute. She couldn't see him properly in the dark, but felt everything in his gaze — attraction, annoyance, a devilish sense of humor, an autocratic need to be obeyed. But it was the heat lurking underneath that made her nervous — and set off a matching heat as she blushed under his assessing eyes.

Finally, he released her. She might have fallen from relief if her knees weren't locked in place. "Madame Guerrier, you have my apologies. I should not have assumed you were like every other actress in London. Your virtue is as superlative as your talent."

She inclined her head, accepting his apology.

Then he stepped closer. "But in case you do not realize what you are denying..."

He pulled her into his arms, brushing a light kiss across her lips. The feel of his hands was like the satin and steel of a corset as they wrapped around her, sensuous and unforgiving. The surprising heat of his mouth on hers made her gasp. Her shoes, higher than she normally wore, unbalanced her, and she leaned into him without thinking. As his kiss grew more insistent, she felt herself melting. This was the kind of kiss she imagined, the kind that made every other man fade into nothingness. Her dream the night before had not prepared her for the reality of Ferguson's touch, hot and hungry for her. She might have even kissed him back...

But then Josephine shrieked in outrage and clouted him on the back with her valise. The force of the blow pushed him against her for one moment before he caught himself and set her back on her feet with a laugh.

"Very well, madame, I shall not attempt to seduce your daughter... tonight," he said, winking at Madeleine.

He let her pull away from him, although she still felt warm and trembly from the need that overrode her caution. "Perhaps I shall seek you out and ask for your company again," he said. Then he picked up her hand and brought it to his lips. "Or perhaps we will find a more pleasurable method of persuasion."

She shivered under his touch as the implication of his words washed through her. "I really mustn't."

He handed her up into the carriage. "Then I live in hope that you will change your mind."

It was a pretty phrase, but his eyes still looked hot and demanding as he stepped away from the coach. He helped Josephine into the coach as well, even though she glared at him like a revolutionary sizing up an aristocrat's neck for the guillotine. Then he tipped his hat to Madeleine. "Until your next performance, Madame Guerrier."

He shut the door and Madeleine collapsed into the seat. She would be ruined. Whether caught by her family, recognized on the stage, or found out by the duke of Rothwell, she couldn't keep the sterling reputation her years as a spinster had gained her.

Ferguson's gaze, the feel of his lips, the heat of his arms around her — she still felt it all, like a brand on her skin. She shifted in her seat as that tiny kernel of desire within her eased some of her fear. If her ruin was inevitable, she suspected that ruin at Ferguson's hands would be the most pleasurable alternative.

Josephine handed her a fan from the depths of her valise. "You must not let yourself be overset, *ma petite*," she said, even though she sounded overset herself.

Madeleine cooled herself with the fan, trying to calm her nerves. Ferguson had made an outrageous proposal — but he did not seem to know who she was, and she must keep him from guessing. She would go to every social event her theatre schedule would permit and sit primly with the other ape-leaders. She would also fulfill her duties as the twins' chaperone, but would only call on them when Ferguson was too occupied to stumble upon her.

She might prefer the duke's touch to a more garden-variety scandal — but she was much too smart to seek it out.

CHAPTER FIVE

The next morning, Madeleine awoke with the dusty, bitter taste of ashes in her mouth and a scream in her throat. Shivering, she pulled the heavy quilts closer to her face. Unless the cold was truly unbearable, she refused to sleep with a fire in the grate. When she did need a fire, she slept badly, waking often and reminding herself that the crackling of burning wood was not something to fear.

There was no fire this morning, but the nightmare had come anyway. It came less frequently than it did when she was a child, and she sometimes wondered if it would fade away altogether, lost with most of her memories of France. But it always came back.

Madeleine turned onto her side and curled around one of her pillows. Her eyes felt gritty, but she no longer cried after the dream. And last night's dream was only a brief series of fragments — the memory of Josephine crushing her hand in her grip as Pierre drove them off into the night, of her family's chateau overcome by towering orange flames. Her parents no longer came to her in her nightmares. She hoped they were at peace, their bones resting quietly somewhere in Paris.

She had much bigger problems than her long-dead parents. Ferguson's attempt to make her his mistress topped the list, followed closely by what would happen when he recognized her — or what her life would be if she survived the theatre to become an unnoticed spinster again. But the old nightmare didn't care about her current problems, just that there were questions she would never know the answers to.

When, after months in England, Uncle Edward and Aunt Augusta had told her that her parents would never come for her, she had a thousand questions and could not find the voice for any of them. They answered some without waiting for her to ask — she would live with them forever, and they already loved her as much as they loved their own children. She never needed to fear being sent back to France alone.

But others they could not answer. Those questions still haunted her, even though her memories had faded. She no longer thought about her parents except after her nightmares, or occasionally when she was standing at the edge of a ballroom feeling like she did not belong. She would never know how they spent their final moments, whether they thought of her — whether they thought their duty to France was worth leaving her alone.

Madeleine rolled onto her back and stared up at the ceiling. The room, painted a delicate blue, was less ornate than her old nursery in southern France, but it suited the woman she had become. She didn't mourn what she might have had at the French court of Versailles, even if it would have been nice to have a life of her own. She should have been grateful — she *was* grateful — that her aunt and cousins loved her, but it wasn't any easier to accept that she would spend the rest of her life dependent on their kindness.

At least she had finally done something wholly for herself. It wasn't something she could build a life on — but she could hope that the theatre would give her something else to dream of.

And if she didn't dream of the theatre, she would prefer to awaken from dreams of Ferguson's kiss instead of old nightmares of France.

She had never spared a thought for how she would react if a man propositioned her; it was too ludicrous. But now that it had happened, she knew how she would react — with shock, dread... and longing.

Perhaps she only felt longing because it was Ferguson. There was something about his eyes that drew her in, made her believe he could cherish a woman for more than her body.

And didn't it say everything that she was more offended when he asked her to chaperone his sisters than when he tried to take her to bed?

There was the briefest of knocks at the door, and it swung open before she could gather the energy to respond. Josephine entered, carrying a pitcher of warm water. Amelia followed, with what was sure to turn into a lecture for the ages.

Madeleine loved them both — and didn't want to face either of them. Her cousin perched on the side of her bed, deep lines creasing her forehead. "Are you ill, Maddie? You never stay abed this long."

Madeleine tried to pull the covers over her head, but Amelia's position kept them in place. "I don't see why you had to come in so early," she muttered.

"Early? It is nearly noon. Mother's holding an at-home this afternoon — did you forget? You surely aren't planning to make me face the wolves alone."

If anyone could handle the wolves, it was Amelia. "Tell her that I am ill again."

Amelia shook her head. "If you keep pretending to be ill, she will be very worried. She said this morning that we should remove to Bath so that you can take the waters. Not that I would mind escaping for the season, of course, but Bath's entertainments are even more hideous than London's."

"I can't go to Bath," Madeleine exclaimed, finally sitting up against the headboard.

Amelia reached out to squeeze her hand. "I know you detest the place as much as I do. I'm glad the play is over so you can 'recover.'"

Madeleine sighed. In her waking moments, obsessing over Ferguson, she forgot Madame Legrand's demands. "The play isn't quite over, Mellie."

Her cousin's grip on her hand tightened. "I thought last night was the final performance? I was sorry to miss it, but you know Mother would have had kittens if neither of us accompanied her to that dinner party."

"Madame Legrand has other ideas," Madeleine said.

When Madeleine finished sharing the details of Madame's threats, Amelia stood to pace the room, sidestepping Josephine on every pass. "I cannot believe that woman has betrayed you! You must tell Alex at once. If anyone can find a way to change Madame's mind, it is he."

"Unless Alex wants to kill her or burn down the theatre, I see no alternative," Madeleine said. "Can you imagine if Alex knew? He often says he is too lax a guardian — this would just give him proof. He would probably send me off to rusticate for the next twenty years."

Amelia grinned. "Rustication would be preferable to London, though. I have begged him to let me stay in Lancashire for at least the last five seasons."

"Yes, but you have your writing," Madeleine retorted. "What would I do in the country? Put on theatricals for the pigs?"

Amelia did not respond. Josephine took the opportunity to order Madeleine out of bed. While Amelia paced, the maid gave Madeleine a cold compress for her head and tea for her dry mouth.

"You know I am not truly an invalid," Madeleine said to Josephine.

"Yes, but with the poor sleep you've had, you look as sallow as an Englishwoman. You are not yet an Englishwoman, are you?"

Madeleine laughed despite herself. "I have lived here for twenty years, and my mother was English. Perhaps a sallow complexion is to be expected."

"You are French. And you will get out of bed in case the red-haired duke calls for you today. At least his mother was Scottish. The Scots are allies of the French, are they not?"

"That was decades ago, Josephine. There are no more Jacobites, and if there were, they would not like Napoleon."

"Pfft." Josephine did not like Napoleon any more than she had liked the revolutionaries.

Amelia stopped pacing. "What does Rothwell have to do with this?"

Madeleine pressed the cold cloth to her eyes, closing herself off from Amelia's suspicious gaze. "He could call. I am chaperoning his sisters, after all."

"You wouldn't look guilty if that was all you were doing," Amelia said. "What happened last night, Maddie?"

She did not want to say the words, did not want to share the best of last night, or make the worst of it real by saying it aloud. But

Amelia would not accept silence. "The duke encountered me and Josephine leaving the theatre," she said, still not meeting Amelia's eyes.

"What?" Amelia shrieked.

"Shh. You'll draw Aunt Augusta's attention," Madeleine hissed, the danger forcing her to drop the compress and glare at her cousin.

Amelia collapsed dramatically into Madeleine's armchair, but she lowered her voice. "Did he recognize you? Have you been discovered? Did he do anything...*untoward*?"

Madeleine paused. Amelia was her dearest friend, more of a sister than a cousin, and they had never kept secrets from each other before.

But for some reason, even though she would tell the truth in all other things, she wanted to keep her memories of Ferguson's kiss to herself.

"No, he was a perfect gentleman," she lied. "And he did not recognize me."

Josephine gave Madeleine a dark look but didn't dispute her statement. Amelia was too shocked to notice. "Are you sure he didn't know you? He did dance with you at Aunt Augusta's ball. Surely that is unusual."

"Because no one ever dances with me?" Madeleine asked, bristling despite herself.

Amelia sighed. "No, you goose, because he is a rake whose one saving grace is that he has never ruined an innocent."

Madeleine felt a twinge of guilt. It wasn't Amelia's fault she had so many suitors, and she knew her cousin would have given them all to Madeleine if she could. "I'm sorry, Mellie. I am just worried about the next month. But Ferguson aside, I've no idea how I shall keep acting without Alex and Aunt Augusta finding out. I cannot keep feigning illness. What am I going to do?"

They debated options as Josephine dressed her, wrapping her in a pretty pomona-green afternoon dress that highlighted her eyes. They finally settled on what they felt was the best course of action. Amelia and Madeleine would insist that they wanted to go on a reducing diet and so could not attend any dinners. Then, Aunt Augusta could attend whatever dinners she wished, retrieving the girls before the usual round of balls and parties. As long as Madeleine returned to the house before Aunt Augusta did, they could keep their secret.

"This is the most harebrained scheme you've ever dreamed up," Madeleine muttered as Josephine fussed with her half-boots.

Amelia looked smug. "It's genius."

"It's suicide," Madeleine said. "Do you have any idea how hungry I shall be?"

"We shall ask Josephine to sneak us sandwiches," Amelia said. "And it's only a month — and only four nights a week at that. We'll be done in no time a'tall, and with better figures as well."

Madeleine looked at her maid. "Josephine, what do you think?"

"If eating sandwiches in your room will save you, I will bring them every day. But you must take care about the duke. Flatter him, flirt with him, until he will do anything you ask him to. If you do not succeed with him, he is a bigger danger than your aunt."

Madeleine's breath caught in her throat. The idea of flirting with a rake like Ferguson...

She did not even know *how* to flirt. At least her utter lack of feminine wiles would make him lose interest in Madame Guerrier, even if a small part of her wished she had more talent in that area.

Josephine tweaked a last piece of hair into place. "You should eat before the callers arrive and you start this reducing diet. But please take care. The marquis and marquise would not want you to live with the Stauntons forever, but they would not want to see you ruined either."

Madeleine tried to push Josephine's last statement to the back of her mind as she and Amelia went down to lunch. Josephine had gradually stopped discussing Madeleine's marriage prospects over the past few seasons. She knew Madeleine did not like the topic, and she probably gave up hope that her behavior would ever change. But if she was more concerned about Madeleine's potential suitor than Madame Legrand's threats, her hopes for Madeleine's marriage were rekindled.

It was a shame, really, that those hopes were destined to be dashed.

But it was more of a shame that she would likely see Ferguson again before making any decisions about what she wanted — or determining if his kisses were worth the danger.

CHAPTER SIX

Ferguson pulled himself up into one of his father's many well-sprung carriages, glad that it would only take ten minutes to reach the Stauntons' townhouse. He was impatient for reasons that went beyond his sisters' debuts, even though those couldn't come fast enough. After his encounter with Madame Guerrier the previous evening — and what he discovered about her after she left — he was oddly eager to be out in society again, if only to ferret out the woman's identity.

It would have been faster to walk. Salford House was on Berkeley Street, almost on Berkeley Square, only five minutes on foot from his Piccadilly mansion. But since he was using the twins as a pretext for visiting, it was more proper to drive.

Maria and Catherine were twenty-one, born to the sweet doormat the old duke had married when Ferguson's mother died. They sat on the opposite seat, draped in black, blonde hair pulled into tight chignons and blue eyes firmly fixed out the windows. Except for their hair, they had little in common with their mother, who had died almost two years earlier. In fact, their contained poise and stubborn chins reminded him of his full sister, Ellie. He hoped the chins were an anomaly. He had never been able to manage Ellie, and he didn't want to try again with two of her. But a bit of spine would be nice, if only to make them more attractive to suitors.

The coach was enclosed and the view unremarkable, but they studiously avoided his gaze. Other than a single awkward breakfast earlier in the week, when he surprised them on his first day back in London, he had not seen them in a decade. Even before that, he hardly knew them. He was shipped off to Eton less than a month after his mother died and he avoided the nursery — and memories of the happier years he spent there with Ellie — on the rare holidays when he came home.

He knew their names were Catherine and Maria, but it was a shame no one thought to introduce one to one's own siblings. He could not tell them apart — and if they never spoke, he might never discover which was which. Imagine if he agreed to an engagement for the wrong one?

He cleared his throat. They ignored him.

Finally, he said, "Ladies, you do know that I shall not hurt you, correct?"

This finally got their attention. They swiveled toward him, each giving him an identical once-over. Then, the one on the right said, "We do not know that with certainty, your grace."

So at least one of them had a bit of backbone. He smiled. "I'm your brother, not a distant cousin. You may call me Ferguson."

"You may as well be a distant cousin, for all we've seen you," the other one said.

They both had backbone. And from the sudden mutinous cast to their mouths, they would use it with him.

Perhaps backbone wasn't a quality to be prized in younger sisters. "I had my reasons for staying away, I assure you."

If he thought his quelling tone would dampen them, he was wrong. "Your reasons were serious enough to leave us to our own devices with Father?" the right twin asked.

"If you were so unhappy in his house, you should have married. It would have at least been an escape."

They both laughed, a bitter sound incongruous with their innocent appearances. "And where should we have found husbands? We still haven't debuted. Other than walking in the park, we never leave the house."

"Surely you go shopping, or calling on other ladies?"

"Father wouldn't let us," they said simultaneously. The twin on the right continued. "With you turning into a notorious rake, Henry drinking himself to death, Ellie making herself the most scandalous widow in London, and something clearly off about Richard, Father was determined to keep us from misbehaving. He found it easiest to keep us at home."

The duke's children had not lived up to their breeding. Richard and Henry, the unstable sons from his first wife, had raced toward death since they were in their teens. Ferguson and Ellie, products of the duke's only love match, were cast aside when their mother died and spent a lifetime making their father pay for it. After his third marriage, the duke declared that his first two children were too strange, his second pair too emotional, but his future children would obey him. The twins must have inherited his stubbornness, though, despite his attempts to corral them.

He sighed. "Well, my dears, I am quite ready to find you husbands. We're going to see your new chaperone now. With any luck, she can get you out and affianced within the month."

If they were mutinous before, now they looked beyond ready

to toss him out of the carriage onto the nearest deserted island. One of the twins rubbed her temples; the other eyed him as though she would happily endure another few months of mourning to be rid of him.

Finally, the more murderous one spoke. "I don't see why you left London. If you are as much of a tyrant as Father was, you must have gotten along quite well."

The other one patted her knee. "Kate, there's no need for insults."

Ferguson's relief at discovering their names almost made him forget that Kate had compared him to their father. "Kate, Maria — my apologies for speaking so suddenly. I thought you would want to be married."

"Because all young women want to marry?" Kate scoffed.

"You do want to marry," Maria pointed out. "Or at least, I want to."

"But not when I haven't even debuted! I haven't been to a pleasure garden, haven't seen the Court, have never even *once* been..."

She cut herself off abruptly, but Ferguson could guess her thoughts. "Father did more harm than good to your characters by keeping you shut away, didn't he?"

The carriage pulled up to the Stauntons' townhouse. Maria looked outside, swallowed forcefully, then looked back at Ferguson. "Can't we delay one more day?" she pleaded. "I didn't even know we were calling anywhere. We assumed we were going to the park."

He was a heel, the worst sort of brother — and in this moment, using them for his own purposes, more like his father than he cared to admit. What he could not tell the twins was that he needed them as an excuse to call on the Stauntons. It was not an errand he would postpone, despite their reluctance.

Because even though he was not proud of his spying, he had followed Madame Guerrier's hackney coach the night before. And he watched her sneak out of the carriage and dash to the service entrance of Salford House.

The actress was in there someplace, disguised — and no mere servant could take several nights a week to act onstage. He was determined to find her, even if he couldn't win her.

But he had never failed in a seduction before.

Maria shivered as she looked at him, mistaking the steely determination on his face. "Very well, we'll go," she stammered.

"You'll quite like Lady Madeleine and her family," he said, attempting to sound encouraging. "You will see, girls — you'll be planning weddings before the season ends, never doubt it."

Kate winced, but he stepped out of the carriage to avoid her accusatory glare. The twins would be fine once they became accustomed to the idea.

And if they didn't make matches quickly, he would need a distraction. The challenge of finding Marguerite Guerrier — and claiming her in his bed — would be just the amusement he needed to survive the season.

*   *   *

Several hours after lunch, Madeleine sat in her aunt's blue and gilt drawing room, staring at the ormolu clock on the mantel. She was trapped for at least another thirty minutes. She had drunk enough tea to float an armada, smiled at so many visitors that every facial movement felt like a grimace, and feigned serenity even though a growing headache rapped out a battle march behind her eyes.

They had received over fifty callers already, all of whom had only one name on their lips.

Ferguson's sudden reappearance in London was the *on dit* of the day. It was universally agreed that he was just as handsome — and just as dangerous to a woman's reputation — as ever. And the rumor mill had already discovered that he had gone to a theatre in Seven Dials the previous evening and abandoned his companions in favor of an actress.

"How very like him," they all whispered, gleeful to witness the start of another scandal. "Not in London above a week and already seeking a new mistress."

From the sharp look Amelia gave her, Madeleine knew her face had drained of color the first time she heard the story. By the fifth, she mastered her response: a slight frown, a small shake of the head, as though nothing the duke did could surprise her.

Now, with only thirty — twenty-nine — minutes left before she could escape the drawing room, and with the happy fact that she would not have to go to the theatre again until the following night, Madeleine thought she might survive yet another at-home.

But when Chilton appeared in the drawing room and announced, "His grace the duke of Rothwell," her careful control slipped. She looked up into those perfectly clear blue eyes, stunned again by his intelligence, by the way he took in everything at a glance.

He held her gaze for a fraction longer than necessary. She felt her breath catch in a quick gasp. With his perfectly molded breeches, tight coat, and elegant cravat, he looked like the dangerous rake she had been warned about — and the bold way he appraised her offered an escape from her prison. If the drawing room was Newgate and he was her jailer, she'd be out of her dress for him at the merest promise of fresh air.

Madeleine winced. That stray metaphor was as overdone as anything Amelia had ever written. She realized that Josephine was right: Ferguson was more of a danger to her than anyone else in the ton.

But the butler wasn't done with his announcement. Ferguson was accompanied by his sisters, the ladies Maria and Catherine. The women were still in mourning for their father and brother, and the unforgiving black of their gowns turned their creamy complexions wan in the late afternoon light.

The girls huddled in the doorway as Ferguson strode forward, frowning as they surveyed the room. They did not look much like Ferguson — their features were too delicate — but they did have the same stubborn chin, raised in identically arrogant postures. Madeleine did not know whether to pity them or dislike them. Without Ferguson's humor to soften their arrogance, they seemed distinctly unfriendly.

"Please forgive me for bringing my sisters, Lady Salford," Ferguson said. "They should not call while still in deepest mourning, but why anyone is still in mourning for my father is beyond me."

It was an outrageous speech, designed to shock. Madeleine took a closer look at the twins. They were equal parts embarrassed and rebellious, as though they might turn and flee.

She had felt the same more than once.

"Lady Maria, Lady Catherine, my condolences on your loss," she said, not waiting for Aunt Augusta to answer Ferguson's question. "Amelia and I delayed our debuts after her father passed, and I cannot imagine how hard it has been to be in mourning for several years in a row."

The sisters exchanged glances before moving as one to sit on the settee that mirrored Madeleine's own perch. They were beautiful girls, but their patent unhappiness muted their appeal. Madeleine's headache demanded her attention again, throbbing even more forcefully. She had agreed to chaperone them, but she had not expected them to be quite so...

"Charming, aren't they, Lady Madeleine?" Ferguson said, as though he could read her thoughts. "I do hope you have not changed your mind about taking them under your wing."

She had discussed it with Aunt Augusta over luncheon. Aunt Augusta thought she was a fraction too young for the role — but if anything, she was pleased that Madeleine might stop hiding in her room and start attending proper functions again. With her aunt's approval, her fate was sealed.

"Of course not, your grace. I am honored to help your sisters find proper matches."

They turned into twin pictures of fury, displaying a depth of emotion they would learn to hide with more experience in the ton. She could not tell them apart, but one of them gasped, while the other clenched her jaw in a most unladylike way. Finally, one of them croaked out, "I was not aware that our endeavors to find matches were so public."

He crossed his arms as he leaned casually against the mantel, obscuring Madeleine's view of the clock ticking toward her freedom. "Kate, we can discuss this at home. But we had to call on Lady Madeleine so she can call on you," he said patiently, as though explaining etiquette to a small child. "And Lady Salford, I assure you my aunt will be at home whenever Lady Madeleine wishes to visit the twins."

The countess nodded. "If I can help as well, I would be delighted. I knew all three of your father's wives, as well as your siblings. If my family can ease your current burdens in any way, do let me know."

Aunt Augusta was unfailingly generous — from small acts like offering to support the twins' debut, to large acts like caring for her niece for over twenty years. Madeleine sighed. She didn't regret what she had done, even if she felt guilty about deceiving her aunt.

But then she thought of the freedom she had tasted these past two weeks. Rather than feeling grateful, she felt more trapped than ever. If Aunt Augusta discovered her secret, it would hurt her greatly — and Madeleine would be on a very short leash. There would not be another opportunity for rebellion until she was too old to enjoy it.

And the idea of remaining a perfect spinster, staying on as Aunt Augusta's companion and sitting through twenty more years of at-homes, was truly appalling.

Aunt Augusta's next words snapped her to attention. "What is this I hear of you venturing into Seven Dials? Surely the theatre scene has not expanded so far beyond Drury Lane."

For some reason, it was Madeleine that Ferguson looked at as he responded. "I went in search of a bit of harmless fun, but I found an actress whose talent is truly astounding. Have you heard of Marguerite Guerrier?"

Madeleine looked away as though she was too prim to answer. "No, I've not heard of her, but I trust your opinion on actresses," Aunt Augusta said, with the perfect blend of amusement and censure. "But our Madeleine loves the theatre. Perhaps we shall attend."

Madeleine wanted to faint — but she had never been the fainting type, even when it would have been convenient. "I'm sure

Seven Dials is not quite the thing, Aunt Augusta."

"Oh, it's not so bad as all that, Lady Madeleine. If you could see this actress, you would know why I feel as I do."

He held her gaze then. She felt frozen, splayed out like one of the scarab beetle amulets her cousin Alex collected. She still didn't think he knew her identity — he couldn't have guessed without saying something — but his appraisal of her was too direct to ignore.

Amelia dropped her pen. "That is inappropriate for our ears, your grace," she said in the same chilling voice that froze a score of suitors.

He raised an eyebrow. "I was referring to Madame Guerrier's acting, Lady Amelia. Is it you whose thoughts have taken an inappropriate turn?"

Amelia flushed bright red. It was very rare to see anyone give her a set-down. If the topic was anything other than a certain actress in Seven Dials, Madeleine would have found it vastly amusing.

Aunt Augusta intervened before either Amelia or the duke could say something unforgivable. "My daughter does let her tongue run away with her sometimes. If you say the actress is excellent, I am sure no one here will dispute you."

Ferguson shrugged, breaking the tension. "It matters very little. I do hope the woman gets the recognition she deserves, though."

He gave Madeleine another assessing look, but he didn't say anything else. She had to hope her composure would throw him off the scent.

The butler brought in another set of callers — Prudence Etchingham and her mother, Lady Harcastle. She had never been so grateful for Lady Harcastle's appearance, since this was Ferguson's cue to take his leave. His sisters had said very little, but he had accomplished their introduction and they were expected to leave when the next guest arrived.

He bid farewell to Aunt Augusta and Amelia before turning to Madeleine. She wished they could talk in private, if only so she could see whether he had guessed her identity. But there was no way to extricate herself from the drawing room without calling too much attention to herself. She let him kiss her hand with a flourish, and the strength of his fingers and the heat of his lips seared her skin. She thought wildly of corsets and prisons before forcing herself to look away. Then, he bowed to Lady Harcastle and Prudence and left, the twins trailing in his wake like forlorn blackbirds.

As soon as they heard the front door close behind him, Lady Harcastle settled into the chair next to Aunt Augusta, ready to dissect every bit of Ferguson's visit to the Staunton townhouse. Prudence sat next to Madeleine and squeezed her hand. She knew about Madeleine's acting — as soon as the story unfolded, she would realize what Ferguson's interest in Marguerite really meant.

Madeleine looked up at the clock. Only ten minutes had passed. She sighed.

After Lady Harcastle heard everything from Augusta, she drew herself up. "He is still a rake through and through," Lady Harcastle declared. "To pay what appeared to be a courting call on Madeleine while lusting after some trollop of an actress!"

Aunt Augusta laughed at Lady Harcastle's unladylike language. "That is harsh, Mary. He may have just liked the play."

"Men like that do not attend plays for the artistry."

"Still, despite his reputation, he never posed a risk to proper ladies. I trust his intentions toward Madeleine, at least, are honorable. And if they aren't, she will put him in his place."

Aunt Augusta sounded so confident in her niece's morals. Madeleine twitched in her chair. Prudence stifled a giggle, which turned into a cough as Lady Harcastle glared at her.

"The duke is not courting me," Madeleine said, knowing her voice sounded too forceful in the serenity of Aunt Augusta's drawing room.

Lady Harcastle frowned. "Asking you to become so intimately involved with his family is suspicious. I wager he wants something from you. If you make just a bit of effort, you can engage his affections."

Madeleine would have said the notion was ridiculous — but she remembered the heat of his fingers on hers, and knew that whatever it was he wanted, it went well beyond needing her as a chaperone. But with Amelia's speculative gaze on her and Prudence holding her hand like she was afraid Madeleine would collapse, she realized she couldn't stay in the drawing room a moment longer.

So she fled, making a barely coherent excuse before bolting for the door. She knew her exit would give them something else to discuss, but with her pounding head and racing heart, she did not particularly care.

The very fact that Madame Legrand's theatre was on everyone's lips was enough cause for concern. Worse, though, was the very real chance that Ferguson would discover she wasn't the well-behaved spinster the ton believed her to be. If he had not already guessed, he seemed to be on a mission to find her out.

But what would the most notorious rake in London do with that knowledge? And if he still wanted her despite her reputation, was she prepared for what he might offer — or demand?

CHAPTER SEVEN

By the following evening, Ferguson needed to escape the mausoleum of his inheritance. He had stayed in the previous evening, but he couldn't spend another night in his study, where his father's presence still lingered. The weight of the place, even after ten years away, had only increased.

So rather than torturing himself by eating with the twins, who had coldly ignored him after leaving Salford House, or lying sleepless in the cavernous ducal bedchamber, he took his coach to the theatre district, giving in to the lure of Marguerite Guerrier. With what he suspected about her, it would be better to leave well enough alone — but seeing her again was the only entertainment he wanted.

As he left his coach, he looked at his watch. It was stupid to flash jewelry after dark, but he was almost itching for a fight. The prospect did not seem likely. There were too many liveried coachmen about, and potential thieves had decamped for less populated areas.

Then he realized the oddity of that — coachmen never loitered in Seven Dials. Only a block from Legrand's Theatre, at least twenty fine carriages waited in the alleys.

Had his first visit to the theatre caused this?

He picked up his pace. He could not prove it, not without

seeing her eyes in the light, but he thought he knew who Marguerite really was. If he was correct, then the best actress in London — the woman he had tried to take as his mistress two nights earlier — was the woman who agreed to help launch his sisters.

If Madeleine was the actress, aristocratic playgoers could only bring her to ruin. And any ruin she faced would taint his sisters' debuts. It was ironic that he had sought out her sterling reputation to help with the rumors about his family, when she might ultimately bring even more devastating gossip down on their heads.

He entered the theatre just as the intermission ended before the final act. He had taken the precaution of sending a footman for a ticket earlier in the day, knowing even then that he would not be able to stay away, so there was no need to haggle with Madame Legrand. He spotted her across the room, though, looking immensely satisfied as she conversed with a gentleman and his companion — a much finer couple than any he had seen on his previous visit.

Ferguson took a sharp look around the theatre, his senses alert under his bored façade. The types he saw before were still there — rowdy off-duty footmen, maids and their beaus, shopkeepers, secretaries, and members of the more-respectable middle classes.

But sprinkled throughout the crowd, looking by turns aghast and titillated, were people who could only be part of the ton. He watched a matronly woman swish her silk skirts away from a pair of footmen who were cracking walnuts onto the floor. But where her anger would have cost them their jobs in her own home, here it made them laugh.

This mixture of rich and poor at the theatre was unremarkable. Even the Theatre Royal allowed footmen in the gallery. But his concern grew. With this many members of the aristocracy in attendance, the actress would surely be found out.

And given his role in bringing them here, it would be his fault if she were ruined.

He settled into a seat and tried to force himself to relax. He had only associated the actress with the Stauntons because he followed her carriage. If she was Madeleine, she was well disguised.

There was one fact to take comfort in: if she had been discovered, the play would have already ended. The audience was enraptured, eager for the final act to begin.

He scanned the crowd, looking for clues. Two rows ahead of him sat Viscount Osborne — a wealthy old roué who had kept a string of the most desirable courtesans for the last four decades. Off to his left, the earl of Westbrook sat with Caroline, Lady Greville, on his arm. Neither looked happy, and Ferguson felt a small pang of remorse. He was involved with Caro before his Scottish exile, and it looked like the intervening years had hardened her. He knew Westbrook from the worst of his days as a rake — if Westbrook planned to replace Caro, he would not wait long before finding a new mistress.

As that thought sank in, his blood went cold. A top actress would be an immediate attraction on the mistress mart. In the darker world of the demimonde, there were no titles or chaperones to protect her.

Ferguson would bet his birthright that whoever Madame Guerrier was, she never seriously considered that actresses usually became mistresses, even if the example of the great Mrs. Jordan and her large brood of royal bastards should have concerned her.

And if the woman was as naïve as she seemed in the alleyway, she would be wholly unprepared for the onslaught of men who would try to claim her.

Damn. If only he had kept his mouth shut about the theatre. If the woman wasn't ruined by the ton discovering her, she would be if Westbrook started sniffing around her skirts.

Or rather, around her breeches — he looked up just as she sauntered onstage, her lithe legs perfectly showcased in the light. He cursed again under his breath.

As he glanced at Westbrook, then back to her, a plan began to form. He couldn't stop the others from wanting her. But he could remove her eligibility as a mistress. All he had to do was get to her first...

*   *   *

Madeleine took another bow, trying to relax in the face of the audience's acclaim. The applause was thunderous. Even with only two days to print handbills and send out announcements, Madame Legrand had sold out the theatre.

However, while the applause was gratifying, her stomach knotted up under her waistcoat. She felt like she could barely breathe with the bindings around her breasts. She had learned during intermission just how many members of the ton were in the audience, and the damp, moist air of the playhouse felt like her ruin closing in on her.

But some secret place, which she would never confess to, was thrilled at her forced return to the stage. In all her years as a debutante, she had never walked into a room and felt — *adored.*

Tonight, they adored her. The sound crashed around her, and the stage reverberated under her with the stamping of their boots. At her next ball, she would be Madeleine again, and these same men wouldn't look at her twice.

Here, they were at her feet.

She mentally shook herself as she bowed a final time and left the stage. She was still in danger of being caught and she needed to hurry if she wished to reach Salford House in time for that night's round of parties. But when she entered the backstage area, a very agitated Madame Legrand greeted her. "Madame Guerrier," she said, using the pseudonym almost warningly. "The duke from the other night. He's back here and we can't get him away. He said he would cause a scene if we tried."

Madeleine compressed her lips. How dare he come back here like this? It was yet more grist for Madame's blackmail — and a temptation Madeleine needed to avoid. "I will send him away," she said forcefully.

"It's not him what I'm worrying over," Madame said, her accent slipping. "It's the line of gents outside waiting to see you."

"What?" Madeleine demanded.

"You must be careful — act like you have been in the theatre all your life," Madame said urgently. "No one will recognize you if you stay in costume, but I forgot what the fancy men will think of a pretty thing like you when you've no high-born name to protect you."

Madeleine's blood turned to ice. "I must find Josephine. She will know what to do." She brushed past Madame, too angry to spare consideration for the woman she once trusted.

But when she shoved open the door to her dressing room, it was Ferguson who leaned against her wall. Josephine was nowhere to be found. She wanted to rail at him for his presumption, but the dark, dangerous look in his eyes stopped her short.

"What are you doing here?" she demanded.

"Saving you," he said, striding toward her. He looked like he should be bare-chested and holding a dagger, like a Grecian marble come to life and ready to do battle for her.

Madeleine drew a deep, shuddering breath. He didn't look like a savior. There was something too primal in the way he stalked toward her, despite the cool perfection of his waistcoat and cravat.

She started to back away from him. His hand shot out to stop her. "Stay here," he grated. "It isn't safe for you to leave alone."

Somewhere at the back of the theatre, she heard a shout, followed by the slow tread of a man's booted feet on the old floorboards. The man was coming closer, but his pace was almost leisurely — as though he did not expect to be denied.

She shivered. Ferguson's hand skimmed down her cheek to lift her chin. He looked hard into her eyes, holding her gaze for a long moment, until he made a momentous decision that she could not fathom. Underneath his resolve, she saw the flickering of something deeper she could not name.

"Trust me, Madeleine," he whispered.

She gasped as he used her real name, too shocked to argue.

And then he pulled her into his arms and kissed her.

CHAPTER EIGHT

The heat of his kiss, the firm pressure of his arms wrapped around her shoulders, and the wildfire of fear from the encroaching footsteps threatened to burn her. She tried squirming away from him, but he kept her trapped against him. So she kicked his shin, and she felt him flinch as her foot made gratifying contact with bone.

But just as she thought he might let her go, she heard the door open behind her. The sound of those booted feet coming to a stop froze her in Ferguson's arms.

Holding her like she was a racing trophy, he looked over her head at whoever had entered behind them. "She's a feisty lass, isn't she?"

She tried to turn, but he draped his arms around her shoulders, a prison disguised as affection. Behind her, she heard a man drawl, "Indeed. I do hope you are prepared to give her up, though."

"Give her up? You are better acquainted with me than that, Westbrook."

Madeleine sucked in a breath. The earl of Westbrook's name was whispered in the ton — more often around her now that she was on the shelf — but he did not frequent the debutante-rich circles Madeleine moved in.

She turned around to face him. It was stupid, but they had never spoken, so the chance he would recognize her was small. Westbrook was quite handsome, in a sinister way, with a physique and complexion not yet devastated by drink. He had dark hair that swept back from his face, and grey eyes that would be lovely when warm — but now, as they stared uncompromisingly at Ferguson, they were cold and intimidating.

He was accustomed to getting what he wanted. And what he wanted now was Madeleine as his mistress.

She might have found it funny if her situation weren't so dire. Ferguson, however, was unamused. He took charge again, sitting in her dressing chair and pulling her down onto his lap. She landed with a muffled gasp, her legs falling astride his thigh, her back pressed to his chest, and his arms quite proprietarily encircling her waist.

He kissed the side of her neck, right over the vein, and she was surprised to discover how sensitive she was there. She arched her neck unconsciously, then realized that Westbrook, still watching from the doorway, would think she wanted more.

Westbrook's grey eyes glittered. Madeleine felt utterly out of her depth.

"Madame Guerrier, I assure you that you would be more secure under my protection," he said, with all the calm of a man conducting a business arrangement. "Ferguson — Rothwell now, I suppose — has been out of London for nearly a decade, and I doubt he will remain for any length of time. You should think about which of us is better placed to support you."

He sounded like he had negotiated with mistresses for years. There was a lot about the demimonde she did not know. But she suspected his argument would sway a high-flying courtesan.

Ferguson cut her off before she could answer. "How does the lovely Lady Greville feel about this?" he asked, his lips still grazing over Madeleine's throat.

The earl waved a hand and his onyx signet ring flashed in the candlelight. "Not that I should like to admit this, but it is the lady's decision to end our arrangement. If she no longer wants me in her bed, I see no reason to delay finding a new companion."

Ferguson's lips pulled away from her and she felt his arms tighten. "I do hope you are not leaving Caro out in the cold."

Westbrook laughed bitterly. "My dear Caroline can shift for herself better than any of us. But I forgot all about your connection with her — it was your precipitous flight from her bed that sent you off to Scotland in disgrace, was it not?"

Madeleine's head snapped up at that. Westbrook met her eyes. "I did not intend to offend you with this nonsense, Madame Guerrier," he said silkily. "But you should know what you are signing up for if you choose to align yourself with Rothwell."

"You are no saint yourself, Westbrook," Ferguson said. He sounded calm, but she could feel his legs tense beneath her as though preparing for a fight.

Madeleine was drowning in this conversation, and there was nowhere that offered safe purchase. Ferguson had behaved abominably by kissing her without so much as a by-your-leave, and apparently his illicit connections from ten years earlier still haunted him — but Westbrook had a reputation as a dangerous predator. Worse, he was a wealthy, titled predator, which made him nearly unstoppable. Without Ferguson there, he may have already carried her off. Josephine had disappeared, but neither she nor Madame could have saved Madeleine from Westbrook without giving her name away.

Westbrook turned his gaze back to her. "So, Madame Guerrier, I must ask why you are throwing yourself away on Rothwell. Even leaving aside the rumors about his brothers, the whole ton knows that he has turned his back on London life. If you choose him, you will find yourself out on the streets within the month."

"Did you offer Lady Greville the same security?" Madeleine asked. She had never played the role of a hardened mistress — but in for a penny, in for a pound.

"Caro got what she wanted out of our arrangement, which is more than I can say for what she got from Rothwell."

She wasn't ready to forgive Ferguson for taking command, but she couldn't express interest in Westbrook just to get revenge. And since Ferguson had guessed her true identity, she could not risk offending him. So she murmured, "I am flattered by your offer, my lord, but my understanding with his grace is of longer duration." Ferguson squeezed her, and despite the distracting nuzzling at her neck, she was glad that he was at her back.

Westbrook was shocked for a single second, but he smoothed his face and put his hat back on his head. "You wound me, Madame Guerrier. But I am quite particular in my tastes. No doubt Rothwell will end this soon — or you will end it yourself, if he proves dangerous. If you find yourself wanting a new companion, I am at your service." He kissed her hand, gave a curt nod to Ferguson, and took his leave.

Madeleine leaned back into Ferguson's chest, not knowing how tense she had been until Westbrook left the room. Talking to Westbrook in the ton could have caused a scandal for an unwed almost-spinster. Accepting his kiss while sitting in Ferguson's lap made her feel like she was already ruined.

She listened to him walk away, and her rage rushed back with every step. As soon as she heard the stage door close in the distance, Madeleine sprang to her feet. "Are you mad?" she shrieked. "What in the world are you doing?"

Ferguson put a finger on her lips. But after his autocratic possession of her body in front of Westbrook, she was in no mood for his control.

She opened her mouth and bit him.

"Bloody hell," he swore, jerking his hand back. "What was that for?"

"Don't shush me like a child! I deserve an answer for what just happened."

"And you shall have all the answers you want as soon as we're in my coach," he said, opening the door to check their surroundings. "But unless you want the whole theatre to hear our discussion — and there will be a discussion — I suggest you accept my shushing and come with me."

She wanted to bite him again, but she knew he was right. He took her arm and ushered her out of the dressing room, pulling her toward the back door. "There may be more outside. Act like you haven't a care in the world."

She glared at him. "I was not born yesterday, Ferguson. If anyone gives us away, it will not be me."

He grinned. "You may be the most vexing mistress I've ever had."

Madeleine sucked in a breath as her fury renewed itself, but they were out of the theatre and into the alley. Several men, all vague acquaintances from the ton, loitered as the glowering doorman watched them. Someone had given him a cudgel, and no one else appeared eager to storm the theatre.

"Madame Guerrier!" they cried with one voice. In the darkened alleyway, she should have been afraid — but there remained that fascinating feeling that *she* was in control, not them. She suddenly understood the Caesars of the world, perhaps better than any woman of her station could.

"You are all too late, gentlemen," Ferguson said.

Their acclaim turned to disappointment. "Rothwell?" one man said. "I see you've lost no time in finding a new mistress."

He shrugged. "I must keep up appearances."

"Damned expensive bauble," another observed. "You could have just bought a new horse and been done with it."

Madeleine couldn't keep herself quiet. They discussed her like she was a commodity, and seeing how men spoke about women when there were no ladies present annoyed her. "I am worth more than a horse, I assure you," Madeleine said, slipping back into her French accent for the crowd.

"And much more fun to ride," Ferguson drawled, pulling her closer to him.

The men roared. Madeleine blushed, wishing she could have controlled her surprise, but Ferguson's ribald comment caught her unawares. Was this what it was to be a courtesan — an object for entertainment?

The crowd was still laughing, some of them shouting suggestions for Ferguson's future happiness with his new mistress. She may have liked their adoration from the safety of the stage, but in the alley, their desires felt dangerous. She was glad she couldn't remember any of their names. It would be bad enough seeing them in the ton, let alone knowing which wives or fiancées they were ignoring in favor of her.

"When he tires of you, Madame Guerrier, I wouldn't mind taking you for a ride myself!" yelled one of the men, sounding drunker than the rest.

Three offers of carte blanche in one night — it must be a record for a spinster of her status. She waved a hand. "Rothwell will not cast me off yet, will you, *cher*?"

He started to speak, but she brushed her fingers over his lips. "Don't tell me here," she said with a wink. "You can tell me in the carriage."

Ferguson scowled at her, displeased by her mimicry, and pulled her fingers away from his mouth to thread them through his. He tugged her away from the crowd, guided her around the corner to his waiting coach, and lifted her in before settling across from her. The coach lurched forward without him giving a direction. Where in all of London could he take her while she looked like this?

And what would he do with her when they reached their destination?

But before she could ask, he exploded.

CHAPTER NINE

"What in the devil were you doing?" he yelled.

"What in the devil was *I* doing?" she asked, her temper flaring to match his. "I was merely making the best of the situation *you* forced me into. You, on the other hand, have gone mad! And now I'm trapped in a carriage with you, bound for an unknown destination, and you ask what I was doing?"

He leaned forward until his face was mere inches from hers. In the flickering lamplight of the coach, he looked grim but determined. "If I had not intervened tonight, you could be in a coach with Westbrook right now — and you would like that much less, I assure you."

"I could have dealt with Westbrook," Madeleine said.

"Bollocks," Ferguson retorted, leaning back into the red velvet seat. "He would have had you out of those breeches before you launched a protest."

His comment reminded her of her costume — and his lingering caresses in her dressing room. She crossed her legs uncomfortably. "You paint such a picture of my honor. Do you think that because I am an actress, and not the paragon of virtue chaperoning your sisters, I must be ripe for the taking?"

It was Ferguson's turn to shift. "Not at all. I just know how rakes like Westbrook act when presented with a challenge."

"Because you act the same?" she asked sweetly.

She had backed him into a corner. He scowled in response. "This isn't about me. This is about you, and the ruin from which I am trying to save you. Which, let me remind you, I must save you from — you are associated with my sisters, and I cannot let you be ruined."

"And your brilliant plot to save me from ruin is to make me your mistress?"

"It is the only way. I saw the men in the theatre. If your actress does not have a protector, half the men there are willing to do the honors."

"So in the time you spent sending away Josephine, bribing the doorman, and arranging whatever else it took to make this plan, you couldn't have just hired a dozen men from the nearest pub to guard the door?"

His mouth opened and shut several times, as though he thought better of every defense he might have offered. Finally, he recovered his resolve. "This is still the better plan," he said. "Even when I am not at the theatre, you needn't worry about another man backstage if they know you belong to me. But it is my fault you are so close to being discovered by the ton — and I intend to guard you until the last performance."

"Why should I not just ask Alex to guard me?"

"Given how well you've kept this secret so far, I suspect he does not know. Do you really want to tell him?" Ferguson asked.

She paused, then gave the tiniest shake of her head.

Ferguson smiled, looking just as predatory as Westbrook. She wondered if the two of them were really so different — if Ferguson had lived in London for the past decade, would he be as hardened as the earl?

He leaned in again. "As far as I am concerned, your reputation is my responsibility now. The sooner you accept that, the easier a time we will have of it."

Madeleine arched a brow. "That is quite a bold statement."

"You either accept my protection, or I will take you to the Stauntons right now and demand they send you away."

Her eyes widened. "You would really tell Alex? He will kill you when he finds out your role in this."

Ferguson shrugged. "If I died, at least I would be rid of this bloody title. And anyway, I think you would rather accept my help. The Stauntons would smother you in their attempts to protect your reputation, but I'm not ready to give up on you just yet."

His voice dropped into a caress on that last line, and she felt a brief, peculiar flutter in her chest that had nothing to do with the bindings around her breasts. The man was insane, and if they were caught it would be the scandal of the decade — but if she had been found out as an actress, it would have been a scandal anyway. The consequences would be the same in any case.

But with Ferguson on her side, she felt a flash of hope that she might emerge unscathed from her month at the theatre, despite the overwhelming odds. It was strange to have a partner in this. Amelia and Prudence were the closest things she had to partners, but even they had voiced reservations about her scheme. Ferguson, however, seemed convinced they could pull through — and his belief gave her hope.

She relaxed slightly into the seat. "Where are you taking me?"

she asked.

"My sister's house, if she'll have us," he said. "It was the only place I could think to take you. I sent Josephine back to Salford House so that no one would recognize her, and her husband will retrieve you when the servants are all asleep and it is safe for you to sneak back in."

Somehow she had forgotten about servants, even though they were often quicker to know of the latest gossip than their masters were. "And your coachman?"

"A bit belated to ask — but you can trust him as well. He came with me from the Ferguson clan, and he does not gossip with the English servants."

Madeleine left her questions at that. The more important question of what it meant to masquerade as his mistress — and how far that masquerade would go — she left unvoiced. It was too mortifying. Better to brazen it out when he broached the subject. Until then, she would pretend she was on the way to a late supper party, or a musicale, or even a boring evening at Court — anywhere but in a private coach with Ferguson, destined for the home of one of the most notorious hostesses in London.

The carriage finally came to a halt. With the shades drawn, she had not known where they were, and she wasn't entirely sure whether to be relieved or worried that they had arrived at their destination. She felt the coach sway as the driver leapt down from the box. The door swung outward and the man pulled down the steps.

Ferguson exited first, then turned and offered her his hand. In her breeches, sliding out of the coach was trivial — a welcome change from the challenges of exiting a coach in full ball regalia without snagging oneself on the doorframe or ruining one's slippers in the mud.

She looked up at the massive townhouse in front of her. It dominated its section of Portman Square, a four-story behemoth nearly twice as large as its nearest neighbor. The surrounding houses were owned by other illustrious members of the ton, including a duke, an earl, and several baronets — all of whom were no doubt appalled by the comings and goings at the Folkestone residence.

A footman opened the door, retreating unseen behind it. The butler was framed by the opening, his unexpectedly young, handsome face illuminated by the sconces on either side of the door. Madeleine eyed the butler and felt another wave of trepidation mixed with curiosity. One of the rumors about the marchioness was that she trawled the theatres looking for the most handsome men and women to serve her, for reasons that no one knew but herself. Madeleine had never believed the rumors, but the butler's looks made her wonder.

Ferguson leaned down to murmur in her ear. "I know Ellie isn't quite the thing in your circles, but she always had a kind heart. I think you will suit each other quite well if you are willing to chance it."

"I am hardly in a position to cut anyone, let alone someone who may be willing to help me."

He placed his hand on the small of her back and they walked up the steps to the door. The butler bowed to them. "The marchioness is waiting for you in her private salon, your grace."

He led them up the staircase to the hall above. The Folkestone house rivaled some of the grandest buildings in London, redolent with the scent of perfume, dozens of beeswax candles, and lavish bouquets of hothouse flowers. Madeleine imagined an Eastern harem might smell similarly — this was a house dominated by its mistress.

The butler opened an oak door near the end of the hall. "His grace the duke of Rothwell and Madame Guerrier," he said, knowing who Madeleine was supposed to be even though her name had not been mentioned.

A woman lounged on a divan in the center of the room, the book in her hand and the serious expression on her face at odds with her daring gown and opulent surroundings. With her dark red hair and striking blue eyes, she clearly shared a mother with Ferguson. She rose from her seat as they were announced and her gorgeous gold gown shimmered around her as she walked toward them. There was such an allure about the way the silk flowed around her legs that Madeleine felt very plain and insignificant in her men's garb.

The woman was taller than Madeleine, even with Madeleine's high-heeled shoes. She also had a larger bosom and smaller waist — combined with her self-assurance, she was everything Madeleine should have hated. But despite the fact that hosting an actress was a clear impropriety, the woman's dramatic blue eyes were so filled with wry concern that Madeleine couldn't help but smile as she was introduced.

"My dear Madame Guerrier," the marchioness exclaimed, taking her hands and kissing her on the cheek. "Word of your talent is spreading through both my staff and the ton like a wildfire."

"Or a plague," Ferguson muttered.

"You mustn't mind my brother — I don't," she said with a laugh. "Now that I've seen you, I know why he claimed you so quickly, even if I am in the dark as to why you are here. I did not think my reputation was so far gone that I could entertain my brother's mistress." She sounded amused as she said this, even though nearly every other woman in the ton would have had hysterics at the thought.

"About that, Ellie," Ferguson said. "We need to talk about why I was so desperate that I brought her here."

"I think we need to talk about the fact that I haven't seen you in ten years and that you did not even attend my wedding, but I suppose we can begin with Madame Guerrier."

She was so pleasant, so cheerful that Madeleine could barely believe she had heard correctly. How could Lady Folkestone act so nice when Ferguson's absence had been so absolute? But before Ferguson could respond, the marchioness glanced to the door where the butler still hovered.

"Ashby, be a dear and have some tea sent up?"

The butler nodded and left, shutting the door behind him. Madeleine wondered what kind of establishment she had entered — she had never seen such a handsome butler, nor heard the mistress of the house address one so fondly.

"You will have to forgive the lack of refreshments with the tea," she said, gesturing them toward the seating area in the middle of the room. "I was just on my way out when I received Ferguson's note, and my chef has the evening off."

"I am so pleased that you read it," Ferguson said, a banal statement noteworthy only for how very expressionless his voice was.

"And I am so pleased that you chose to call," she retorted. "And now that we are all so pleased, please do be seated, Madame Guerrier."

Madeleine perched in one of the two armchairs flanking the divan, not trusting Ferguson enough to take a place on the settee where he might join her. A fire burned brightly in the grate between two tall windows, and the flames threw shadows on the elaborate chinoiserie screen and tall Oriental urns. A table with a lacquered writing box stood in the corner, below a painted scene of a Chinese dragon. On the other wall, a large gilt-framed mirror reflected the room and its occupants. It was a luxurious room, but smaller and more intimate than the hall — likely not where the marchioness accepted casual callers.

"This is a lovely salon, my lady," Madeleine said, careful not to lose her French accent.

Ellie nodded her thanks. "The current marquess is enamored with the Orient. Maybe he will find this to his liking if he ever returns."

Ferguson waited for his sister to take her place on the divan, then sat down in the armchair across from Madeleine. "You will have the devil to pay if he does come home — where in the world did you unearth that butler? It's unseemly."

"Well, doesn't someone sound like our dear father tonight?" Ellie said. Ferguson flushed, but didn't apologize. "And besides, the current Folkestone is not my husband. If he comes back, I'll pack up Ashby and the rest and move elsewhere."

"You can always come to Scotland. Our clan would be thrilled to have you."

Ellie sighed. "Can we leave our endless family drama for another time? I was supposed to be playing whist with the delicious Lord Norbury and his cronies tonight, and instead I am hosting you. What do you want, Ferguson?"

Madeleine saw him clench his jaw. "Ellie, I know this is deuced awkward. I should have called on you when I first arrived, but I did not know what to say to make up for not being here for you."

This time, Ellie's voice betrayed her. "There is absolutely nothing you can say," she said, sounding frozen.

"Quite. But you are still the only person in London I trust. And I know that as much as you might hate me — and rightly so — you are still best positioned to help my actress friend."

Ellie turned an appraising eye to Madeleine. "From what the servants tell me, she hardly needs assistance. Her debut has set the theatrical world alight. Even I can hardly make her more well-known."

Ferguson glanced at Madeleine too. Before she could stop him, he said, "The problem is that she is not Madame Guerrier. She is Lady Madeleine Vaillant, and she is at serious risk of being discovered."

Ellie looked at her sharply, as though she could peel away Madeleine's disguise with a glance. The silence turned awkward. Madeleine would have kicked Ferguson for sharing her secret if he were not seated so far away.

Finally, Ellie nodded slowly. "Lady Madeleine, your talent is even greater than I have heard. I would never have thought Madame Guerrier was of such noble birth, or that my sisters' proper chaperone would be so daring."

"Did the twins tell you about Madeleine?" Ferguson asked.

"I haven't seen the twins since Father's funeral," Ellie said. "But I heard you approached Lady Madeleine with the request, no doubt because I cannot chaperone them."

She didn't sound upset — but other than that one bleak moment, Ellie hadn't divulged any emotion other than amusement. Madeleine unexpectedly sympathized with her, but her own predicament outweighed her concern. "No offense meant, Lady Folkestone, but I did not intend to share this with you. It must remain a secret if I am to avoid ruin."

"Please, call me Ellie — we are surely already familiar enough for that," she said with a little laugh. "You needn't fear that anyone in this house will divulge your secret. My servants are known for their discretion even more than for their physiques."

Ashby returned with a footman pushing a teacart. The conversation halted as Ellie unlocked her tea caddy and measured leaves into the beautiful silver teapot. She filled it with hot water from the urn, then occupied herself with cups, cream and sugar.

When the servants were gone and the tea was handed around, Ellie said, "Now, Ferguson, tell me why the two of you are here and how you want my assistance. I won't betray your confidence, but I still have not decided whether to help you or toss you out on your ear."

Ferguson explained what happened at the theatre — Madeleine's would-be suitors, his actions to secure her, and their eventual escape. "This was the only place I could think to take her. I cannot take her to the townhouse with Aunt Sophronia and the twins in residence, and she cannot return to Salford House like this."

Ellie sighed. "I do hope you both know what you are about — this will not be a garden-variety bit of mischief if you are discovered."

"From what I hear in Scotland, you are no longer one to steer away from scandal yourself," Ferguson said.

Her blue eyes darkened. "I am a widow. It is different than being a debutante."

Madeleine had heard all the rumors about Lady Folkestone. Madeleine and Amelia would have debuted the same year as Ellie, but Amelia's father died that spring and sent them into full mourning. Ellie had made a glamorous match, culminating in a June wedding to the marquess of Folkestone. Some gossips claimed that she loved someone else, but if that was true, she had forgotten him by the time she walked down the aisle. Everyone said that her smile as she said her vows was absolutely radiant.

Then the marquess died three days later in the arms of an opera dancer. And if Ellie had been pleased to marry him, she was more than happy to bury him.

She mourned him for an eyebrow-raising four weeks, and then set about becoming the most high-flying widow in London. Since the marquess's cousin and heir had left for the Orient just before the wedding and stayed there, Ellie was free to do whatever she desired.

And right now, it appeared that she desired to help Madeleine. "My dear, you are indeed lucky that my infernal brother brought you here. If anyone can help you navigate the ton and the demimonde with your reputation mostly intact, it is I."

Madeleine noticed the "mostly" that qualified Ellie's offer, but the risks were too high to hope that she might remain spotless.

"What do you propose we do?" she asked.

CHAPTER TEN

Ferguson thought it was a mad plan — but if all went well, it wasn't any madder than Madeleine's decision to become an actress in the first place. Her onstage disguise would keep anyone from guessing who she was, and setting her up as his mistress would keep others from pursuing her.

In fact, as he followed her down the back stairs of Ellie's townhouse, he knew that the only real danger Madeleine faced was him.

She seemed completely oblivious to that aspect of their masquerade. She looked like the perfect spinster the ton knew, wearing one of Ellie's most demure gowns for her quick journey back to Salford House. He watched her hips sway under the white muslin, more obscured and therefore more tantalizing than the revealing breeches she wore on stage. When she reached the bottom of the stairs and glanced back up at him, her green eyes brimming with laughter, he nearly groaned.

Perhaps he was the one in danger, not she. Whether she was dressed as his sisters' chaperone or his supposed mistress, she had the same effect on him.

It was not a connection he would be able to discard lightly

when both arrangements ended.

But she wasn't thinking of the future. Her eyes only held the pleasure of the present. "If I knew that becoming a mistress would win me a house of my own, I should have done this ages ago."

Ellie had suggested that Ferguson rent a house for Madame Guerrier so Madeleine would have someplace to return to. With a house of her own, no one could follow her coach to the Stauntons' as he had. He suspected his sister took malicious pleasure in suggesting a variety of expensive options to make their arrangement look more believable, but in this instance, he agreed with her.

Still, he had to warn Madeleine that this was not just a lark. He caught up to her and took her arm. "You would not want to be a mistress, Mad."

She tilted her head, considering. "There is something appealing about one's own house — and I must say I love the stage."

"You cannot have the house without the man who provides it," he said, stepping closer until she was boxed in against the wall of the small passage.

"Perhaps that would not be so bad either." But her voice betrayed her, and he heard the tremor of nerves. She wasn't nearly as provocative as she wanted to seem.

He tilted her chin up with his hand, a demanding gesture to prove his point. "Would you really want to trade your body for a house? Take a man into your bed so you can eat?"

She clamped her lips in a rebellious line.

"I do not think you would like that lifestyle, Lady Madeleine," he said, running a finger down her cheek. "You're destined for a proper marriage, not a string of protectors."

She finally looked away from him. He knew she recognized

the truth of his statement, even if she was too stubborn to admit it. "Surely my carriage is waiting outside, your grace."

He heard the derision in her voice when she said "your grace," and he found himself aching to prove his point. "If you were really my mistress, Mad, you would only go when I said you may. The life of a mistress isn't nearly as free as you seem to think it is. In fact, if I wanted to take you up against this wall like a common streetwalker, there would be no other choice for you."

He wanted to shock her, and he succeeded. Her mouth formed a small "o" of surprise at his harsh tone, and seeing those moist, parted lips made him think of something else his mistress might do if he desired.

But he had not shocked her in the way he expected. "Is that really possible? Prudence and I saw an engraving once that made it seem so, but we could not fathom how it would work."

The woman was a menace. But her curiosity — and the slight tinge of pink as she realized what she had just asked — took the edge off his anger. "It is possible, minx," he said, "but not something we should discuss if you want to go home tonight."

Madeleine stopped smiling. "All humor aside, Ferguson, I hope you know how much it means that you are willing to help me. I cannot tell you how wonderful it is to have an ally."

"If there is anything I can do to protect you, I will do it — and would have done it for your own sake, not just because you are now linked to my sisters."

He wanted to kiss her then, to thread his fingers through that glorious brown hair, which had been freed of its wig only to be stuffed into a tight chignon. More, he wanted to make her see that his desire to help her was more than just chivalry.

But she was still an innocent. And if there was any hope of letting her walk away at the end of the month, he had to ensure she remained that way.

He escorted her out the door and handed her up into the waiting coach. Josephine's husband Pierre would deliver her back to Salford House, and Josephine would sneak her in through the gardens. She was safe for the night.

She would be safe the following night as well. Her next performance was two nights away, giving him time to put their plans into motion. It also gave him time to consider his intentions toward her — and whether she might be willing to entertain those intentions.

He walked slowly back up the stairs to Ellie's salon. Madeleine was like no other woman he had ever met, either in the ton or the demimonde, but her real identity meant that he could not seduce her as he wished. She was the type of woman one would have to marry, even if he suspected she could be just as passionate as a courtesan if partnered with the right man.

But he didn't want to think of marriage now. Seeing Ellie again only reminded him of the price they had paid for a marriage gone bad. Their childhood was happy, until their mother died and took every ounce of their father's heart with her.

Ferguson did not intend to turn into his father, but it wasn't lost on him that the worst of his father's actions were always related to his title. After all, the man enjoyed spending time in Scotland when his wife was alive. But when the woman died, only a few years after he unexpectedly inherited the dukedom, he had cleared the Scottish tenants, devastating the estate he once loved for the riches it could add to his ancestral English lands.

Ferguson had just inherited the title unexpectedly himself. The last thing he needed was to ruin his heart over a woman like his father had, even if Madeleine made him mad for her.

When he reached Ellie's salon, he pushed open the door, wanting to thank her for her assistance. She still lounged on her divan, just as he had left her five minutes earlier. But she pressed one of her pillows to her face, and the silent shaking of her shoulders told him that she was sobbing.

He didn't know what to do, how to comfort the sister who had grown into adulthood without him. He felt the same helplessness as when his mother died, a feeling that had only grown as his father turned colder, until he finally realized their family would never be more than a menagerie of damaged creatures.

That was the day he decided to get himself banished to Scotland so he could escape.

But the cost had been leaving the rest of his siblings behind to fend for themselves. It was a price he was willing to pay at twenty-four, when he was too stubborn to seek a way to stay in London. Now, nearing thirty-five and responsible for them again, he only felt shame.

Ellie noticed him before he could leave. She hurled the pillow at him. "Go away!" she screamed, pulling herself upright and dragging a shawl around her shoulders as though preparing to chase him out.

He crouched next to her divan. "Ellie, I did not mean to hurt you like this."

She choked back another sob. Her face was splotchy with a redhead's unmistakable flush, her eyes puffy and rimmed with smudged kohl. He tried to offer her his handkerchief, but she swatted his hand aside and blew her nose into her shawl. It was an ugly, unladylike gesture, a measure of her contempt for him that she would rather ruin her garment than accept his help.

"You should have been here, Ferguson. How could you leave us with him? The twins needed you. I needed you," she said, her voice breaking on another sob. "And if you had been here, maybe Henry wouldn't have drunk himself to death and Richard might not have been so unbalanced."

He withdrew slightly, sitting on the carpeted floor with a hard thud. "I wasn't any better at dealing with the old man than the rest of you. And our mother's estate needed me too. If you had come with me when I asked you to, you would have seen how dilapidated it had become with the old man's neglect…"

"She's dead, Ferguson, and half the clan emigrated to America before you ever moved there," Ellie spat out, cutting him off. "Your leaving had nothing to do with that, and everything to do with feeling that saving yourself was more important than staying here with the rest of us and waiting for him to die."

He couldn't deny it, couldn't explain how the last six months he had spent living in his father's house before achieving his banishment had felt like he was being flayed alive by every disappointed stare. Ellie surely knew that look just as well as he did — and she had stayed in London to endure it.

"Why didn't you leave?" he asked. "If you didn't want to come to Scotland, you could have gone to the Folkestone estate after you were widowed, taken the twins in when their mother died."

"Don't you dare tell me that I could have behaved differently," Ellie said, blowing her nose into her shawl again. "Father wanted me to remarry, had started the arrangements before Folkestone was even cold. I merely followed your lead and made myself too notorious to be married off again so easily. Besides, until the current marquess finally decides to show his face in London, there's no need for me to leave this house."

"You had best hope he never returns, if you're spending as much of his money on this house as I wager you are."

"The trustees have never stopped my spending. I'm sure Nick will know why I'm draining his coffers," she snapped.

He raised an eyebrow. "Did you know him before you married Folkestone? I thought he left for the Orient before your wedding."

"If you had bothered to come to my wedding, I would have told you," she said. "I loved him once — almost eloped with him. But Father found out, and instead of merely forbidding me to run away, he knew he had to make me ineligible. Arranging for me to marry Nick's titled cousin was his idea of humor."

Ferguson felt the same cold rage he had always felt around his father. The man was a tyrant, an iron fist in a glove of ice rather than velvet. "So Nick left to avoid seeing you marry his relative?"

"Then the cousin died, leaving me a widow and Nick the heir. But Nick has never returned."

"Ellie," he said.

"Don't say anything," she said, her anger flooding back. "You should have been here, and there is nothing you can do to change the fact you weren't. I will help Lady Madeleine — but for her sake, not yours. Unless you promise that you will stay in London and be the head this family needs, I do not want to see you again."

He thought of his plan, of his desire to go back to Scotland and leave the English properties in the hands of his stewards. "I cannot say anything yet, Ellie. Once the twins are married..."

"So you intend to get rid of them through marriage? I never

thought I would see the day, but you are becoming our father after all."

The words cut into him like a lash. He rose stiffly to his feet, not willing to acknowledge the truth behind the insult. "I will not turn into him, but I won't sacrifice my life for his estate either. I need time — and I think we all need time — to understand what to do."

"Don't kill yourself like Richard did," she said nastily. "At least he took Father with him. Your death would just be selfish."

He bowed. "I will endeavor not to disappoint you again. Now, if you will excuse me, I shall continue my metamorphosis into our evil father by going off and sacrificing a goat."

Her lips quirked at their old joke about the duke's satanic ways. He was glad to see the glimmer of a smile before she curled back into herself on the divan. His hand hovered above her hair, wishing they could say goodbye properly — but he had not said goodbye when he went to Scotland. She clearly did not want to hear it now.

So he left, ambling down the stairs so he didn't feel quite like he was fleeing. He had to find a way to make things right with Ellie — with all of his family — but that was not something he could achieve in a day.

First, though, he had to decide whether to truly be the duke. Every instinct screamed for him to return to Scotland, take up the life he had built for himself rather than the life that his inheritance thrust upon him. Every moment he stayed in London felt like he was being bound more tightly to his title — and if he was already using the old duke's favorite tactic of marrying people off to control them, how badly might he behave if he became the duke in earnest?

But returning to his old life would not make things any better for his siblings — and it wasn't enough to offer a woman like

Madeleine.

He cursed as Ellie's indecently handsome butler showed him out the door to his waiting carriage. He couldn't think of what to offer Madeleine because he couldn't offer her anything — he needed to focus on getting her through the month with her reputation and virtue intact. Then, he would find husbands, or barring that, a better chaperone than Sophronia for his sisters, and go back to Scotland where he belonged.

And he needed to stop thinking of Madeleine as though she was already his, before the temptation to keep her overwhelmed his tenuous ability to be a gentleman.

CHAPTER ELEVEN

The next afternoon was Friday, and as usual, Prudence called on Madeleine and Amelia while their mothers shopped. It was an arrangement they made several years earlier, after all three girls mutinied and demanded one afternoon a week when they might be free of the usual house calls and shopping excursions to Bond Street.

Lady Harcastle had declared that Prudence was wasting all her other chances to make a decent match, so she might as well lose her Friday afternoons as well. Aunt Augusta was more tactful, but she felt the same. Either way, the girls had won — and their little club was born. They dubbed themselves the "Muses of Mayfair," and each week, they shared a bit of their recent work: Amelia read from her novel in progress, Prudence shared bits of her latest historical treatise, and Madeleine recited a monologue.

As the years progressed, though, the meetings paled for Madeleine. Amelia published several novels under a male pseudonym with increasingly large sales. Prudence wrote to a variety of historians, again as a male — and they had all laughed uproariously when she started corresponding with Alex, who never guessed that many of those letters were composed in one of his own sitting rooms.

Madeleine, though, could rarely act, and she could only suggest charades at house parties so many times before people declined. It was with Prudence and Amelia's encouragement that Madeleine finally sought out Madame Legrand and a real stage.

But this Friday, Madeleine didn't want to discuss the latest developments with her friends. How could she tell them she had expanded her repertoire and become Ferguson's mistress? It was hard enough lying to Aunt Augusta at breakfast about why she had "confined herself to her room" the night before, when she had promised to attend the Locktons' ball.

Amelia would not let her keep secrets, though. As soon as Prudence arrived and they were all ensconced in the small back sitting room that overlooked the Staunton gardens, the inquisition began.

"Where were you last night?" Amelia demanded. "I know you weren't in your room before we left the house, and when I returned after two, your door was locked."

Madeleine had heard someone try the handle as she tossed away another sleepless night, but she had not wanted company. "It took longer to leave the theatre than I expected."

"Nonsense," Amelia said. "We have timed that route exactly. When I left for the ball, you were already over an hour late. And since Josephine was here to make your excuses to Aunt Augusta, you were somewhere without an escort."

Madeleine couldn't say anything without incriminating herself further. "What were you thinking?" Amelia continued, starting to pace. "London isn't safe for any of us alone at night. And the danger is not merely our reputations — any number of things could happen in Mayfair, let alone in Seven Dials. Highwaymen, procuresses, white slavers from the Barbary Coast..."

Madeleine sighed as she watched her cousin pace the room.

Amelia always paced when she was agitated, or just thinking things through. Since this was the room she wrote in, there was a well-worn path for her in the carpet.

"Isn't the Barbary Coast a bit far from Mayfair?" Madeleine asked.

"Yes. They would never be suspected," Amelia said triumphantly. Madeleine sighed again. Amelia would be easier to reason with if she didn't occasionally lapse into thinking that the events of her Gothic novels could happen to them.

"Madeleine would never be so careless," Prudence said soothingly, assuming her usual role of peacemaker. "The logical answer is that she was not alone."

Amelia stopped pacing to stare at Madeleine. "Then if Josephine was not with you, who escorted you home?"

Madeleine looked at both of them. They were her dearest friends and she trusted them completely — but they would not be pleased with her next words. "Pierre brought me home after retrieving me from the duke of Rothwell."

Prudence gasped. Amelia's jaw dropped. They could not have been more surprised if Madeleine claimed she was rescued by Shakespeare's ghost. As much as Madeleine had not wanted to tell them, this reaction was worth it.

Finally, Amelia pulled herself back into some semblance of order. "Why on earth did you take Rothwell, of all people, into your confidence? The man is a scoundrel, and we know just how unstable his family is!"

Madeleine held up her hands. "I had no choice. Ferguson came back after the play was over and discovered me."

"Oh, so he's Ferguson now?" Prudence teased. "I do hope he

hasn't taken unwanted liberties."

Madeleine flushed.

Prudence laughed delightedly. "So he has taken unwanted liberties! Or were they not so unwanted after all?"

"Prudence!" Amelia gasped.

Madeleine frowned at her cousin. "Why are you so upset about this, Mellie? I thought you would react like Prudence did. Weren't you the one who always thought we needed to embrace new experiences to improve our art?"

It was Amelia's turn to flush. "I may have said that, but I never expected you to dally with a duke. You, who wouldn't even kiss the dancing master when I dared you."

"You didn't precisely enjoy kissing the dancing master, did you?" Madeleine retorted.

Prudence dissolved into giggles, quickly smothering her laughter after a glare from Amelia. Madeleine would have laughed too, but Amelia turned back to her with an unusually hard look in her eyes. In that moment, Madeleine saw what Amelia would be if she decided to marry one of her suitors. As she aged, and with the right husband, she could rival any of the most fearsome hostesses in the ton.

"Perhaps it would be helpful if I explained everything," Madeleine said, knowing that Amelia wouldn't stop questioning until she did.

Amelia sank onto the settee next to Prudence. They both looked at her, Amelia with angry concern, Prudence with expectant amusement.

She didn't want to start, but she somehow managed to stumble into the story. As uncomfortable as it made her, she told them everything: the earl of Westbrook's offer, the men in the alleyway, her introduction to the marchioness of Folkestone, and the help Ellie had provided with her wardrobe.

But when she needed to tell them about Ferguson's plan for keeping her safe, her voice faltered.

Amelia noticed when Madeleine broke off abruptly. "What are you not telling us?"

She never was good at delivering bad news, so she just said it in a rush. "Ferguson made me his mistress."

Prudence shrieked, bouncing in her seat and sloshing a bit of her tea onto the delicately patterned saucer. "What was it like? Was it anything like those engravings we saw?"

Madeleine shook her head, grinning at Prudence's reaction despite herself. "He did not really make me his mistress — we are just making it appear that Madame Guerrier is his mistress. It's genius, actually. As long as Madame Guerrier has a protector, she is safe from the likes of Lord Westbrook."

Amelia did not find any humor in the situation. "Madeleine, you cannot keep this charade going any longer. You might have been able to survive being found out on stage, but if your role as Rothwell's mistress is discovered, you will be irrevocably ruined."

"You have always wanted to set up a cottage in the country. Aunt Augusta will surely send me someplace to rusticate if I am discovered," Madeleine said. As consolations, it wasn't much. But she was still surprised by the vehemence of her cousin's reaction.

"I never intended to be forced to move away. If you are exiled, Mother may not let me go with you. She will try to marry me off, if anyone will take me after the amount of time I have spent with you."

Prudence looked ill, as if Lady Harcastle had already walked in to call her on the carpet. "If your mother does not take this well, imagine how my mother will react."

"Yes, and what will happen to our club if you are forced to move away?" Amelia said.

Madeleine looked down into her teacup, untouched during their discussion. Amelia was right. Her acting would have been scandalous enough, but if anyone found out she pretended to be Ferguson's mistress, no one would believe she was still a virgin. Men like Ferguson did not take innocents under their wing — and if they did, the women did not remain innocent for long.

But the question Amelia had not asked, and the one that had given Madeleine such a sleepless night, was why Ferguson intervened at all. Perhaps it was only because she was his sisters' chaperone. If that was the reason, though, she could not explain the blast of heat she felt from him when he cornered her in the stairwell, or the sensation that he wanted to do all the things he was warning her against.

She took a sip of her cold tea, wiping the thought out of her mind. Amelia was upset enough by what had happened. She did not need to know the full depths of the danger Madeleine courted.

"I still do not think I shall be discovered," she said. "Ferguson only caught me because he followed my coach to our house, not because he recognized me outright. He will arrange things so no one else may follow me here, and my secret should stay safe."

"You have to tell Alex," Amelia insisted. "He could put an end to all of this, or at least make sure Rothwell's protection isn't necessary."

Madeleine hesitated just a bit too long. "Methinks the lady doth protest too little about 'Ferguson's' involvement in her affairs," Prudence snickered.

Prudence had always had the most shocking sense of humor,

at odds with her dry interest in the ancient world. Madeleine did not appreciate it now, particularly not with Amelia's gaze weighing on her. "I am not concerned about ending Ferguson's involvement," she lied. "But Alex would put an end to my time at the theatre. I am not sure I am willing to give up these last few weeks prematurely."

It was the same reason she hadn't told Ferguson that she was being forced to continue acting — if anything, he was even more likely than Alex to take drastic measures to ensure her safety, with or without her consent.

Amelia looked stunned. "You would rather risk being sent away forever than stop acting at Madame Legrand's? You didn't ask for this — the woman forced you into it. Why is continuing so important to you?"

"You know why," Madeleine said, feeling a kick of anger that matched Amelia's temper. "You can hide behind a male name to publish your books and Prudence can pretend to be male in her letters, but I cannot act without going out in public. It isn't fair for you to deny me that when you can still do everything you please with your own art."

She stood then, setting her teacup onto the cart with a dangerous amount of force. "If you will excuse me, I believe I shall rest until it is time to attend the Leynham affair tonight. I will do my best not to cause a scandal before then."

Her cousin tried to call out to her as she left, but she didn't want to hear the words. She walked as fast as she dared up the stairs to her room, locking herself in against any attempts Amelia might make to gain entrance.

She lay down fully clothed on the counterpane and stared up into the canopy over her bed. She had not told the entire truth to

Amelia and Prudence — but she knew she could not, not after seeing Amelia's reaction to what she did share. It was true that she did not want to stop acting, but she had feigned a carelessness toward Ferguson that was the opposite of how she felt.

Even though she knew better, knew that both her reputation and her heart were in danger, she was not ready to cut ties with Ferguson. Once their masquerade was over, he would have no reason to pay attention to an orphan with passable looks, and he didn't need any of the riches that would come from marrying her. He had a title to think of now, even if he didn't seem to want it. Eventually, he would put his duty above his feelings. While it wouldn't cost him his life, unlike her father's convictions, it would force him to marry an appropriate lady — and he could reach higher than her, both for rank and fortune.

Until then, though, the next few weeks might be the only time she would ever feel adored — by the ton, by the audience, by the duke who promised to save her.

She just had to hope a few weeks would be enough.

CHAPTER TWELVE

That night, Madeleine wished she could have attended anything but Lady Leynham's ball. The woman was a notorious skinflint and the refreshments were dreadful — the ham was even thinner than at Vauxhall, if that was possible, and the lemonade tasted as though it had made only the briefest acquaintance with the rind of one fruit before being delivered to the ballroom.

Her stomach rumbled under her blue and cream striped ball gown. She sighed and eyed the buffet, but the footmen must have been trained to handle people of her hungry ilk. She had already eaten four sandwiches, and they avoided her gaze so that they would not have to offer her another one.

If her reputation survived the month, the reducing diet she feigned to throw Aunt Augusta off the scent might still kill her.

She scanned the ballroom, realizing after her eyes were already moving that she was searching for a particular shade of burnished hair amongst all the blondes and brunettes. Ferguson would never attend a ball such as this. Even if he did attend, he would not express more than passing interest in her when she was in her spinster garb.

But she still wanted to see him. And she still had enough sense to be scared by the impulse to find him.

Alex strode up to her, catching her as she surveyed the trays again. "There's no harm in having a sandwich," he remarked as he joined her. "Those little things look like they've been reduced themselves."

Madeleine laughed as she saw one of the footmen bite back a grin. "Don't you have better things to do than keep us poor females company?"

"It does Mother good to see me at these functions occasionally. If she thinks I might stumble into wedlock on my own, she only mentions it once a week instead of once a day. The same would be true for you if you weren't avoiding the ton so assiduously."

His tone was still light, but his dark eyes were serious. "The ton does not amuse me as it used to."

"I can't say I blame you. But is anything else amiss? You haven't dropped by my study in weeks."

She read there occasionally, a habit she had continued since childhood, when Uncle Edward's presence was sometimes enough to keep her nightmares at bay. But she couldn't do it now, not when she was deceiving Alex so thoroughly.

"Everything is fine," she said. "I just feel less eager to play the social games this season."

"If anything is wrong, promise you'll tell me?"

She nodded, unable to say the lie aloud.

"Then if you'll forgive my desertion, I think I shall escape to White's. I will think of you with pity while I take my supper there."

His remark merited a swift retort, but she froze when she saw the man who appeared behind him. Ferguson leaned against a pillar, wearing cool, unrelenting black, with his arms crossed like an impatient warrior. He stared directly at her, a man who didn't care that the gossips tracked his every glance.

Madeleine regained her senses just enough to laugh at Alex's jest, but her eyes were still locked on Ferguson's. Everything else fell away — the music faded, the bright silk and velvet gowns dimmed in the candlelight, the hum of conversation disappeared, and even the feel of Alex's lips brushing against her gloved hand in parting failed to register.

Alex pulled her back into reality with a shake of her shoulder. "Are you sure you don't need to eat something? You are as pale as a sheet."

She waved a hand. "No, go to White's. I shall survive another hour."

"Let me take you to Amelia," he said, turning to take her arm. It was only then that he saw Ferguson still leaning against the pillar.

"Surely you aren't in such a state over him?" he asked, his voice dropping into an incredulous whisper.

She shook her head, more to clear the thudding of her heart than to answer his question. Ferguson pushed himself away from the pillar and strode toward them. She felt Alex's grip tighten on her arm. Her sober cousin would not like the type of man Ferguson had been.

"Lady Madeleine, a pleasure to see you again," Ferguson said, kissing her hand. She had barely noticed when Alex did it, but the ritual gesture from Ferguson was enough to awaken something in her blood. She curtsied for him, and for the first time, the dip felt like a seduction.

"Salford," he continued, turning to her cousin. "Do you mind if I steal Lady Madeleine for this dance? You surely see enough of the fair lady at home."

Alex didn't look happy, but he couldn't say no — not when Madeleine had already pulled away from him. He stalked off without saying goodbye, headed straight for the exit as though he needed to leave before changing his mind.

Madeleine thought it unfair of Alex to judge Ferguson for actions that happened a decade earlier, but she forgot her cousin as Ferguson took her hand and tucked it into his arm. She felt his muscles beneath the fine, smooth cloth of his jacket and she wondered again how he had become so hard.

"Thank God I found you," he said as they skirted the dancers who awaited the first strains of the waltz. "I was in no mood to come here and discover you already gone."

"Is everything all right, your grace?" she asked.

"Do not call me your grace," he bit out. Then he saw her face and softened his tone. "I'm sorry, Mad, but I've no wish to be reminded of what I have inherited."

His tone was bitter. She speculated that he was upset about more than just the title. "Do you want to talk about it?" she asked.

Ferguson looked out over the crowd. "Not here. I would take you out to the garden, but I doubt we could escape undetected."

He was right. Too many speculative eyes tracked their progress through the ballroom, looking for any indication of an understanding forming between them — or of the moody, unstable brooding his older brother had exhibited. "Can you tell me tomorrow?"

"There is nothing to tell," he said, with a smile that did not reach his eyes. "Merely boring family business. Would you care to dance? I think we can waltz without giving the harpies too much to sink their talons into."

Madeleine laughed as he pulled her onto the floor. The rhythm came easily for them and she forgot her hunger as a different kind of need slowly worked through her. She relaxed into him, simply enjoying the feel of his arms around her. That belief that everything would come out perfectly stole over her again, and she was struck by how safe she felt with him — as though he could protect her from anything.

"Do you think I shall ever see your hair as it really is?" he asked.

"What?" she asked dumbly, startled out of her dreamlike state.

"Your hair. I've only seen it in a wig, or pulled up tight under one of these awful caps. Do you think I shall see it in all its glory?"

It was a dangerous question. "The proper response would be 'no,' of course."

"Of course," he said. "But even though I knew I would be seeing the spinster tonight, I could not stay away. You are the only reason I came out. If not for hope of seeing you, I would have remained shut up in Rothwell House, cursing my inheritance."

"I am pleased that you wished to see me," she said, keeping her voice cool. She wasn't ready to admit that she had hoped he would attend as well. "I do wonder if it was an intelligent desire."

That statement made his head snap up. "You would prefer not to see me?"

"No, definitely not," she said hastily. "But the way the gossips watch us when we dance — it is bringing me a type of renown I've never had before. Renown that, I might add, I would rather not have while handling my current... difficulty."

"So you want to keep me in a box and just bring me out when you need me?"

All lightness was gone from his voice, sucked away and replaced by something far darker. She sought out his eyes, trying to reassure him, but he kept them focused over her head. "Ferguson, it isn't like that. I must have a care for my reputation."

"And that reputation will be made worse by dancing a single waltz with a duke in a full, well-lit ballroom?"

She stopped talking then, unable to think of anything that could explain her position without angering him further. When he phrased things as he did, it did seem like she was using him for her own gain — something that no one had ever been able to accuse her of before. It wasn't her intention, but that did not make his feelings on the matter any less real.

When the waltz came to a halt, he bowed over her hand. She started to pull away, eager to escape to the other spinsters, but he held her firm in his grasp. "Mad, I'm sorry. I did not come here tonight to start a fight."

"Then why did you come, Ferguson?"

"You," he said. "Regardless of what you're wearing or where you are, I wanted to see you. And now that I have, I shall take my leave."

He strode away then, moving through the crowd without a backward glance, acknowledging others' greetings with just enough of a pause to avoid causing mortal offense. He reached the door before she even remembered to close her mouth.

"You are more attractive when you do not look like a gaping fish," someone said beside her.

She turned and found Sophronia, duchess of Harwich, staring at her with undisguised interest. She liked the old woman, despite her tongue. "Thank you for the reminder, your grace."

"If you become my niece, you won't be able to stand about looking confused," Sophronia said. "Not that anyone would blame you. Ferguson is one of the more confusing men in my acquaintance."

"Whyever do you think I would become your niece? Ferguson hasn't the slightest interest in me, I'm sure."

Sophronia swatted her with her reticule. "Do not play dense with me, young lady. Everyone in London just saw him come to this ball, drag you out of the crowd, dance with you once, and leave. What other sign of interest do you need? A proclamation written in his own blood and read by the lord chamberlain?"

"I have always appreciated your imagination, your grace. It is quite a gift," Madeleine said drily.

"I do hope the boy is intelligent enough to offer for you and you have enough sense to accept," Sophronia said, ignoring Madeleine's last sentence. "You have more to recommend you than most of the other fools of your generation. It is a shame that he seems taken with that actress in Seven Dials, but then, men will be men. Don't let the gossip about her bother you. He knows he has to make a proper match, and a common strumpet like her isn't it."

Madeleine choked back her laugh. "I will remember, your grace."

Sophronia walked away, no doubt to torment someone else. Still, her conversation had given Madeleine two important bits of information.

First, everyone knew that Ferguson had taken Madame Guerrier as his mistress. If the duchess of Harwich felt comfortable discussing it with the woman she thought would be Ferguson's future wife, then everyone else in the ton knew too.

Second, and more alarming, Sophronia thought Ferguson would offer for Madeleine. Regardless of how she felt when she was with him, she absolutely did not want to be a duchess. Being dependent on Alex was one thing. Being the inferior bride of a duke was quite another.

But if she was a topic of conversation within the ton, people would be looking for her at social events — and would notice that she was routinely absent. A girl who hoped to land a duke would not spend half her evenings quietly at home.

Which meant that, regardless of why he had sought her out, Ferguson had just made their masquerade more difficult.

CHAPTER THIRTEEN

After he left the ball, Ferguson went to White's. Not that he wanted to socialize — he still didn't intend to stay in London, and so didn't want to waste time either rehabilitating his reputation or gambling with his old cronies. But after hearing Madeleine's concerns, he realized that he needed to reenter society. It was vitally important to hear any rumors about her when they first arose, if only so he could try to change their course.

He examined his surroundings as he entered. His shoulders tensed, and he felt like he was walking into a battle, but he maintained his usual poise. White's was still the same club he had known ten years earlier. Ferguson supposed that they must have reupholstered chairs and refurbished rooms, but the atmosphere was the same — the same sodding aristocrats playing cards and placing wagers.

The only change that mattered was that his father no longer presided over the older Tories, gathered as always in one corner of the main room. Their gazes were calculating, either wondering how to curry his vote in the Lords or betting on how long it would be before he snapped like Richard had. He felt like he had returned to his first days at Eton. He felt too young for a dukedom, and his thick red hair made him an outcast in this bastion of English society.

Thank God it had darkened as he grew older — but in moments like this, he felt ten again, and utterly out of place. He hadn't belonged at Eton initially either, but he learned how to manage, using his fists when he couldn't humor his way out of a problem.

Those same fists had earned him his name. The boys had called him Avenel, his father's surname — and the first act of rebellion in his life was to abandon his father's name and demand to be called by his mother's. Even the teachers gave in, until his father was the only one in the world whose mind he couldn't change.

Fists wouldn't help him now, particularly not if everyone was waiting to see him lose control. He could try humor, but he held little hope for success. Most of the peers were braggarts, dullards, or popinjays, and the remainder were too stiff with protocol or too wasted by drink. That left the smarter rakes, like Westbrook, or the sober, intelligent lords like Alex Staunton. Neither of those groups would be charmed by Ferguson's drawled quips.

Speaking of the devil — he heard Madeleine's cousin hail him. He felt that childish flare of hope that someone might want to befriend him despite everything — but when he turned, the man was bearing down on him with the look of a sea captain about to keelhaul a sailor.

"Rothwell," Alex said again. He was the earl of Salford now, having inherited sometime after Ferguson left; relearning titles and names alone could take Ferguson an entire season. "Would you be so kind as to spare me a moment of your time?"

"At your service, old man," Ferguson said in a jovial tone that made Salford grit his teeth. He shut down the desire for friendship and seized the initiative. "You're not still sore over that widow from so many years ago, are you? I saved you a great deal of trouble by winning her, if you must know."

Salford's face turned even more forbidding as he steered them into a private room. "I see the past decade has not improved your comportment, your grace."

"I thought you were an art collector, not a Puritan," Ferguson retorted. "Will you be calling in the ghost of old Cromwell to read me my sins?"

The briefest flicker of amusement passed through Salford's eyes. "'Tis a shame you had the father you did — you might have been worth knowing otherwise."

Other men might have called Salford out for such a remark, or at least cut him. Since Ferguson agreed with the sentiment, he ignored the insult. Still, it would not do to give him ground until it was clear what he wanted. "Cut line, Salford," he said, taking a pinch of snuff for appearances even though he hated the stuff. "Why are we here?"

Salford shut the door, looking uncomfortable, but his determination did not lessen. "You will tell me what your intentions are toward my cousin."

Ferguson was surprised by the question, but he had been confronted by too many angry husbands in his earlier career as a rake to give anything away. He made a show of inhaling his snuff and brushing his spotless coat, buying time while he tried to pull his thoughts in order. What had Salford discovered? And how should he play this, when not even he knew what his full intentions were?

Finally, he decided to prevaricate. "Ah, your cousin — my sisters' proper chaperone? It was Sophronia's idea, not mine. If you are not happy that she has taken up the role, I can find another spinster for the task."

He had hoped nonchalant ignorance would lead Salford off the scent, but it just infuriated him. "If she is your sisters' chaperone, you hardly need to dance with her. Yet the gossips maintain that she is virtually the only woman you have danced with since your return."

Ferguson shrugged. "Your cousin is a good dancer and adequate conversationalist — more rare than one might expect."

Salford slammed his hand down on his own thigh, fully betraying his temper. "You had every widow and courtesan in the ton panting at your feet ten years ago, and yet now you only have eyes for an orphaned spinster who has been too long on the shelf. I will know why that is."

Hearing Salford's assessment of his cousin, the same instinct that had driven Ferguson backstage to save Madeleine from ruin flared up again. He leaned forward, muscles tensed, all hints of his reprobate's façade replaced with a predator's calm. "If you only see the lady as an orphaned spinster, you do her too little honor. At least I see Mad in terms of what she could be rather than what she lacks."

Salford's eyes turned deadly. "Who gave you leave to address her so familiarly?"

"You must not know your cousin very well. The girl is not a mere 'Maddie,' regardless of how you see her."

Most men quailed under the glare Ferguson used, but Salford held his ground. "I only want what is best for her. You are not the one who will make her happy, regardless of how familiar you have made yourself. Consider this your only warning, Rothwell — I would rather see you join your father in hell than allow you to marry Madeleine."

Ferguson should have left well enough alone, let Salford walk away believing he had made his point. But giving someone else the last word was not his forté.

"I have no intentions toward the lady at the present," he said, pausing long enough that Salford's face began to soften. "But I assure you that if my intentions change, Mad's desires are the only ones I will accommodate."

Salford leaned against the door, putting on the same nonchalant air as Ferguson. But the slight tic in his jaw gave him away. The earl was rumored to be a masterful negotiator in the antiquities markets, but his temper was harder to control when discussing his family.

Finally, he said, "Do not hurt the lady, or I will kill you. Hiding your death would be beyond tedious, so I hope it shan't come to that."

Ferguson finally smiled. The image of Salford burying him in the back garden was too entertaining to ignore. The earl gave him another hard look, then decided the conversation was over. But just as he reached for the door handle, he turned back to Ferguson. "If your intentions toward my cousin do change, it would behoove you to set aside that actress chit. I will look even less favorably on your suit if you are still carrying on with the high flyers of the demimonde."

Fortunately, Salford left before Ferguson's face could betray him. He was accustomed to handling irate family members, but the situation with Madeleine was unique. The earl still did not suspect Madeleine's acting — but given the display of temper Ferguson witnessed tonight, there would be hell to pay if he ever did find out.

Worse, though, he had forced Ferguson to consider what his intentions toward Madeleine were. He still did not have an answer — not that it was possible to think of the future with Salford glaring at him. But if he and Madeleine continued down the road they were currently on, he would need to make a choice.

Could he offer for the only woman who might make his title bearable? Or was a love match — and the possibility of turning into his father — too much of a risk?

CHAPTER FOURTEEN

In Ferguson's carriage the next night — her first night pretending to be his mistress while leaving the theatre — Madeleine could not meet his eyes. Being alone with him in a closed carriage was very different from dancing with him in a crowded ballroom.

Ferguson seemed similarly lost in thought. He stared straight ahead, at a point somewhere just to the left of her head. The cadence of his fingers tapping out a rhythm on his knee was the only indicator of his mood.

But then she noticed his eyes occasionally flicking over her, a gesture she wouldn't see unless she was trying to read his face. It was an attempt to reassure himself of something — her mood? Her acquiescence?

The next time he glanced over her, she caught his gaze. "I really cannot thank you enough for your help."

He shifted in his seat. "Do not thank me yet, Mad. Wait until I have survived the next month without touching you, and then you may be grateful."

She felt the same powerful kick that she always experienced on the stage. Those were words of adoration, hinting at a need for her that he could not easily control. And *she* had created that need, even though he knew who she really was.

Marguerite Guerrier won over all who saw her, but no one had wanted Madeleine Vaillant before.

The knowledge that he wanted her, combined with her own desire to feel everything she might have done if she had ever married, added a dangerous fuel to her actions. She leaned back into the seat, still holding on to his gaze. "You are not the only one who will find our masquerade challenging."

He arched a brow at her, an arrogant look he must have perfected long before he became a duke. Her lips curved into a smile. Men like him had never attracted her before — but then, she had never known how it could feel to have one such as him at her feet.

Her heart beat faster and she lowered her voice. "Perhaps we should practice how we might appear together in the demimonde."

She was useless as a flirt, but he was smart enough to grasp her meaning. "You want to practice being my mistress?"

"I find my acting improves with experience," she said, hoping she sounded like a coquette but fearing that she sounded like a fool.

He laughed. She flushed bright red as the heady bubble of attraction burst. She was indeed a fool... she didn't know how to play these games... he was helping her out of charity, not desire. She turned away from him, wishing she could hide in a carriage as easily as she did in ballrooms.

He reached across the carriage to stroke her cheek. "Mad — it's not you I'm laughing at. Imagine my predicament, though. I have the most beautiful, talented woman in London as my mistress, and I cannot touch her without ruining her."

She looked back at him. Several emotions flickered across his eyes in the dim light of the coach, but mockery was not one of them.

"And I have the most notorious rake in London in my carriage to save my reputation. Aren't we quite the pair?"

He watched her for a long moment. She saw the battle play out on his face. Abruptly, the darker side won, and he shifted his hand to her wrist and pulled her toward him.

She landed in his lap, too astonished to do more than squeal with surprise. With her face mere inches from his, she could see the banked, smoldering look in his eyes — just as he tilted her mouth and kissed her.

Where their first kiss was interrupted by Josephine and the second kiss performed for the benefit of Westbrook, this kiss, their first real one, was pure possession. His mouth slanted over hers, and he didn't wait for an invitation to take the kiss deeper, to suck her breath away as he claimed her tongue.

Madeleine tried to gasp but it merely sealed him to her, fusing them together with the heat of their kiss. She knew she should push him away, that she had pushed him too far. But his arms pulled her closer, gathering her up until she was entwined in his embrace. Without her usual froth of skirts and petticoats, there were no barriers between them. Down the entire length of her body, her skin burned with the touch of his muscled limbs. Only her breasts were denied the sensation, bound as they were to fit under her jacket — and she squirmed slightly in his arms, wishing she could get closer to his chest.

He didn't stop the kiss, but while one hand stayed firm against her back, the other caressed her cheek before dipping lower to attack her cravat. The length of lace came away from her neck, and she felt a single moment's coolness before he broke away from her mouth. He trailed kisses down her throat, lingering on the sensitive pulse point until she was arching against him, held in place by his hand and her own desire. He brushed aside her cloak, made quick work of the buttons on her jacket, and tore the fastenings of her shirt in his haste — only to be thwarted by the bindings on her breasts.

She saw the hunger on his face and knew it mirrored her own. In all her years as a spinster, and despite all her illicit reading, she never imagined a man could drive her to this level of need with nothing more than a few caresses.

"This is a crime, Mad," he said, in a hoarse voice she barely recognized.

She pulled her jacket shut to protect herself from his gaze. "Ferguson..."

He cut her off and flicked her jacket open again. "Not us... *this*," he said, gesturing at her breasts. He ran his hands over the tightly contained mounds, and even through the yards of linen, her nipples strained to respond. There was the barest swell of flesh above her bindings, and he leaned in to kiss the slight hollow where it disappeared under the cloth. "When I kiss you again, I will set them free and make up for how you've tormented them."

Then he gathered her back into his arms. This time she was ready for his touch, and she opened for him as their lips came together, eager for that moment when the distance between them was wholly erased. She was no longer a passive territory for him to claim — she met him halfway, resting her arms on his shoulders and twining her fingers through his silky hair. There was something building inside her, matching the heat she felt from his embrace. She pressed him closer to her, hoping that with enough kisses, the fire would flare up and consume them.

Finally, though, he pulled away, leaving her burning, gasping, desperate for something she had never felt before. "Ferguson," she whispered, trying to pull him back toward her mouth.

He drew a deep, shuddering breath. "If I don't stop now, I might never quit."

He hoisted her off his lap and deposited her across the carriage from him before she could voice an objection. Still, his admission that he was just as aroused as she was took the edge off her temper. She sighed as she looked at him across the carriage. He looked more frustrated than she had ever seen him. Their kiss had done that — *she* had done that — and she felt a giddy rush of power.

He slid open a curtain just wide enough to ascertain their whereabouts, then snapped it shut. "You should right yourself, Mad — we will arrive in a minute or two."

She looked down. She might not be his mistress, but with her shirt and jacket hanging open, baring the bindings around her breasts, she looked the part. "Where are we?" she asked as she retied the broken laces of her shirt.

"I found a house for you that was already part of the duchy's holdings in London. I had to pay the tenants an extravagant sum to vacate within the day, but when you see the location, you will understand why."

She had just arranged her cravat into some semblance of a proper knot when the carriage rolled to a stop. Ferguson helped her out, and she looked up at the trim edifice of the house he had found for her. It was smaller than the grand townhouses of Berkeley Square, but it was only a street away — one of those respectable addresses that only the highest mistresses of the demimonde ever aspired to. Madame Guerrier would not be received by her neighbors, who would be scandalized at Ferguson's actions in depositing her there, but she would be accessible to the males of Mayfair.

"Everyone will think you are here to be close to me — Rothwell House is at the end of the street, where Dover and Piccadilly meet," Ferguson said, seeming to read her thoughts as he took her arm. "But the true advantage is that the back garden adjoins the Salford House mews. You can sneak back and forth undetected if you time it properly."

It was a brilliant plan, and she was impressed that Ferguson had arranged it so brilliantly. There was no time to thank him, though. The door to the house was flung open from the inside, and a young butler with unusually artistic brown hair bowed deeply to her. "Madame Guerrier, welcome home. My name is Bristow, and I look forward to serving you."

He stepped aside as Ferguson ushered her into the hallway. "My sister provided the staff, thank God. It was the only way I could fill the place with discreet servants in time."

Ellie's involvement explained the handsome butler, whose dark eyes twinkled as he took her cloak and Ferguson's hat. Madeleine paused in the hallway to examine her surroundings. The house was smaller than those of most of her peers, with only four rooms on the first floor, but the entryway was perfectly respectable. There were no traces of personal effects that would make the house a home, but it was sparklingly clean, and Ferguson had spared no expense on lighting.

Ferguson took her arm and led her up the stairs. "Bristow can give you a tour of the lower rooms tomorrow, but you should change if you wish to return home in time for tonight's ball."

Madeleine had of course never had a house of her own; she always lived wherever the Stauntons or her parents were in residence.

And while this wasn't her house, she already found herself thinking about replacing the drapes, hanging artwork — making it hers.

She shook her head to dislodge her dangerous thoughts. This house, this life — this man — weren't hers. If she survived the next month, she would go back to living her staid Staunton life. If she was ruined, she would find herself in exile. Either way, her time in this house was limited, and she would do well to remember it.

Ferguson led her past the second floor sitting room and pushed open a door to a room facing the rear courtyard. A gorgeous fourposter bed dominated the center of the chamber, the dark green coverlet partially obscured by the gauzy light green chiffon bedcurtains. A sensuously curved chaise-longue, covered in gold velvet and similar in design to the one in Ellie's salon, angled out of the corner, positioned to take advantage of the fireplace. An armchair in the same velvet stood across from it, with a table between them where a pair of lovers could take a private meal. A dressing table on the opposite wall held a variety of small glass vials and ceramic pots, no doubt filled with perfumes and cosmetics, with another door leading to the dressing room beyond.

Something about the room, whether it was the dramatic greens and golds or the seductive glamour of the furnishings, appealed to her deeply, in a way that her light, innocent room at Salford House never had. And she felt a very real flash of regret that she would never sleep in the bed, or read a book on the chaise, or explore all the potions on the dressing table.

Ferguson shifted beside her. "Do you approve?"

She looked up. His eyes were anxious, as though her approval mattered. "It is a wonder you created the perfect room for me in a single day. If only I could take it with me at the end."

He relaxed, grinning at her. "You will just have to enjoy it while you have it, Mad."

The statement could have been a motto for the entire month — until it was over or she was ruined, she had to enjoy it thoroughly, before her old life claimed her again.

He pulled the bell cord. In a few moments Lizzie, her temporary lady's maid, hurried in. She had the lush figure of an opera dancer, and Madeleine wondered again where Ellie found her servants. Ferguson left her to her toilette, promising to wait and see her safely across the alley to her real home.

As she let Lizzie dress her in one of the evening gowns Josephine had sent over, Madeleine thought back to the carriage and the heady demand of Ferguson's kiss. He had controlled himself, but it was a close thing.

She watched in the mirror as Lizzie removed her wig and began piling her hair up in an acceptable chignon. It took only a few minutes to transform her from a renowned actress to an unnoticed spinster. If she didn't get caught, she would pack away all memories of the theatre and store them in one of the deepest recesses of her heart, where she wouldn't have to remember what she had achieved and lost.

She would lose Ferguson too, just as surely as she would leave the stage. He wouldn't offer for her, not after the thrill of their charade died and he remembered just how improper she was.

She had debated telling him about Madame Legrand's threats, if only to warn him that the woman might hold gossip over his head as well. But she didn't say a word. When the play ended, their arrangement would end too. She wouldn't mourn until it was over — and she certainly wouldn't do anything to shorten it.

Her reflection smiled back at her with all the daring she had failed to find in the carriage. She had a month to live the life she secretly dreamed of — and she would live it, whether it was the smart thing to do or not.

CHAPTER FIFTEEN

Later, at Lady Blexham's ball, when Mad was Lady Madeleine again, wrapped up in muslin and weighed down by her spinster's cap, Ferguson pulled her into his arms for their waltz. They had parted ways less than an hour earlier, but he didn't want to waste any opportunity to have her to himself. If all went according to plan, the twins would debut soon, and she would spend her evenings escorting them.

And when her acting career ended, their illicit, stolen time together would end as well.

"If only I could have more than one dance a night," he murmured.

"Do try to be generous," she said, tapping his arm with her fan in mock reproof. "You cannot go about monopolizing all my time."

"Even if we could practice new forms of entertainment?"

It was an obvious gambit, and her eyes sparkled with laughter. "I do find it easier to learn from an excellent instructor, your grace."

He flashed back to the image of her in his carriage, dress open and eyes full of heated wonder. No one in the ton would guess that she was capable of such abandon.

But he knew. And the more nights he spent with her, the more he doubted his ability to let her go.

They fell silent. There was nothing more they could say to each other in public that would not give them away. When he held her, though, that silence was a gift. Within their dance, he didn't have to worry about titles, or the vast estates he had inherited, or the wreckage he had made of his sisters' lives. There was just Madeleine, and the belief that he could be the man she needed — even though he had failed with everyone else.

Spending time with her was also turning him maudlin, he thought.

At least maudlin and lovesick were preferable to bitter and ashamed.

The dance ended well before he was ready to let her go. She looked up at him, some unreadable look on her face — perhaps her thoughts had taken the same turn as his.

Then she looked over his shoulder and her gaze turned wary. He swung around, ready to protect her even though the notion of a physical threat in a ballroom was ludicrous.

"Hello, Ferguson," Caro said. His former mistress — now Westbrook's former mistress, he supposed — was dangerously seductive, in a dark blue gown that clung to her like she had been sewn into it. Her blonde hair was piled high on her head and her face was cleverly painted. Despite her fashionable attire, he noticed the hardness beneath her appearance and felt another flicker of guilt.

She wanted something from him. Whether it was love or revenge, he didn't know. Either way, he didn't care to find out with Madeleine on his arm.

"Lady Greville," he said. Giving her the briefest possible bow, he fixed his gaze at a point above her head. He wouldn't cut her —

he still wished her happy, after all, even if neither of them had any illusions about love when they were together a decade earlier — but he did not want to give her the slightest bit of encouragement.

Even without eye contact, he could tell she was startled by his coldness. Still, she pressed on. "I thought I would see you at all the usual haunts. Don't tell me you've become the sober duke your father was? Or, worse, that you've taken to your chambers like Richard did in the last year of his... illness?"

He didn't like the insinuation, and he met her eyes. "Caro, I've no desire to hurt you, but I am no longer the man you knew ten years ago. I do wish you all the happiness you deserve, but I shan't be the one to provide it."

It was an abrupt remark. He didn't want to waste time on a thinly veiled conversation when one statement could give her the answer she needed. She blanched, and her blue eyes moistened. But just as he thought she might leave, she turned her gaze on Madeleine, who still held Ferguson's arm. "My apologies for interrupting your time with the duke," Caro said. "I know how precious these moments must be for one who is desperate to snare a husband."

The venom in her tone surprised him. Ten years earlier, he was more than willing to provide the sexual satisfaction she could not achieve with her husband, particularly since her heart was not engaged — but any wildness within her had turned to something darker. "I suggest you leave before you embarrass yourself further, Lady Greville."

"Is that why you left London after our affair? You were too embarrassed about being caught in my bed to come back?"

"You know why I left, Caro. It had nothing to do with you."

She tilted her head as though trying to remember, but her

glittering eyes never left his face. "Oh, of course — getting caught with me was just the scandal you needed to get your father to banish you. You cared about your freedom more than anything else, even though it nearly destroyed me. If Greville hadn't died within the year..."

Caro broke off before revealing what Greville might have done — or what he likely did, when he discovered his young wife in the arms of his best friend's disreputable son. He had been too much of a coward to call Ferguson out over it, and as far as Ferguson knew, the affair had been hushed up. But just because Greville was a coward with other men did not mean he ignored a disloyal wife.

She turned back to Madeleine. "You're not young, Lady Madeleine, and so I understand if you are pinning your hopes on the duke making good with you. But there are worse things than being an ape-leader. Ferguson will show them all to you if you stay with him."

"I appreciate your concern over my age and status, Lady Greville, but you need not trouble yourself," Madeleine said smoothly, ever the actress. "I suggest you take this conversation elsewhere if you don't have the sense to end it, though. The next dance is about to begin."

Caro narrowed her eyes at Madeleine's astonishing directness. "Have a care, Lady Madeleine. If you let your claws show like that, Ferguson will run off to that mistress of his. What is the name of that girl from Seven Dials? I would wager she's not even French — probably just a little workhouse rat. Ferguson likes them desperate, after all. And if he does turn into his brother, better that he does it in the slums than in the ballrooms."

A small crowd had gathered around them, pretending to prepare for a quadrille, but they all listened avidly. No surprise there — the ton always circled at the slightest hint of blood.

But everyone was shocked when the earl of Westbrook emerged from the crush to grasp Caro's elbow. Westbrook was the last man Ferguson expected to see at Caro's side, particularly at a boring affair such as this one. "You've made enough of a show of yourself for one night, don't you think?"

Caro tried to pull away from him, but he held her fast. "Leave off, my dear," he said in a low voice. "This isn't who you are."

She blinked up at him, and the tears she had hidden during her verbal attack came back to the surface. Ferguson watched her soften, saw the girl she had been beneath the woman she had become, and felt something uncomfortably like guilt replace his annoyance.

Westbrook looked right at Ferguson, his eyes holding a deadly glare. "Stay away from Caroline, Rothwell. You've damaged her enough for one lifetime."

The earl turned away then, dragging the woman with him. He may have claimed that he wanted to take a new mistress since Caro had left him — but his feelings for her went beyond what he pretended at the theatre. Ferguson never expected to see Westbrook give up his bachelor life, but he seemed ready to throw it away for Caro.

Madeleine coughed in an artificial way, drawing him back to her. "Can we leave the dance floor?" she whispered.

The sharks still watched them. He plastered on his most disaffected look. Forcing his features into some semblance of boredom was even harder than talking to Caro. "Shall I procure you some refreshment after that shocking display, Lady Madeleine?"

She inclined her head, having an easier time of maintaining vacant pleasantry than he did. He escorted her through the throngs, found a glass of champagne — and watched her down it, then a second one, like she was a sailor at the grog barrel.

He took the empty glasses away and handed them to the startled footman, taking two more glasses from the tray. "Slower this time, Mad," he said as he gave her another glass. "We wouldn't want you to choke to death."

"At least I wouldn't have to see Lady Greville again," she muttered. But she sipped this one — still faster than most ladies would, but not fast enough to raise eyebrows.

Then she stared at him over the glass, eyes filled with questions. The one she asked was not what he expected.

"How many other women will treat us to a display such as Lady Greville's?"

He looked around. They were mostly secluded, still in full sight of the ballroom, but far enough from other guests to talk freely. "Are you asking how many mistresses I've had?"

"Consider it a matter of academic interest. If I'm to chaperone your sisters, I need to know which ladies might cause them trouble."

"Is it only academic interest, Mad?"

She drained her glass and gestured for his, still full in his hand. "I never overindulge, but you have driven me to it," she said. "And yes, it is only academic interest. Why should I care what kind of man you were in the past?"

He gave her the fourth glass of champagne. Other than in his carriage, he had never seen her this close to losing her composure. "You seem overwrought."

Madeleine waved her glass. "Why would I be overwrought? Your decision to leave that poor woman to face Greville alone while you went about your life in Scotland doesn't affect me at all. But between that and leaving your family under your father's thumb, it's important for me to know who else you've disappointed if I shall help your sisters navigate the ton."

He didn't like that she claimed this had nothing to do with her — as though she had no feelings at all for him beyond the assistance he provided. And he especially didn't like the implications she made about his character. "I was desperate then. I'm not desperate now. And I will not abandon you, Mad, no matter how badly this all turns out."

"How many?" she asked, ignoring his excuses. "A handful? A score? Enough to fill this ballroom?"

"Caro was the only one with whom I parted badly," he said, sidestepping her request to count his past mistresses. She would run into some of them — it would be impossible not to — but they were all too discreet to mention it in front of her.

She sighed into her champagne. He could tell from her flushed cheeks that she was already feeling the effects. "I wish I could believe you, Ferguson," she said softly.

She turned on her heel and walked toward the chairs along the opposite wall, taking another glass of champagne as she went. She swayed slightly as she walked, no longer steady on her feet, and he watched until she made it safely to her seat. But even though he didn't want to leave, wanted to tell her he was a different man than everyone thought, he did not follow her. She didn't want to listen — and she would not be pleased if he drew any more attention to them than Caro already had.

So he turned on his heel, striding out the door with her condemnation still ringing in his ears. He couldn't promise her he would never leave her. That would require giving up his dream of returning to Scotland, and he was not prepared to take that step. If he stayed to fulfill his duties, he would inevitably get bound to the dukedom as well — and there would be no freedom for him, despite his power.

Of course, he could protect her just as easily in Scotland, if Mad agreed to marry him.

He stood in the cold April night, feeling everything tilt into place. As Sophronia reminded him nearly daily, he would have to marry someday, if only to produce an heir. Madeleine was the perfect candidate — excellent reputation, equally excellent dowry, and a secret rebellious streak that would make his father spin in his grave. If he took her to Scotland and stayed there, he could risk marrying someone he cared for. After all, it would be hard to turn into his father if he never stepped foot on a ducal property again. And Scotland wouldn't be so dull with a woman like Madeleine at his side.

All he had to do was convince her that he wasn't the man the ton saw — and that life as his wife would be a suitable replacement for the theatre.

CHAPTER SIXTEEN

The next morning, in the breakfast room, Madeleine had a revelation.

Gin may have been called "blue ruin" by the lower classes, but champagne was the devil's drink.

At least she was still feigning her reducing diet to avoid dinner parties. Even the smell of the rasher of bacon on the sideboard made her stomach heave. She nibbled a dry piece of toast, for once grateful that she was confined to bread. She still felt unsettled, though, like the room would start spinning again if she moved her head.

"Can I bring you anything else, my lady? Kippers, perhaps?" Chilton asked.

She put her hand to her mouth at the thought. The butler had already given her a once-over when she arrived for breakfast; he must have seen her come home the night before. But the end of the ball was a hazy, champagne-drenched blur, and she did not remember preparing for bed.

She declined the offer. The unusual good humor on his face suggested that he knew what was wrong with her. Chilton had been a fixture in the house since she arrived in London, and he sometimes betrayed an amused, affectionate nature at odds with his choice of careers. She should have been mortified — but of all the things she had done in the past few weeks, arriving at the breakfast table still suffering from the effects of too much champagne was the least of her sins.

Aunt Augusta entered the breakfast room, her forehead wrinkled with concern. She did not take a plate from the sideboard; it was well past the time she usually broke her fast. She sat down across from Madeleine and gave her a searching look. "Are you feeling well, my dear? I heard about your encounter with Lady Greville at the ball last night."

No doubt everyone had heard about their conversation. A notorious widow confronting a prim spinster about the most eligible bachelor of the season was too juicy to ignore. "Lady Greville said nothing I could not deal with."

Her aunt frowned. "Then why were you foxed when we came home last night? I wanted to ask you then, but you were not in any state to answer questions."

A wave of nausea hit her, but she couldn't evade Aunt Augusta's questioning. "I may have been a bit startled by Lady Greville. The duke sought to calm my nerves and I had more champagne than I intended."

"You must have drunk a whole bottle to leave you in the state you were in," Augusta said. Then her voice softened. "I cannot blame you, though. Lady Greville used to be a sweet woman, but she is not someone I would recommend knowing now."

"Then you aren't angry that I had so much champagne?" Madeleine asked, feeling a little like she was nine years old again, new to England and this house.

Aunt Augusta laughed. "I've had too much champagne before

myself. There's no harm in it occasionally, but you should not do it every night. It would be hard to chaperone Rothwell's sisters if you develop a reputation for overindulgence."

Madeleine did not want the reminder of her responsibilities. She was supposed to go to Rothwell House in a few hours to make plans for their debut, but she was not eager to see the twins if they were still openly hostile.

Augusta interrupted those thoughts, and her tone snapped Madeleine back to attention. "I do hope you know that if something is troubling you, you may always come to me? You have not seemed yourself in weeks..."

She trailed off, hoping that Madeleine would open her heart in the silence. Madeleine smiled tightly, nodding her agreement. If she could take Aunt Augusta into her confidence, it would all be easier — but Augusta would never permit her to act, let alone spend time with Ferguson as his supposed mistress.

Her aunt sighed. "Very well. If I can be of help, though, do let me know? Perhaps you can retire to Lancashire early this summer if you are still bent on avoiding society."

It was the kind of reward that Amelia would want, not Madeleine — particularly not when this was the most exciting season she'd ever had. But Augusta didn't suspect that. "Thank you, Aunt Augusta. I will be fine, I am sure."

Her aunt stood, rounding the table to pat her fondly on the head. The gesture usually comforted her, but not this time. If she couldn't tell the family her secret, she would have to be more careful — with Alex and Augusta both asking questions, it would be even harder to maintain her ruse.

Augusta left and Chilton replenished Madeleine's tea. She sat quietly, hoping that if she sat long enough she might be able to stand again without the room spinning. It took longer than she anticipated and she finally sent Chilton away, earning an impertinent smile from him when she said she wanted to be alone with her thoughts.

But her solitude was soon interrupted again, this time by Amelia. Her cousin sank into the chair Augusta had vacated, and Madeleine noticed how much Amelia's frown was beginning to match Augusta's.

"What happened last night?" Amelia asked. "I've never seen you drink so much in a week, let alone at a single event."

Madeleine shrugged. Even that movement was too much for her head. "Can we discuss this another time, Mellie? I have the devil's own headache, and I must somehow recover in time to go to Rothwell House this afternoon."

"Should you be spending any more time with the man than you already are?"

"I likely won't even see him. I am visiting the twins to discuss their debut." She paused, not sure she wanted to continue the conversation, but knowing Amelia would whether Madeleine wanted to or not. "But even if I were seeing Rothwell, what does it matter to you?"

Amelia lowered her voice. "I do not like that your life is in the hands of someone we do not know — someone who has a terrible reputation. Do you not think it is time to tell Alex so he can find a solution that does not involve Rothwell?"

Even though her encounter with Caro the previous evening had raised doubts about Ferguson's past, she did not like Amelia's characterization of him. "That is just like you, isn't it? You've judged him and determined he is not worthy without even a single real conversation."

"That is unkind," Amelia said, her spine stiffening. "He isn't one of my suitors — he is someone who I fear could really hurt you."

"And how does it feel that he is not one of your suitors?" Madeleine asked, her headache driving some malicious desire she couldn't acknowledge. "Are you jealous that he chose me instead of you?"

"Jealous? I would sincerely wish you happy if I thought the man would come up to snuff," Amelia exclaimed. "But men like Rothwell do not change. He could hold this over your head for the rest of your life. You cannot stand against one of the most powerful men in Britain. You need to end this now before anything happens."

"He is not as bad as you make him out to be, Mellie. He can be quite amusing and considerate..."

Amelia cut her off. "He is courting you. Men are always at their best during courtship. But he will turn into what he has always been — a rake. There is a chance he will instead turn into his father, since most men do. But that would be even worse, and neither outcome would make you happy."

"He's not courting me. He is helping me avoid detection so that his sisters are not ruined, nothing more."

"I saw the way he looked at you last night," Amelia insisted. "He has his own interests at heart, not yours. You have to tell Alex everything."

"No. If I tell Alex, he will force me to stop, and I am not ready."

"Not ready to give up acting, or not ready to break off your relationship with Rothwell?"

"Acting," Madeleine replied, even though she suspected the real answer was some combination of the two.

Amelia wore a defeated look that Madeleine rarely saw on her strong-willed face. "Please do not get caught," she said, reaching across the table to squeeze Madeleine's hand. "I could not bear it if you were banished."

Madeleine watched her leave, not sure if she wanted to hug her or hit her. Amelia had always been the domineering type, but her insistence that Madeleine tell Alex everything was surprising. After all, Amelia had been perfectly willing to support Madeleine's desire to act before Ferguson became part of her disguise.

She picked up her tea, realized it was cold, and sighed as she set it down. She was not proud of how she had spoken to Amelia, and for the first time, she truly saw the selfishness of what she was doing. At first, playing Hamlet in male garb was a grand lark — but as the ton discovered the theatre, the stakes rose, and her acting threatened to bring down her entire family. No one had recognized her, and she now doubted that anyone ever would, but there was still a chance someone would discover her.

And yet even with that risk, she refused to quit, refused to sacrifice the last handful of nights when she could feel the worship of the crowd — and, more than that, feel like she had a life of her own. Those same nights were also her last chance to see the adoration in Ferguson's eyes as he collected her backstage after each play, to seize the opportunity to kiss him again as they had done in his carriage.

Selfish or not, she was not ready to give him up.

CHAPTER SEVENTEEN

A few hours later, Madeleine stood outside Rothwell House, wishing she could refuse Sophronia's invitation to plan the twins' upcoming debuts. She had barely spared a thought for the girls since the night Ferguson took her as his false mistress. But it wouldn't be wise to irritate the dowager duchess, even if Madeleine did not want to be a chaperone.

As she ascended the steps to the imposing front door, she wondered how quickly she could find suitors who would remove the girls from her care. With their dowries and looks, it could be accomplished well before the end of the season. She may not have had success on the marriage mart herself, but she knew how most matches were accomplished. As long as the twins were more amiable than they were during their visit to Salford House, they possessed everything necessary to make brilliant matches.

The door swung open just as she reached it. An old butler greeted her with the proper degree of deference and led her upstairs to the family wing. As they walked, she was glad her acting abilities covered her fascination — of all the houses she had visited in London, this was perhaps the nicest.

It felt more like a palace than a house, really. She had been once before, to a ball the old duke and his third duchess gave to celebrate Richard becoming the heir to the dukedom. The timing was odd, since Richard was an erratic man not given to elegant parties, and he was replacing an alcoholic older brother who had drowned in the Serpentine — but the general sentiment was that the duchess had seized on it as an excuse to give a party. After all, there had been little to celebrate since Ferguson's banishment and Ellie's disastrous marriage.

At that party, Madeleine had seen only the ballroom, which was impeccably decorated and could hold nearly five hundred people when opened into the drawing rooms around it. If anything, the rooms on the second floor were even more elegant. Most families devoted all their wealth to the public spaces, but it shouldn't have surprised her that the old duke cared as much about the private rooms, particularly since he rarely offered entertainments. For a man obsessed with status, and with ready funds available, it made a sort of twisted sense to create lavishly appointed rooms that no one else would see or use.

They passed through room after gorgeously decorated room — a library, galleries full of family portraits, and several drawing rooms. A fire burned in every grate, and Madeleine could hardly guess the expense of heating every room in a house this size. As with many older houses, there were few passageways. The large rooms all connected to each other, which gave Madeleine the opportunity to see more of the house than she otherwise might have.

She was distracted from her discreet perusal of the furnishings by the music wafting toward her, becoming more distinct as they progressed. The song began to take shape for her as they walked. It was an old melody, a version of the folk song "Greensleeves," but as it was played in this house, it sounded like a dirge. The pianoforte was mournful, and the harp had all the cheer of Juliet in her tomb. It was sad music, expertly played, and she guessed that the musicians had spent much time practicing with each other.

Despite the tone, Madeleine could not remember ever hearing something so beautiful. She didn't want it to end, and so she was grateful when the butler silently ushered her into the room without the usual announcement. The twins sat at the instruments, facing each other and ignoring everything beyond the bubble created by their music. Sophronia was nowhere to be seen, but Ellie was present. A rapt expression lit her face and temporarily stripped away the veneer of easy humor that Madeleine had seen her display in her own home.

Whether by coincidence or as a direct reflection of Madeleine's arrival, the threads of the song slowly rewove themselves. As Madeleine hovered in the doorway, she felt the music change, gain speed, as something more akin to anger entered the melody. The girl at the piano looked grimly at her fingers as they rushed over the keys, while the other twin was nearly on the verge of tears. By the time they brought the piece to a close, Madeleine felt almost like she was under physical attack, even though it surely had nothing to do with her.

Then they turned to her, and she took an involuntary step back. The looks they gave her matched the music completely — sadness overlaid with hatred.

Ellie chuckled. "You will have to do better than that in the ton, my dears, unless you want the whole world to know your thoughts."

The pianist smoothed her expression first. "Lady Madeleine, what a wonderful honor to receive you," she said. If her eyes weren't still filled with anger, she might have sounded sincere.

Madeleine's champagne headache pounded back into her consciousness. The urge to turn tail and flee was an almost physical thing. Their talent was impressive indeed to rework the song with their changing emotions, but that didn't make her feel any better about bearing the brunt of their anger.

She sternly reminded herself of her role — she was their chaperone, not their friend. "Shall we dispense with the pleasantries and move to the matter at hand?" she asked, taking a seat in the armchair across the teacart from Ellie. "The sooner we can settle on your debut, the sooner I can leave you in peace."

They shot her matching looks of resentment, and she didn't bother trying to hide her sigh. At least she had a night off from the theatre — this could well take all afternoon.

"Maria and I do not wish to debut," the pianist declared. "You may take yourself off now that we've settled it."

So Kate was the angry one and Maria the sad one. "Why do you not wish to debut?" Madeleine asked.

"We *do* wish to debut," Maria said, twisting her fingers in the folds of her black gown. "Just... not yet."

"Is it the mourning period?" Madeleine asked gently. "There may be some raised eyebrows for coming out so soon, but everyone knows your circumstances. I do not think many will find fault."

Kate snorted. "We would have already left off mourning if we had bought any gowns in the last four years that were not black, grey or lavender. It is the old man's fault we still have not debuted — we do not miss him."

"Then why not come out? If your dancing is as superlative as your music, you will be the sensation of the season. Your poor brother will be inundated with requests for your hands before the first ball even ends."

Maria and Kate exchanged looks.

"If you do not believe me, you should see the other ladies out this year — not a single one could hold a candle to either of you."

She wanted to flatter and encourage, if only so she could finish with them and leave, but as Maria's lip started to tremble, Madeleine knew something was amiss. "Will you tell me what is causing your concern?"

The twins glanced at each other again, the instinctive gesture of two girls accustomed to having only each other for support. Then it all spilled out — in a torrent of words, interrupting and finishing each other's sentences, Kate and Maria compared their previous life to the worst sort of prison. All they wanted was a reprieve before being forced to seek out husbands.

"Did you tell Ferguson this?" Madeleine asked when their words petered out into silence.

"We tried, but he is just as bad as Father," Kate said bitterly. "He cares only for settling us quickly so he can return to Scotland."

Madeleine felt her face drain of color. Ferguson had never mentioned a desire to return to Scotland — but then, she had no reason to demand his confidences despite the role he played to protect her.

Ellie noticed her pallor. "Tea, Lady Madeleine? You do not look quite the thing today."

Madeleine turned toward the woman, expecting mockery from one who so overtly hated Ferguson, but there was only sympathy on her face. As Ellie poured, she said to the twins, "Our brother is not quite like Father yet, although he shall be someday. I can assure you that he will not arrange your matches just to teach you a lesson. He wants you off his hands, but I doubt he specifically seeks your unhappiness."

"Is that what happened with you and Folkestone?" Kate asked, as though a grand mystery had been resolved. "Father never mentioned it, save to say that Maria and I were not under any circumstances to emulate you."

Maria gasped at her twin's directness, but Ellie just laughed. "Good — I hope I made the old devil lose some sleep. My story does not bear repeating, except to say you would be wise to choose a man who can give you the kind of family you want. Ours always seems to find a way to fail you."

The words struck home for everyone in the room. The twins were both speechless, stunned by their sister's blunt wisdom and the anger beneath it. For Madeleine, though, the impact was different. She had spent her life wishing her parents had lived for her, and marriage was the only way to build a family that was hers. No man had ever lived up to that expectation, and she had all but given up hope that it would happen.

The only man who made her reconsider her spinsterhood was Ferguson.

And that same man planned to return to Scotland at the end of the season, once again leaving his family behind.

She sipped her tea to calm her churning stomach. They continued discussing the debut, and she reassured them that she would not pressure them into marriages they did not want. The twins ultimately agreed to debut a month later, giving them time to plan the festivities and also purchase the full wardrobes necessary for their stations.

Sophronia finally arrived, and the talk devolved into invitations, catering, and remedying the twins' wardrobes. Through it all, Madeleine's thoughts kept returning to how they all felt about Ferguson. Their condemnation did not match the man she knew — just as her actions in Seven Dials were far removed from the paragon of virtue the Stauntons saw. She knew better than anyone that blood did not always breed familial loyalty. If it did, her parents would have left France with her rather than giving their lives to her father's country.

The evidence pointed to Ferguson leaving London again. Whether it was a stubborn desire to thwart his father from this side of the grave, or the cowardly abandonment that Ellie hinted at, she didn't know.

But what if his family was wrong? Could she risk believing that he was really a hero bent on saving her from ruin? Or was ruin inevitable — and would he abandon her the moment she became inconvenient to him?

CHAPTER EIGHTEEN

A week later, Madeleine thought she might emerge from the month-long run of the play with her reputation intact. There was not even a breath of suspicion that Madame Guerrier was not who she claimed to be. The ton was enthralled by the French actress, clamored to see her on stage, and never hinted at an alternative explanation for her identity.

The constant praise slowly alleviated the fear underscoring every performance. The aristocrats saw what they wanted to see, oblivious to the deception playing out under their collective noses — so oblivious that Madeleine began to wonder if she could maintain the deception forever.

She said as much to Ferguson as he escorted her into "her" house after yet another standing ovation and no hint of recognition from anyone. "Wouldn't it be lovely to always live like this?" she asked as Bristow took their coats, hats and gloves.

Ferguson stalked over to the solitary card on the console table and ripped it in half without opening it. "If Caro doesn't stop writing to you with dire warnings about my character, I don't know what I shall do."

"At least she's confining her warnings to Marguerite. She must know that the mistress is in danger where the spinster is not."

He paused in front of her, opened his mouth — then clamped it shut as though he had thought better of his statement. Finally, he said, "Do not doubt that my intentions toward you are honorable, Mad."

She had no idea what he meant. Did he simply mean that he would not touch her again? He had behaved like a proper gentleman over the past week, even though she wanted him to kiss her again. But as the nights progressed, he grew increasingly agitated, seeking her out at every ball, talking with her as long as he could in their secret house before sending her back to the Stauntons.

They had talked of all manner of things — books, art, the gossip he missed during his absence. And he listened too, as though her opinions were all he cared to know. She had even told him everything she felt when she was on stage, how the act of performing excited her in a way that nothing else in her life ever had.

But even though she loved their conversations, she thought Ferguson's interest had cooled. From what she had heard, a rake never talked to a woman when he could have her in his bed. She started to think that their first carriage ride, when he kissed her breathless, had been just a bit of fun to him — but his talk of "intentions" brought all those feelings rushing back.

She wanted to know what he meant, but he pulled her forward and they climbed the stairs in silence. If they succeeded in their masquerade, both of them would be free to return to their old lives. A discreet conclusion to her acting career should be her sole goal, particularly since any further liaison with Ferguson would be impossible.

In all their conversations, the one topic he never discussed was the future — and he avoided all mention of Scotland. After talking to his sisters, she'd wanted to ask him whether he was staying in London. But she had no claim over him, and she wouldn't risk revealing the feelings slowly growing in her heart. The thought of a lifetime without ever seeing Ferguson again saddened her more than she cared to admit. And when he inevitably left, she would lose her chance to experience everything Ferguson's touch had awakened in her.

It might be worse to know, to ache for those feelings for the rest of her life — but once their month together was over, she might never have the opportunity again.

So when he swung open the door to her chamber and released her arm, she reached out to him. "Won't you come in? I have heard it is all the rage for mistresses to allow men to watch their toilettes."

His eyebrows slammed together. "Where the devil did you hear that?"

"I have been in the theatre for weeks, Ferguson. Surely you don't think me that innocent?"

It was the wrong thing to say. She recognized the implication immediately. He pushed her into the room, and her waiting maid squeaked in protest.

Madeleine was too arrested by the fierce gleam in his eyes to spare a thought for Lizzie. "Get out," Ferguson said, his words directed at the maid even though his gaze never left Madeleine's face.

Lizzie disappeared, closing the door behind her. Ferguson broke away and turned the key in the lock. Madeleine heard the bolt slide into the hole with a metallic whisper, amplified in the silent room — a sound that was dangerous and exciting all at once.

He turned back to her, slipping the key into his coat pocket.

"Now, Lady Madeleine," he said, in a dark drawl that made her flush, "do you care to explain why I am here?"

She blushed even hotter, ashamed of the desire that tempted her. "You may leave if you wish, your grace," she whispered.

He stepped toward her, cupping her chin in his hand and nudging it up so she was forced to meet his eyes. "I never thought I would like to be called 'your grace,' but you could make me crave it."

She swallowed, her mouth dry as she saw the raw need in his eyes. She took a step back, and he caressed her face as she pulled away. His touch was soft, almost tender, and there was no doubt that he still wanted her — he closed the distance between them, placing his hands low on her hips as he guided her into his embrace.

"I am sure you are still an innocent, despite your profession," he said, grazing a kiss on her forehead. "And I don't believe you would throw yourself away on any of the bounders loitering at the theatre," he continued, sliding his hands down the curve of her hips to rest on her derriere.

"But I'm not a saint, Mad." He pulled her even closer toward him, and she could feel the hardness of his arousal against her belly. "I could be more dangerous to you than anyone if you don't take care."

This was madness. The very name he called her should have been a warning. But her desire to experience all those delicious feelings that his kisses created overrode her prudence. "I don't want you to be a saint, Ferguson."

She watched the battle between honor and hunger play out on his face. Honor was on the verge of winning, and some instinct drove her forward, arching into him and offering up her mouth. She would die of embarrassment if he set her aside...

...but then she felt his right hand leave her bottom to rest on her neck. "You are going to be the death of me," he muttered.

His lips claimed hers. She opened for him immediately, wanting the heat of his mouth to reignite all the need still smoldering within her. His hand at the base of her head held her tight. She couldn't move away from him — but she wouldn't have moved away from him even if she was free to go. She wanted to get closer, until there was nothing left between them. She had the strangest desire to twine around his body, like ivy on a lamppost, supported by him and yet capable of pulling him down.

She wrapped her arms around his shoulders, using her hands to press him deeper into the kiss. He groaned in response, and his free hand caressed her bottom, running across the curves encased by her tailored breeches. The heat was building again, and she moaned as the seam of her breeches rubbed against that increasingly sensitive bit of flesh between her legs.

He broke away at the sound and she opened her eyes. He grinned at the disappointment on her face, grazing one last kiss on the corner of her mouth. The grin made him seem younger, less cynical, and her heart ached for the man he might have been.

But Ferguson wasn't focused on introspection. He fixed his eyes firmly on a different prize. "I told you that the next time I kissed you, I would punish you for this abuse."

She didn't understand his meaning until he started to unbutton her jacket. Then she remembered his reaction to her bound breasts in the coach and blushed. "How do you intend to punish me?"

He ignored her question, making quick work of her jacket, waistcoat, cravat, and shirt. Tossing them aside, he skimmed his hands down her sides, exploring the contrast between her bindings and her soft flesh. She shivered as he splayed his hands across her belly, his thumb tracing a line around her navel.

Then his hands came back up. He ran his thumbs over her nipples, still trapped within their linen prison. She felt them hardening, coming to life for him, and she arched toward him, hoping this time he wouldn't stop before she understood what was building inside her.

He dipped a finger into the hollow between her breasts, and she gasped as his callused skin rubbed against her soft flesh. He retreated slowly, teasingly, pulling the end of her bindings with him, and her breath hitched as the knot came free.

"Turn," he commanded softly.

She looked up into his face. His eyes were sharp with need and his mouth glistened in anticipation of their next kiss. But there was a playfulness to his smile that told her everything she needed to know.

Her heart might be in danger.

She certainly hoped her virtue was.

But Ferguson wouldn't hurt her, regardless of what transpired between them.

So she turned away from him, and the top layer of linen came away in his hands. She felt like she was dancing a new kind of waltz, and he partnered her perfectly, pulling the cloth with just the right amount of tension to keep her turning in place. And when she faced him again, he caught her chin, tilted it, and gave her a languorous kiss that kept her blood simmering.

"Again," he whispered, pulling away and tightening his grip on her bindings.

It took six slow, torturous revolutions before the last bit of cloth fell away — six long, aching kisses that brought her to a boiling point of need. He kissed her again, pulling her into the circle of his arms, and this time her bare, sensitized nipples grazed against his jacket. She gasped into his mouth as first one hand, then a second, came up to cup her breasts.

He shifted away from her, pulling back to watch as her flesh came back to life under his gaze. She always felt hot pinpricks of sensation as the blood rushed back after her bindings were released, but this time the feeling was heightened as his hands warmed her skin.

"God, Mad, if you knew how I've dreamed of this," he said, his voice reverent.

Her desire was so high she could barely think, let alone be shy about standing in front of him in only a tight pair of breeches and her high-heeled shoes. But still, she was shocked when one arm slid underneath her to lift her up against him. "Put your legs around me," he ordered, and she did as he asked, her breeches dangerously tight against the center of her need. She didn't understand, dimly thought of protesting — but then his mouth claimed her nipple, and in the fire of her response, it all became clear.

He tormented her slowly, first one breast and then the other, until she was moaning incoherently in his arms. She leaned in, nearly sobbing in his ear as her moans turned to inarticulate pleas. He didn't stop, and the combination of his tongue and teeth toying with her still-recovering flesh made her understand the madness he had warned her of.

His punishment — which had long since turned to worship — ended before she reached the mysterious peak he was driving her toward, and she didn't know whether to be disappointed or grateful for the reprieve. But when he set her on her feet and tried to renew his assault on her mouth, she broke away. She had dreamed of him too, and she reached out greedily to tug at the first button of his jacket.

He didn't move to help her, but he didn't make her stop. He played with her hair as she worked on the buttons, and she felt her hairpins falling to the floor as he pulled off her wig. Before she could finish untying his cravat, he was running his hands through the mass of her hair, letting it tumble down her naked back.

"I've waited to see your hair too," he reminded her, brushing it from her face before attempting to kiss her again.

She stood her ground, placing her hands on his chest and pushing him the smallest fraction away from her lips. "Your jacket first, if you please."

He chuckled, shrugging out of his tight jacket and letting it fall to the floor. He tossed his creased cravat on top of the jacket before unbuttoning his waistcoat. Soon it was gone too, and she reached up to tug at the drawstring of his shirt. The shirt came open, and she brushed her thumb across the Adam's apple that had been hiding behind his neckcloth. He groaned and captured her hand in his, kissing it before pinning it to her side.

But then he tugged the tails of his shirt from the waistband of his trousers. She swallowed as the hard planes of his stomach were revealed. He pulled the shirt over his head in one motion, and everything rippled in a most delightful way.

He was a Greek statue come to life, a god disguised as a man, slipping out of his costume to claim his maiden. She had felt his muscles when they danced, knew he was strong by the way he held her suspended in his arms while he tormented her breasts, but nothing had prepared her for this. He wasn't overly large, nothing like a farmhand — he was perfectly proportioned for his height, the kind of specimen a painter would kill to have as a muse.

His chest was broad and sculpted, crowned by tiny nipples that she wanted to torment as much as he had tortured hers. His trousers were slung low on his hips, and she swallowed as she saw the indentations of his pelvis below the well-defined muscles of his abdomen... and the slight trail of dark hair that led her gaze to the unmistakable bulge in his trousers.

"Those green eyes will be my undoing," Ferguson said, kissing them closed to stop her exploration of his body. Before she could protest, he picked her up again, cradling her in his arms and striding toward the bed.

She should have been nervous, but in that moment, his arms were the safest place in the world. He shifted her weight against his chest so that he could pull back the coverlet, and then he laid her on the sheets.

He lay down beside her, propped on one arm as he examined her naked breasts. He seemed fascinated by them, as though he had never seen anything so perfect — and she knew she misinterpreted his gaze if she believed that, since he'd surely had mistresses more well endowed than she. She tried to turn onto her side, to cover herself with her arm — but he placed a hand on her belly and kept her flat on her back beside him. "Stay still, Mad. I only want to give you pleasure."

He leaned over her, kissing her again as his hand fumbled with the fastening of her breeches. The placket came free and she felt his hand sliding under the loosened waistband to tangle in her curls. But his movement was constrained by her men's garb, and she whimpered in his mouth as she tried to tilt herself up toward his hand.

Ferguson laughed. "If you didn't look so damned delectable in these breeches, I would insist you burn them."

She flushed at the compliment. He didn't linger over his words, moving to kneel at her feet. He pulled off her bejeweled shoes, then removed her breeches and hose. She imagined herself from Ferguson's vantage point — hair tossed wildly around her face, lungs heaving as she gasped for air, breasts straining for his touch. Her legs had fallen open as he stripped her, and he was staring at her sex. She felt moisture there, like she was somehow hungry for him, and she blushed as his gaze intensified. She tried to close her legs, to draw his attention away from that private part of her, but his hand shot out to grab her ankle.

"Madeleine," he groaned. He knelt between her legs, pulling her ankle up as he sank into the mattress, nudging her other leg away with his knee, until she was spread before him like an offering. He leaned down and placed a kiss on her navel, and her hands balled into fists. The thin scrap of sanity she still possessed told her she should push him away, but her blood was thrumming with the need to pull him closer.

But he didn't move up her torso to kiss her. He slid lower, skimming his hands up to her hips as though he intended to hold her in place.

"What are you doing?" she asked, propping herself up on her elbows to watch him. The need was still there, but whatever her body wanted, she hadn't expected this.

He lifted his head, and his blue eyes were hazy with the same desire that flooded her veins. "Do you trust me, Mad?"

She nodded slowly, hypnotized by his hunger.

He grinned at her. "Then trust me when I say you will love this."

She watched his head dip again, his dark hair stark against her pale skin.

Then he kissed the very center of her need. All her thoughts shattered, her mind wiped clean as every nerve focused on what Ferguson was doing to her.

He wasn't slow, and he wasn't quick — he somehow found the exact tempo that would have her begging in his arms. He flicked his tongue across her aching nub once, twice, ten times, until she tried to arch off the bed under the hands that held her down. Just as she reached the pinnacle of the need building inside her, he slipped away, laving the folds around her entrance, his tongue dipping into her slick passage and adding to the moisture his ministrations had wrought. And when her breathing grew a fraction less ragged, and her thoughts began to return, he restarted the process, returning to torment her until she was writhing beneath him again.

She lost count of how many times he did this, but she felt like her whole body was flushed, her legs quivering around him as he continued his onslaught. She had long since fallen back onto the bed, biting her lips to quiet the moans she couldn't contain. She didn't know how much more she could take...

...and then his wicked tongue stopped, just long enough for him to breathe a command. "Come for me, Madeleine," he whispered, his breath hot against her sex. Then he stroked her with his tongue, harder and faster than before, and she felt all of her need coiling for him, spiraling up, tighter and tighter to a point that almost felt like pain. Just as she reached the top, his hand found her breast, and the unexpected caress was enough to push her over the edge.

The world exploded around her, and she screamed his name as her whole body shuddered in climax. Without his hand to stop her, she drove up toward him, almost violent in her need — and he followed her movements, kept his lips locked around her as he wrung every last sensation from her.

When it was over, when his movements had subsided to a few feathery kisses on her inner thigh and a slow circling of her nipple with his thumb, she floated in the warmth of her flushed, sated body. She could have stayed there for hours, content as long as he still touched her. But he placed a final kiss low on her belly, right above her thatch of curls, and the kiss felt like a goodbye.

He started to pull away, but she caught his hand before it could leave her breast. "Why are you stopping?" she asked, her voice sounding hoarse and breathy even to her ears.

"For you," he said shortly.

She threaded her fingers through his. From the bulge in his breeches, he must be desperately uncomfortable. She and Amelia had read enough risqué poetry and scandalous picture books when Aunt Augusta was away to know what that bulge meant — and what was supposed to happen next.

"Don't stop for my sake," she whispered, pulling him toward her. "I do not want this to end until you've had all of me."

CHAPTER NINETEEN

Ferguson felt the resolve in her fingers, heard the need in her voice, saw the way her eyes focused with fascinated greed on his manhood. He had even tasted how much she wanted him, drenched with desire and already opening for him.

But he couldn't deflower an innocent, no matter how much she wanted him to — or how much his cock ached for her.

He rose to a kneeling position on the bed, still between her legs, his hand extended since she refused to let him go. "Mad, I won't ruin you, regardless of what we want."

She sat up, her legs spread wide around his thighs, uninhibited by her nakedness. "What you did to me was the most pleasurable experience I've felt in my entire life," she said, reaching up to pull his lips toward hers. "If that is what it means to be ruined, then I accept my fate."

He allowed her to kiss him, knowing it was suicide but unable to deny the temptation. She was still inexperienced, but her wild enthusiasm made up for her artlessness. His past mistresses were well versed in giving a man pleasure — but he had never been harder than he was at this moment.

She was going to kill him. He groaned and pulled away, grabbing her shoulders with his hands so she could not follow. "Ruin doesn't just mean a quick fuck and a bit of pleasure," he said, harsher than he meant to be. "Ruin means being cast out of society. Ruin means destroying your life, destroying your family. It may even mean raising a bastard child who will be punished for your mistakes. I sincerely doubt you are willing to accept any of that."

Madeleine set her jaw, and he knew that he was lost. "I am acting on a public stage, pretending to be your mistress, and at constant risk of someone with half a brain recognizing me. All it takes is a moment, and I will suffer the exact fate you so kindly predicted. And if I'm not ruined, I will grow old as Alex's spinster dependent, with nothing but memories of these few weeks to feel like there was a reason why I lived."

Her green eyes filled with tears, and before he could think, he brushed her hair away from her eyes. "Don't pity me," she snapped.

"I feel many things toward you, but pity isn't among them," he retorted. "You are the bravest, maddest, most beautiful creature I've ever seen, and why you think you are destined to be a spinster, I will never know."

She started to deny his words. He shook her shoulders. "If you truly want me to take you, I will. But after tonight, you will never again claim that you are meant to grow old alone. Is that clear?"

She met his gaze straight on, her tears replaced by a need that scorched his soul. "I want to believe you. Show me, Ferguson."

He kissed her, his mouth devouring hers as though he could brand her, as though he could make her feel his intentions in their kiss.

She kissed him back, and he lost himself in her. He wanted to touch all of her at once, and his hands were everywhere — kneading her breast, sliding down her spine, skimming across the cleft of her derriere, gripping her hair to pull her deeper into his kiss. She was writhing in his arms, and he could feel the tension building in her body. This was the kind of passion one might go a whole lifetime without ever finding — and he felt a savage thrill at the thought of making her his.

He stopped his exploration of her body only to unbutton his trousers. Without breaking their kiss, he fumbled until the cloth fell away and his manhood sprang forth, the tip already moist. The need to bury himself inside her was urgent, unstoppable — only his rapidly evaporating control kept him from slamming into her like a beast.

Madeleine felt that control in the way he stretched her out on the bed, in the quick, spare movements he took to peel off his trousers and toss them aside. His fingers found the nub of pleasure that his tongue was so well acquainted with. He stroked her, building her need even hotter as he slid one finger, then two, inside her. And he somehow kissed her with the same measured intensity he used to stoke her pleasure, the same tempo and masterful movements thrusting her closer to that delicious edge.

Finally, she broke away from the kiss. "Ferguson, please," she begged, moving against his hand. She looked into his face, and even though his eyes were as hot and demanding as she felt, the grim cast of his jaw told her just how much his control was costing him.

She reached down for the manroot that strained toward her touch, but he captured her wrist. "Not tonight," he grated out. Pinning her hands above her head, he looked directly into her eyes. "Are you sure?"

She nodded, too far gone to think.

"I want to hear you say it."

She didn't hesitate. "Please, Ferguson. This is all I want."

His eyes flashed. She leaned up to kiss him, but he denied her. "I want to see your face as I take you."

The heat within her soared at the harsh, possessive note in his voice. She closed her eyes as he kept stroking her, one hand holding her wrists in an iron grip while the other drove her to the very brink. His fingers moved away, and she moaned — but then she felt the tip of his shaft against her entrance, and she went deathly still beneath him.

He brushed a kiss over her lips. "After tonight, I won't hurt you again." He slid into her, one careful inch, then another. He was so large, so hard, that she felt he might rip her to pieces, and she gasped as he slowly pushed forward.

She could feel his hand tightening over her wrists as he tried to control his movements. He entered another inch and she stiffened under him. The slow torture was quickly killing her desire, but the memory of that explosive pleasure made her want to see this through.

He pulled back, and even though the pain eased, her frustration grew. "Just finish it!" she cried, arching her hips up in an instinctive need to follow him.

Her offering was his undoing. He drove into her, one breathtakingly smooth stroke that seated him fully into her core. She gasped as he filled her, and when he released his grip on her wrists, she wrapped her arms around his neck to keep him from pulling away again.

He did pull back slowly, only to thrust again. As the pain ebbed and his clever fingers toyed with her flesh, she felt the crest of the wave start to rise, driven by the feel of him moving within her.

He thrust harder, his control slipping, and she moaned as the pleasure grew. His head dipped down and he captured her left nipple in his mouth, the scrape of his teeth and the stroke of his tongue matching the tempo of this thrusts. She wanted to stay there forever, to ride at the very peak of that wave — but he was too skilled at what he did.

She screamed again as her orgasm overtook her. It was more powerful than her first climax, and she felt herself contract around him as though she could trap him within her. He pulled away from her breast, thrust hard and fast, once, twice, three more times, extending the force of her climax. Just as she thought it would never end, he went still, and she felt his seed spill within her.

He collapsed onto her, his breath harsh against her ear. She was strangely glad to have his weight on her, as though the feel of him pressing her into the mattress could help to ground her.

When he finally rolled over, he cradled her against him as he brushed kisses through her hair. She ran her hand lightly over his muscled arm, content to explore now that their lovemaking was done. But the heady rush of finally having Ferguson in her bed had exhausted her, and she soon drifted off into her first peaceful sleep in weeks.

*   *   *

Madeleine awoke slowly, lingering in a half-dream state as long as she could. Not only was she more relaxed than she had been in an age, she couldn't remember the last time she had felt this sated. It was so delightful...

...until she heard the clock in the stairwell start to chime the hour. She counted out of simple curiosity at first, but as the number grew, her alarm escalated. When she realized it was already eleven, she shrieked. She should have been home over two hours earlier. Hopefully Josephine had explained her absence to Aunt Augusta, but she needed to sneak back into Salford House.

She tried to roll out of bed, but Ferguson caught her wrist and pulled her back into his arms. "Where are you off to in such a rush?"

She let him kiss her one last time, but she stopped him before he could continue. "I have to go home before my family returns for the evening. If they catch me, it will be a disaster."

Some deep emotion lurked in his eyes, and she realized she might not want to hear what he was about to say. She tried again to leave, and he let go of her wrist — but his words stopped her. "Perhaps they would be easier to manage if you told them we are engaged."

Madeleine sucked in a breath. She was too shocked to control herself. "Are you *offering* for me?" she blurted out.

"Would you prefer that I didn't?"

He was grinning, the smile of a man who thought he would get the answer he wanted. He had propped himself up on his elbow, leaning in to her, a sheet sliding low across that point where his muscles tapered toward his pelvis.

She swallowed convulsively. This man, this wonderful, insane man, was asking her to marry him. She tried to comprehend it, to understand it and categorize it, and her mind stumbled on the only explanation that made sense.

"If you think we should marry just because we... er..." She trailed off, waving her hand in the air between them as she pulled the coverlet more firmly around herself. She regained her voice, and said in her most dignified tone, "I did not do this to trick you into marrying me. You do not need to sacrifice yourself on the marital altar for my sake."

His smile didn't waver. "Don't fall back on formality, Mad. You know me better than to think I would marry a girl simply because she fell into my bed."

He leaned in to kiss her again, but his flippant statement turned her shock into annoyance. She pulled away, trailing the coverlet in her wake as she left the bed to stand over him. "Yes, I forgot just how much of a rake you are, your grace. How silly of me."

Ferguson's smile switched to stormclouds. "I am utterly serious about you, Madeleine. Ruining you is reason enough to marry you — you're hardly the soiled dove type a man can use and leave behind."

She opened her mouth to object, but he silenced her with the dark look in his eyes. "But beyond that, my dear, I am in love with you. And now that I've found you, you can't expect me to let you go."

She was well and truly shocked by his declaration. She blindly sank onto the small footstool by the dying fire, twisting her hands into the coverlet she still used as a dressing gown. "But we've known each other less than a fortnight. How can you be in love with me?"

He strode around the bed, taking considerably less care wrapping himself in sheets than she had, and she caught a tantalizing glimpse of one muscled thigh before he stood in front of her. "I know you probably hate my past, and I can't say I'm particularly proud of it myself — but if there is one thing I learned, it is how rare it is to find what we experienced tonight. In fact, I can safely say that I have never, ever found a woman who could compare to you."

He paused for an endless moment. "What is your answer, Mad?"

She looked into those blue eyes, read the mixture of hope,

sincerity, and hunger, and felt a slamming in her chest as she realized he told the truth. She couldn't call the abruptness of his affections into question — not when she was surely at least half in love with him herself.

A collapsing log in the fireplace jarred her out of the dream. Any debutante would swoon at such a declaration of love, particularly from a duke.

But she knew from bitter experience that love wasn't enough. The fire, and the nightmare it embodied, was enough to remind her. Her parents had loved her, but they still sent her away to fulfill their duties. Augusta and Alex loved her, but they wouldn't accept her desire to act in public. Amelia loved her too, but even that love seemed to be reaching its limit.

People in their spheres could marry for love, but love was not what drove the ton.

Ultimately, Ferguson would embody the title he had inherited, whether he desired it or not. The duties of a dukedom would slowly pave over any hope of a pure, committed love. Or he would go to Scotland to avoid it — but she had never romanticized life as a hermit, and saw no appeal in spending the rest of her life on a remote estate.

If he stayed in London and was not corrupted by the title, she would still be a duchess. If her life felt constrained as a spinster, it would be awful when she was expected to be a grand hostess.

The panic started to rise. She had slept safely in his arms, even with a fire burning in the grate. But awake, with her mind overruling her heart, she couldn't face him. He stood in front of her, one hand fisted in the sheet he used to cover himself, looking like the powerful lord he was. She had successfully tricked her family to pursue her own pleasure, but Ferguson wouldn't be fooled — she would never again have the freedom of the past few weeks.

Marrying him could mean jumping from the boring but comfortable prison of her current life to a trap of her own making. She was sure Ferguson would be more exciting — but the risks were higher. If she married him, there would be no escape.

And his love might not last long enough to compensate for her freedom.

She reached the end of that line of reasoning before the last sparks subsided in the fireplace. Her heart raced and her palms were wet as she clenched them in the folds of the coverlet, but she knew her answer.

"I can't marry you, Ferguson," she whispered.

She forced herself to watch as the hope in his eyes turned to disbelief. He gave her a long, assessing look that made her want to take everything back, but she bit her tongue. He didn't plead his case, and he was not a man who would ever beg. His hand shot out and pulled her to her feet, his arm wrapping around her to hold her against his chest. She made a sound — either of protest or sadness, she didn't know — and he silenced her with one swift kiss.

The heat stayed on her lips even after he stepped back, and she somehow managed to stay on her feet. He snagged his coat from the floor and fished the door key out of its pocket. "I will send the maid up to dress you so you can return to Salford House," he said, as nonchalantly as if they had been discussing the weather instead of marriage.

But then he pinned her with his gaze. With his bare chest and the sheet slung low on his hips, he looked like a warrior roused from bed, ready to do battle at a moment's notice. "Some night soon, though, I will hear a different answer from you," he said, with a subtle assurance that made it sound more like a promise than a threat. "And I will hear you confess to what I suspect you already feel, even if you're pretending otherwise."

He gathered his clothes and left. The door slamming behind him was the only proof of just how frustrated he was.

She sighed, wondering if she should have said yes, or if she could have said no in a kinder way. But there was no way to have an independent life as a duchess, particularly not a duchess who would have to watch her lover turn into the very type of man he did not want to be.

She just had to hope her independence was worth Ferguson's wrath — and that her resolve wouldn't crumble in the face of his love.

CHAPTER TWENTY

Ferguson wasn't in the hallway when she finished dressing, and Madeleine didn't seek him out. She slipped out of the townhouse and through the door cut in the Stauntons' high stone wall, hurrying across the darkened gardens toward Salford House. It was a clear night and the path was easy to find, but she still shivered in her thin gown. She couldn't risk wearing a cloak — it would already raise enough eyebrows if a servant saw her wandering around the lower floors long after her family left for the evening.

But even though she was freezing, and even though she wanted to avoid seeing Ferguson, she wasn't eager to return to her room. With the events of the last two hours — losing her virginity, and then refusing a marriage proposal from a man she thought she might love — she knew she would not sleep easily.

Still, she couldn't delay. Her family could return at any moment. Josephine had surely made excuses for Madeleine, but with Aunt Augusta growing increasingly concerned about Madeleine's health, Madeleine needed to be in bed before anyone came home. Light filtered through the curtains of Alex's study, but it was several rooms away from her preferred entrance — he wouldn't hear her. Otherwise, the back of the house was dark, with a low lamp shining in the small sitting room the girls used during the day. Josephine would be there, loitering to keep the butler from locking the French doors. Madeleine pushed the door open, stepped over the threshold — and shrieked as a man's hand grabbed her arm.

She jerked away, every instinct screaming at her to flee, but his grip was unbreakable. He swung her around to face him, and she relaxed as she realized Alex was the one who had caught her.

The worst of her panic drained out of her, but a different kind of fear replaced it. She saw the grim set of his jaw and the hardness in his eyes — like nothing she had ever seen there before — and her need to flee surged again. There was nowhere to go, though, not when her cousin had just caught her sneaking into the house hours after she had supposedly taken to her bed.

"Where have you been?" he demanded as he marched her out of the sitting room and down the hall to his study.

She had dreaded this moment, almost more than the possibility of being ruined in the eyes of the ton. She didn't say a word, not willing to incriminate herself until she discovered what Alex already knew. If he only thought she had been outside alone, she could talk her way out of it, claim she'd had a nightmare, play on his sympathy. She had already betrayed them so deeply — would another lie hurt?

But if he knew she was acting as Marguerite Guerrier, he would guess her connection with the duke of Rothwell. Everyone knew about his mistress. At least Alex would understand her passion for the theatre, even if he would be annoyed that she had done it without his permission. But if he knew she was acting as Ferguson's mistress...

He opened the door to the study and pushed her inside, gently enough that she didn't fall but forcefully enough to show he was taking over. Every lamp was lit and the brilliance made her blink.

When her vision cleared, she saw Aunt Augusta and Amelia sitting on the small settee beside Alex's desk. Aunt Augusta was ramrod straight, with a severity to her expression that Madeleine hadn't seen since those first awful weeks after Uncle Edward's death. Amelia huddled beside her, her knees drawn up under her chin as though she were five years old. Amelia was thoroughly miserable — and the look in her eyes was something between an apology and a warning.

"Sit down, Madeleine," Alex ordered. There was no invitation in his voice; it was pure command.

She sank into an armchair across from Alex, angled to look at him rather than Augusta and Amelia. She still didn't want to answer his question, so she slowly peeled off her gloves and tossed them onto the table next to her. Her guilt was probably written on her face, but at least her maid had reset her hair and clothed her completely. Despite Ferguson's lovemaking, she knew she looked innocent.

Anxiety and fear still flooded her veins, but she was an actress — she could get through whatever this conversation brought. With that reminder, she took a deep breath, folded her hands in her lap, and looked up at Alex with an expression of utter innocence.

Alex frowned. "You seem remarkably composed."

"Is there a reason I shouldn't be composed?"

He exploded. "I just caught you sneaking into the house a mere half hour before midnight and you ask if there is a reason why you shouldn't be composed? If I were a better guardian, I would whip you for this."

Alex was usually so mild — but he looked half-tempted to follow through on his threat. She swallowed, her mouth dry. "Shall we have some tea as we discuss this?"

"No tea," he said flatly. "All the servants have the night off. We couldn't risk having one of them overhear this discussion."

"Surely Josephine is here?" she asked. If she could just see Josephine and find out what Alex knew, she would know how to handle him.

"She's packing her things."

"What?" Madeleine gasped. "What have you done to her?"

"You could hardly expect me to keep her when she's far more loyal to you than she is to the rest of the family. She said she would rather be turned off than tell me where you disappeared to all these nights, so I granted her wish."

Madeleine rubbed her throbbing temples. "You can't send Josephine away. It was my decision to act the way I did. She merely helped me when she realized I was going to do it with or without her."

"And what, precisely, have you been doing?" Alex asked. "You still haven't answered that question."

She paused, not ready to plunge into explanations, defenses, and denials, not sure she could meet Aunt Augusta's eyes as she lied to them.

Amelia shifted in her seat. "You may as well tell them about the theatre," she said.

The strained, urgent tone of Amelia's voice meant that her cousin was trying to tell her something else — perhaps that Madeleine's acting had already been discovered, but they hadn't realized Ferguson's role in it. She relaxed into her chair, trying to put all thoughts of Ferguson — and what they had done in the little house across the alleyway — out of her mind so that she could convince Alex that acting was her only sin.

"What do you already know?" Madeleine asked.

Alex pulled a playbill out of his desk drawer and slid it across to her. "I know you are Madame Guerrier. In fact, I even know how talented you are. I was in the audience tonight and discovered it for myself."

"You attended the play? You don't even like the theatre."

"I've known something was wrong with you for weeks, and it wasn't the headache you kept pleading. Mother and I agreed that we needed to discover what was wrong before there were any surprises. And once I found out what you were doing, we knew just how unpleasant those surprises would be."

Aunt Augusta hadn't said a word since they entered the room. Madeleine would have noticed such unusual silence if she had not been so concerned about what Alex knew. She looked over at her aunt and was horrified to see the glimmer of what looked like tears.

Madeleine hadn't seen Aunt Augusta cry since Uncle Edward's funeral.

And then Madeleine knew their ambush was about more than just her acting.

"You know about Ferguson too, don't you?" she whispered.

"Ferguson?" Alex said, his brows slamming together. "So now you're calling that bounder by his nickname instead of his title?"

Damn. They didn't know about Ferguson — and she had given herself away. "He made it clear at every turn that he prefers not to use his title."

Alex ignored her explanation. "And yes, we know. Everyone in London is talking about how the duke is back to his old tricks, taking the most desirable actress of her generation as his mistress."

She heard Aunt Augusta sniffle, but she kept her gaze locked on

Alex's. He was turning positively feral. She had a very real suspicion that he had never been angrier in his life. She held her breath, waiting for his next words.

But they were even worse than she could have imagined. "You have thirty seconds to convince me you haven't become his whore, or I'm going to kill him."

Madeleine felt dizzy, and a dull roar in her ears almost drowned out the end of Alex's threat. Aunt Augusta finally intervened. "Alexander, there is no need for such vulgarity. Madeleine is still ours, despite whatever she has done."

Madeleine had felt guilty about rejecting Ferguson's proposal, but it was nothing compared to what she felt now. She used to wish for her real family to come back and take her away, dreamed of what it would have been like to grow up with them in France. But Aunt Augusta had never treated her as anything less than a daughter — and Madeleine had just repaid the kindness by disappointing her more than any of them could have imagined.

Alex didn't back down. "Thirty seconds, Madeleine."

She could barely breathe, let alone come up with a coherent, non-incriminating sentence. Finally, she just held up her hands. "Ferguson offered to protect me from others who might try to seduce me, and I thought it best to accept his help. By pretending that I am his mistress, he's kept other interested men away from me while I am at the theatre." Then she steeled herself for the lie. "But I would never do anything improper with him, and he is too much of a gentleman to take advantage. He is only helping me to keep me from ruining his sisters by association."

Alex snorted, then demanded more detail. She explained it all — the desire to act, Madame Legrand's blackmail, how Ferguson had saved her, and even the earl of Westbrook's attempt to make her his mistress. Her cousin scowled at that, and she suspected Ferguson wasn't the only man in danger. But when she reached the end of the story — mentioning the house Ferguson had procured so she could return to Salford House safely, but leaving out what they had done in that house just hours earlier — Alex leaned back, looking satisfied.

"At least your story matches that of your conspirators. If you lied to my face, I would be much less inclined to forgive you."

Madeleine ignored the possibility of forgiveness. It was probably too late for that. But Alex said "conspirators," which meant he had talked to someone besides Josephine. Someone who would know of her acting — someone who, when Madeleine glared at her, looked like she was trying to swallow her own tongue.

"What did you tell them, Amelia?" she asked. It wasn't a nice feeling, the way something inside her saw her cousin as the enemy — but anger felt better than guilt.

"I couldn't keep your secret anymore," Amelia said, sounding both sad and defensive. "I was prepared to help you act in the theatre, but this business with Rothwell is dangerous. We should have gone to Alex as soon as Madame Legrand blackmailed you so he could help you."

"*We* should have gone to Alex?" Madeleine repeated. "Do you forget that I am the one who is in trouble, not you?"

Aunt Augusta cut them both off. "Everyone in this family is at risk because of what you both have done. And I simply cannot understand what on earth possessed you to do this — I let you put on plays twice a year at our country estate specifically so you wouldn't take such a foolish risk."

Madeleine couldn't answer. How could she explain to the aunt who raised her that she felt trapped by the life they gave her? "I am truly sorry," she finally said. "I did not think I would be caught. And other than you, I still haven't been found out."

"It is only a matter of time," Aunt Augusta snapped. "The first lesson anyone should learn in the ton is that every scandal eventually comes out. Someday, someone will recognize you. When that happens, my reputation won't be enough to save you."

"I won't be caught," Madeleine said, although she wasn't nearly as confident as she sounded. "It is only another fortnight before Madame Legrand releases me, and then you will never hear of the theatre again."

"And will Ferguson release you when the play ends?" Alex asked, his voice silky and dangerous.

Madeleine lifted her chin. "Ferguson will not hurt me. If it weren't for him, this may have ended much worse than one would hope."

Aunt Augusta sighed. "Alex, we can discuss Ferguson later. But first, we must decide what to do if Madeleine is caught."

"You can always send me to the country," Madeleine said, not liking the sad, hard tone in Aunt Augusta's voice.

Alex cleared his throat. "We discussed some possibilities while we waited for you to come home from the theatre. Sebastian will come home for a visit this summer. If your identity is discovered, it would be best if you returned to Bermuda with him."

"Bermuda? What would I do in Bermuda? I would prefer to live out my ignominy in Lancashire."

"And we would prefer to have you there. But as much as it pains me, I must marry someday. If your role as Ferguson's mistress is discovered, your reputation will be so far gone that my wife and daughters could not share a house with you."

Alex sounded regretful — but resolute. Her palms felt clammy, and she wiped them on her gown. She turned to Amelia, knowing her cousin had always wanted them to move to the country together if their spinsterhoods continued. "'Tis a shame you do not like warm weather. We must hope I do not get caught."

Amelia retreated into herself, shrinking away from the conversation in a way so unlike her usual mode of direct confrontation. In contrast, Aunt Augusta drew herself up. "Amelia will attend every event I can drag her to this season. If you are caught, no one can think she was at the theatre too," she said. "Unless Madame drops dead — and we considered helping her to that end, but I cannot bear the idea — we can't see a way to extricate you from her blackmail. But it seems wise to limit the possibility that Amelia would be caught up in this scandal too."

Madeleine felt like she had been punched in the chest. Her breath seized up, her heart shuddered — and she felt a flash of heat as every nerve lit up with rage.

"You would send me away to protect Amelia?" Through the ringing in her ears, her voice still sounded almost calm.

"If the roles were reversed, I would send Amelia away to save you," Aunt Augusta said. "Regardless, the most important thing now is to contain the damage."

Damage. As though Madeleine was already a spoiled good who might spread her blight to the family.

If that wasn't stunning enough, Alex's words were enough to make her heart stop. "And by the way, Madeleine, you can't fool me into thinking you spent the past two hours playing charades with

Rothwell and half a dozen proper chaperones. If by some miracle no one ever catches you, I will see Rothwell marry you — or I will call him out for it."

Alex was better known as an antiquities collector than a dueler, but he wasn't a milquetoast, and the look in his eyes said he would happily kill the duke if given the opportunity. "There's no reason for Ferguson to marry me since I haven't been compromised," Madeleine said, looking him straight in the eye as she lied to him.

"I would castrate him and send him to a monastery before I saw you tied to him, but we are too civilized in the modern era to give him what he deserves," Alex said. "But if I have reason to suspect he has touched you — and another night like tonight would be enough — you will marry him, whether either of you want to or not."

Madeleine couldn't defend Ferguson without arousing even more suspicion. She was exhausted, too emotionally devastated by everything that had happened in the past few hours to start an argument about her future marital state. Her legs shook as she stood, but she masked the tremor by swooping to grab her gloves from the table. "Before I *damage* you any more, I shall go to my room."

Aunt Augusta moved toward her, but Madeleine flinched away from her embrace. Her aunt could not have looked more shocked if she had slapped her. "There's no need to explain," Madeleine said in a brittle voice. "I must keep from getting caught, or I will be forced to spend the rest of my life on Sebastian's godforsaken plantation. If I do get caught, I must not, under any circumstance, risk Amelia's reputation or the reputations of Alex's unborn daughters. And if I successfully keep from getting caught, I will be forced into a marriage I do not want. Is that correct?"

No one answered. She wanted to smash Alex's decanters against the wall just to startle them out of their silence.

She turned and left, her steps becoming a run before she even reached the top of the stairs. She heard Amelia call her name from the hallway, heard the pain in her cousin's voice, but she didn't turn around. She ran to her room and locked herself in before collapsing onto her bed. The Stauntons may have seen her anger, but she didn't want them to see her tears.

CHAPTER TWENTY-ONE

Ferguson was turning into his father after all. The night before proved it — when Madeleine refused his proposal, his first instinct was to kidnap her and drive straight for Gretna Green. Or, even easier, drag her to Salford, still wrapped in his coverlet, and prove that she needed to marry him. She was lucky he was still new to his inheritance. His father would have forced the issue before she even left his bed.

But he wasn't quite his father yet, and he had tamped down the desire to claim her long enough to let her flee. After he watched from a window until she safely crossed the alleyway, he returned to their bed, still warm from their bodies, and stared at the ceiling as he waited for sleep to take him. He couldn't let her go, couldn't lose her. He would just have to find a way to win her.

That would require finding out why she said no. When he had awoken to sunlight streaming through the windows of their little house, he realized he hadn't even asked her for a reason.

He cast another glance at the clock across from his desk and sighed. After coming home and changing clothes, he had succumbed to duty and met his London steward for their daily exercise in overseeing the vast estate. They were in his father's study, and the clock, like every other object in the room, was intimately familiar to him — either from his boyhood, when his father used to let him play with the exotic objects, or later, when he stared at anything but his father during the endless lectures. He swore the clock was rigged to make time seem like it had stopped — and it still felt that way, even though he was the master.

Berrings, the steward, coughed discreetly. Ferguson sighed. The London house's steward also oversaw the duchy's city holdings. If Ferguson could concentrate, there was more than enough work to distract him from the topic of Madeleine.

"What are your thoughts on the lease for Legrand's Theatre, your grace?" Berrings asked. "Have you thought any more about the establishment?"

The man had a knack for raising controversial subjects in the blandest possible voice. He surely knew how well Ferguson was acquainted with the place. Anyone smart enough to survive nearly two years in the old duke's service would pay close attention to his master's actions.

"You must know I've attended, but the proprietress did not seem nervous about my presence. Does she not know I own her theatre?"

Berrings shook his head. "Places of that ilk are leased through a subsidiary so that your grace's name is not besmirched by their entertainments."

At least the gossips did not know of Ferguson's ownership. It would look positively feudal for him to sample the charms of the theatre's top performer. "We can leave the theatre alone for now, but I may wish to revisit the matter at the end of the season," Ferguson said. At least he would have leverage if Madeleine continued to refuse him.

He winced. That was exactly what his father would have thought.

Berrings made a notation in his ledger. Then he looked up, awaiting more orders. He was nondescript, a man with a medium build, standard brown hair, and a moderate tone of voice — the type who would blend into the backdrop and work himself to death without complaint.

"How do you feel about your work, Berrings?" Ferguson asked.

The man carefully set his pen on the traveling desk he used to the left of Ferguson's chair, and his face paled as he looked up from his writing. "Have I done anything to displease you, your grace? I know we've not worked together for long, but I assure you I hold your interests dearer than my own."

"No, you've pleased me quite well. With your knowledge, I would be a fool to cut you loose."

Berrings's shoulders slumped just slightly, like a man given a reprieve he did not expect. "You are very kind, your grace."

Ferguson laughed. "'Kind' is not a word I am accustomed to hearing. But I do intend to treat you fairly if you choose to stay on."

Berrings was not likely to leave of his own accord. The position as a Rothwell estate manager would be very hard to eclipse. Although another steward oversaw the grand Rothwell estate on the Dover coast and a third managed the industrial interests in the north, Berrings was responsible for a substantial portion of an income that totaled more than £150,000 per annum. Rothwell rivaled Devonshire as the greatest non-royal duchy in England and made Ferguson's comfortable inheritance in Scotland look like the meanest poverty. Berrings would be a fool to leave it. He said as much, stammering over his words, somehow navigating a course between pride in his work and abject flattery of the dukes who had hired him.

Ferguson waved all that aside. He would need to see if the other two stewards were as loyal, but since his father would have had them transported at any hint of fraud, he guessed they were more than competent. "Since you've no intention of leaving, I am relieved that the duchy will be under your expert care when I return to Scotland. You will still send reports, of course, but it is good to know I do not need to be involved."

Berrings compressed his lips, looking down at his ledger as though searching for a new topic of conversation.

"You are far too easy to read," Ferguson observed. "How did you ever survive my father with such a distinct inability to hide your thoughts?"

He laughed for the first time since Ferguson had met him, a rusty sound that left him mortified. "His grace asked me to sit behind him, your grace. He thought it easier to sign papers and toss them back to me, and he had no need for my opinion."

Ferguson remembered the last time he had seen his father — ten years earlier, in this very room. The duke did not ask Ferguson's opinion either. But he made sure his son stood right in the center, feeling like an insect pinned to the carpet, while he castigated him for being an insult to every ancestor who had conducted themselves honorably since the days of the Conqueror.

Then he ordered Ferguson to get out of his sight and never return. It was the victory Ferguson had fought for. So why had it hurt when his father did not see him off?

"Perhaps you were lucky he did not seat you before him," Ferguson said, pulling himself out of the memories.

Berrings nodded. "If you will forgive me for being bold, your grace, may I offer my opinion?"

So the man did have a voice of his own — even better, if he were to manage the duchy during Ferguson's absences. "I am not my father. Your job is to offer me counsel on the estate."

"Then my counsel is that you should remain in England," Berrings said in a rush, determined to get the words out before his courage failed. "There are thousands of people on your estates who would benefit from your leadership. You could do much good if you were directly involved in your affairs."

"I hardly think anyone is clamoring for my leadership. As long as the estate's coffers don't run dry, they would be just as satisfied if a monkey sat at this desk. Maybe more, since the monkey wouldn't be out making scandals." Ferguson said.

Berrings had an obstinate set to his jaw that Ferguson hadn't seen before. "The previous duke was very astute. It is why this estate prospered when so many are on the verge of failing. But he did not have a gift for talking to the lower classes. The tenants would appreciate knowing that you are both qualified to lead and approachable enough to consider their requests."

"Are any of the tenants starving?" Ferguson demanded, feeling his temper spark.

Berrings shook his head.

"Then they will be fine without me. If they survived my father's presence, it will be even easier for them to survive my absence."

"Very well, your grace," Berrings said stiffly. "But if you will pardon my boldness one more time, I believe everyone is relieved to have you, and not your brothers, at the helm. Your father wanted it too, although not in these circumstances."

"I very much doubt he wanted me to inherit," Ferguson said

with a bitter laugh.

"He only said it once, your grace — when another of his letters to you came back unopened."

Ferguson scowled. The letters had started several years after he left, shortly after Henry's funeral, which he refused to attend. The first two offered to let Ferguson back into the fold if he would apologize to his father for the trouble — as though that would ever happen. He never read the letters after that, sent them all back with their seals intact. He wouldn't have even read the one telling him about his father's death had Sophronia not sent four footmen with it to drag him back to London if necessary.

If his father wanted him to inherit, it could only be because he thought Ferguson stood a better chance than Richard of being a "proper" duke — cold, aloof, obsessed with winning. All the qualities that served the Rothwell dukes on ancient battlefields were a nuisance now — but Ferguson had them in spades, if his autocratic need to steal Madeleine away could be used as proof.

He gave Berrings a look that said the conversation was over. At least his ducal tendencies put a quick end to Berrings's meddling. "Is there anything else to discuss this morning?"

The steward picked up a pile of envelopes. "Your correspondence, your grace. I sorted the invitations, requests, and the like, but there was one I thought you should see now."

Ferguson took the note from his hand, recognizing Caro's handwriting even upside down. He frowned as he slipped the inner sheet free of the wrapper.

Another threat, this time written on a caricature from a cheap newspaper. The drawing was poor, but it was obviously him — wearing a kilt that looked like a dress — and Marguerite, dressed in men's trousers. He was speaking gibberish, and Marguerite said, "Alas, poor duchess!" — an allusion to the line about Yorick from *Hamlet*, and to his family's rumored insanity, with a jab at his masculinity that insulted him more than all the rest. The pile of jewels she sat on made it clear why she stayed, and the footmen standing guard behind her showed how little she thought of his stability.

The caricature was ugly, but he had been caricatured before. Caro's note was worse. "The artists will have much to savor if I publish a memoir of our time together. May I suggest you leave both Lady Madeleine and your mistress before either of them are pulled into the scandal?"

Damn. He crumpled the cartoon and tossed it toward the fire. Her threats were becoming more direct, and he did not think she would listen to reason. He had to get Madeleine to accept his proposal. She would be safe from the ton's curious eyes if she went to Scotland with him.

"No response, Berrings," he said flatly. Then he looked at the clock again. It was still too early to call, but he couldn't wait any longer.

"One more task — I need you to retrieve my mother's jewels. I assume they are in the vault at the bank?"

Berrings made a note. "I will bring the entire casket, your grace. But if you are looking for her engagement ring, I am afraid his grace had the stone reset into a ring for himself. He was wearing it when he died. Since you were not here to decide how to proceed, I took the liberty of returning it to the vault rather than burying it with him."

Why would his father have remade the ring? He was not a sentimental man. Years earlier, he had burned everything of his wife's that it was possible to consign to the flames, including the crofters' huts on her Scottish estate. Any feeling that demanded the displacement of an entire clan to assuage his grief was not sentimental. Still, he may not have lost all feeling for her if he had decided to wear her ring.

Ferguson would have to find another option. He dismissed Berrings — and his remarkably perceptive suspicion about why Ferguson wanted the jewels — before striding up the stairs to his chambers. If he were to embarrass himself by calling too early and demanding an explanation for her refusal, he would at least look presentable.

He just had to hope that Madeleine's objection was something he could overcome — and as Ferguson, not as the duke he would otherwise become.

CHAPTER TWENTY-TWO

Madeleine heard yet another knock at her door and rolled her eyes. It was only noon, but she had already had visits from Alex (once), Augusta (twice), and Amelia (every half hour since eight in the morning).

Or rather, attempted visits — she refused them all. Since none of them would shout at her from the hallway and risk the servants overhearing them, they left without pleading their cases.

But her stomach was making little gurgling noises and her mouth was parched. She had used what was left of the water in her basin to scrub away the lingering traces of last night's tears. Sieges usually ended when someone ran out of supplies. She should have thought about provisions before making her stand.

"Who is it?" she called, disgruntlement clear in her voice.

"Josephine," came the response — along with the much-welcome sound of china rattling on a tray.

She leapt up from her seat by the empty fireplace and flung open the door. "I thought you had gone without saying goodbye," she exclaimed. Josephine was part of the reason for her morning rebellion, since it wasn't fair for Alex to punish her old nursemaid when the decision to act was Madeleine's own.

The maid carefully set the heavy tray on Madeleine's writing table. "Pierre and I have nothing to return to in France. The earl lectured us, but Lady Salford was too kind to put us on the streets."

Madeleine hugged her impulsively, feeling for a moment like a joyful child even though she was a head taller than the other woman. "Thank goodness. When I thought you would lose your position because of me, I cannot tell you how awful I felt."

"Do not thank goodness yet," Josephine warned, lifting the covers from a plate of eggs, ham and tomatoes, with toast and tea besides. "They have ordered me to be more strict as your chaperone. You are not to spend any time alone with the duke as Marguerite."

Madeleine poked at one of the poached eggs with her fork, her stomach making insistent noises as the yolk burst forth. "I am twenty-eight, Josephine. I do think I can chaperone myself."

Josephine fixed her with her best glare, the one that would have terrified Madeleine as a child if she had ever misbehaved enough to see it. "You stayed with him far too long last night. The marquise would have been very unhappy to witness your behavior."

Her mother had been dead for twenty years, but Josephine's words still hurt. "I never intended to embarrass anyone."

"I know," Josephine said, her tone softening. "Your mother would not have approved of your dalliance with the duke, but I think she would be happy to know that you made a life for yourself here. And if you marry him, it would not matter what you did with him, correct?"

Madeleine didn't answer. Josephine was loyal to her, not her aunt — but after last night's debacle, she would report Madeleine's future activities to her family. Besides, the maid was nearly as marriage mad as Aunt Augusta. She would do whatever she could to see Madeleine married to Ferguson.

So she stayed silent, keeping Ferguson's proposal — and her response to it — a secret. Until she knew what to do, she didn't want anyone else to try to sway her.

She toyed with a piece of ham, her appetite gone. She had already said no to Ferguson. He could well decide not to ask her again. Why beg her when another debutante would say yes so easily?

But why was she rethinking her decision? It hadn't felt right at the time, but it hadn't felt wrong either — it was too hard to feel anything with that unbearable panic overwhelming her. She thought the panic was as good a sign as any that she didn't want to marry him — imagine waking up to that panic daily, dreading the hour when she would finally lose him to his estate.

She stabbed hard at the ham with her knife, ruthlessly cutting it into small pieces. At least Ferguson had never threatened to send her away. He didn't care overly for protocol, and he had never been shocked by her acting. There were very few men who would turn a blind eye to the kind of scheme she was playing — and even fewer who would support it.

And there was one undeniable fact — his skills in bed were something that not even the most detailed engravings could prepare her for.

"Are you feverish, *ma petite*?" Josephine asked, returning from the dressing room with the day's garments. "You look flushed."

She blushed harder and shook her head. Josephine looked at her skeptically but didn't press the subject.

Someone tapped on the door, and she glared at it. If it was Amelia again...

But the person opened it without waiting, since she had

forgotten to relock it after Josephine's arrival. It was a maid with a message from the butler. "His grace the duke of Rothwell asked if you would accompany him for a drive in the park, my lady," the maid said.

She wasn't ready to see him. The haze of her daydream dissolved into panic once again. "Is he downstairs?"

"Yes, my lady. Shall I take your reply to him?"

She looked at Josephine, who avoided her gaze. The decision was hers alone. At least seeing Ferguson would be preferable to seeing her family. "I will be down directly," she said.

It was a bit longer than that before she was ready. She was still in her dressing gown, and Josephine needed a few moments to lay out the appropriate accessories for a carriage dress. But by the time Madeleine was properly clothed and coiffed, in a smart russet-colored dress with a jaunty hat trimmed in pheasant feathers, she had at least succeeded in calming her nerves.

He wouldn't ask her again so soon. And if he had come to break off their arrangement, she would know she was right to turn him down. Either way, she could survive their meeting, even if she anticipated it with dread rather than excitement.

She took one last sip of tea, then picked up her reticule and walked out the door. Josephine followed close on her heels, serious in her commitment to keep a watchful eye over Madeleine's dealings with the duke. Down the hall, Amelia sat in a chair she had pulled out from her own room, a book lying facedown in her lap as she stared off into nothing. When Madeleine emerged, Amelia turned to look at her — and it was clear she had passed a sleepless night.

"Maddie, can we talk?" she asked in a hoarse voice, sounding less confident than Madeleine had ever heard her. Her blue eyes were dry, but her nose was red and swollen and her blonde hair looked like it hadn't been brushed.

Madeleine felt a vicious kick of pleasure at Amelia's unhappiness. She felt guilty as soon as she recognized it, but guilt wasn't enough to make her willing to listen, not after Amelia's betrayal. Amelia never admitted she was wrong. She likely felt bad about last night, but she would probably tell Madeleine it was for the best.

Madeleine couldn't stomach the thought of Amelia's excuses. "Not now, Amelia," she said, her voice sounding frigid even to her own ears. "I'm much too busy attempting to control the 'damage' to have another tiresome conversation."

Amelia reeled back as though she had been slapped. "I didn't mean..."

Madeleine strode past her, and whatever Amelia intended to say died in her throat. She knew she had shocked Amelia — they had never had a serious argument before. But the truth was that Amelia nearly always prevailed, and this was one argument that Madeleine could not let her win.

So she walked down to the main drawing room, shoving the thought of Amelia's stricken face out of her mind. Ferguson was waiting for her when she arrived, holding an extravagant bouquet of white roses. She didn't want to react to him, intended to maintain her composure in case he was there to cut her, but her heart still leapt in her chest at the sight of him. As their gazes locked, she had the dizzying sense that, in that moment, they were the only two people in the world. Nothing else mattered — with him, in their private bubble, she could be whoever she wanted to be.

He stepped forward, never losing eye contact. "I've decided I should court you properly," he said in a low voice, the syllables coursing through her blood to jolt her heart again.

So he didn't intend to break things off. She wished she knew how to respond. If she didn't intend to marry him, prolonging their involvement would only make it harder to leave him at the end of the month.

But despite her panic, she wasn't ready to let him go. She took the flowers from his outstretched hand, running a gloved finger lightly across the blooms. At first glance, the petals were white, but the outer portion of each bloom bled into a pink center.

"They reminded me of you," he said, still watching her.

The reference to an innocent façade hiding a secret wildness was unmistakable. She studied him again over the roses. As usual, he wore perfect riding breeches, a morning jacket, and highly polished boots. He carried his hat under his other arm, one of those social niceties that said he was prepared to leave if she commanded. The only imperfection was the slight messiness of his auburn hair — as though still tousled from her fingers tugging him toward her.

She swallowed a sigh. He grinned, and she hoped he couldn't read her face. She turned abruptly, nearly tossing the flowers at Josephine. "Would you find some water for these?"

Josephine looked at the duke, frowned, and looked back at her charge. "I should not leave you alone."

Madeleine set her jaw. "I will be safe here for the two minutes it takes to deposit the bouquet. You shan't take advantage, Ferguson?"

He tried to look appropriately somber as he gave Josephine his assurances. Madeleine thought he failed miserably, but the maid left them alone, her smile undermining her admonishment for Madeleine to behave herself.

As soon as she was gone, Madeleine ignored her advice. "Did

you come in a curricle or a closed coach?"

"A curricle, of course. If I had any hope of seeing you without a chaperone, it had to be an open carriage."

"Then shall we leave at once?" Madeleine asked. He raised an eyebrow at this; it was painfully obvious that she was evading her maid. However, he did as she requested, escorting her out the door and to the curricle before Josephine returned.

Luckily, Chilton was not aware that Madeleine required a chaperone. The Stauntons would wish to maintain the appearance of normalcy, after all, and so they could not take the butler into their confidence. He might have thought it unusual for Madeleine to leave with the duke — but only because men so rarely called for her, not because an afternoon ride in an open carriage was improper. Perhaps comparing her old life to a prison was unfair — it was remarkably easy to escape, after all.

Ferguson handed her up into his curricle, a smart, well-proportioned two-seater hitched to a pair of perfectly matched blacks. He tucked a blanket around her skirts to protect them from the dirt of the London streets, then settled in on her left. Releasing the brake and taking the reins from the waiting footman, he urged the horses forward at a smart pace toward Piccadilly, which would lead them to Hyde Park's nearest gate.

When they turned the corner, safely away from anyone sitting in one of Salford House's windows, Ferguson said, "I did not expect to win your attention so easily. I was prepared for you to give me another setdown."

She couldn't look directly in his eyes, but she felt an edge to his voice despite the lightness of his tone. "I do not wish to end our acquaintance, Ferguson."

He did steal a look at her then, necessarily brief as he navigated the curricle through the delivery wagons, coaches, horses, and darting pedestrians thronging the midday street. "So you can admit that we have something between us that should not be lost?"

She hesitated. It had taken her ten years to finally, temporarily pursue her passion for the stage, and it felt like she had only known Ferguson for ten minutes in comparison to the decade that had gone before. She needed to know the risks and understand her heart before deciding. The thought of declaring some half-formed sentiments of how much she liked Ferguson made last night's panic rise again. She could not say she wanted to be his duchess, but she couldn't say goodbye to him either.

She took the coward's path. It was the only one she could choose without fainting. "Must we talk of this now? Unless you have changed your mind, we need not part ways until I am done with the theatre and your sisters have made appropriate matches."

"What I do not understand," he said, ignoring her obvious prevarication, "is how you could turn down my offer so quickly. I'm not such an ogre as the ton makes me out to be, after all."

"I've never thought that," she said with a laugh. "You are an arrogant scoundrel, not an ogre."

He smiled, a sad sort of grin that pulled at her heart. "You're the first, Mad. How could I not want to marry the one woman who sees beyond my reputation?"

She turned away, not willing to let his face move her. "You will find another. You've only been in London a month. In another season or two, you will discover that there are many women who are better suited to be your duchess."

"People do not change, no matter how long I stay away. The

women are all featherbrained beauties without an ounce of sense, shrill harpies who would seek to reform me, or dead bores whom I would wish to abandon within a fortnight. I've met hundreds of women in London, and you are the only one who doesn't fit into one of those categories."

"Amelia isn't a featherbrained beauty," Madeleine said, more for the sake of argument than anything else.

"I suspect she is a shrill harpy when she doesn't get her way."

Madeleine laughed despite herself. "Still, you are surely expected to marry an heiress with better connections than mine."

"Your excuses don't wash, Mad," he snapped, finally sounding frustrated. "I've more income than I can ever spend and your connections are impeccable. I even checked *Burke's* this morning to see if that was your reason — your mother and Augusta are descended from William the bloody Conqueror, not a swineherd. And a French marquis is good enough for me, even if he is dead and cannot give you a dowry."

It was a callous thing to say. Allowances could be made for his temper, but it didn't stop her from retorting, "You shouldn't place too much weight on *Burke's*. Your bloodlines are perfect too, and yet your father was a notorious autocrat and your brothers were unstable."

He stiffened and she immediately regretted her words. "Is that why you said no? Because my brother shot my father and killed himself?"

Madeleine gasped. "Is that rumor true? I am very sorry, Ferguson. I should have thought before I spoke."

"No need to apologize. I am not insulted by the truth. But is that why you won't marry me?"

"No," she said, snatching at the excuse closest to the surface. "I won't marry you because I've no desire to trap myself into being a duchess."

He laughed, louder than normal, but at least his stiffness subsided. "What woman doesn't want to be a duchess?"

They turned into Hyde Park, making for the driving path along Rotten Row. It was too early for the crush of carriages that would arrive later in the afternoon, but they should not have gone somewhere so public — it would draw attention their relationship, which Madeleine did not want. But if the choice was between being examined by the grandes dames and sitting at home with the Stauntons, she knew where she preferred to be.

Then again, with Ferguson's increasingly persistent questions, perhaps she should have stayed locked in her room. "You do not want to be a duke. Why do you assume I would want to be a duchess?"

"Fair enough. I should remind you, though, that being a duchess would be far more exciting than staying on as Salford's dependent."

"Who says I must stay on in Alex's household forever?" she asked, bristling despite the inevitability of that choice. "If I do not marry you, it does not mean I cannot marry someone else."

He colored slightly, and she congratulated herself on winning the point. But then his voice dropped as he said, "If you do marry another, you might wish it over — I doubt any man could equal the pleasure I gave you last night."

He sounded so smug that she wanted to swat him with her reticule. But they were in public, so she plastered her best false smile on her face. "Someone must have drawn all those engravings I've seen. It may be I just need to move to Italy? Or the Orient?"

She won another point, watching his cocky smirk turn into

a scowl. "You'll move nowhere until we've settled what's between us, Mad."

She had awoken the autocrat within, and she shivered at the dark note of promise in his voice. Still, she held her chin up, pretending not to be affected by the way his sideways gaze raked across her. "And you wonder why I would not wish to be duchess. Why should I marry an all-powerful duke who has demonstrated such little regard for his family?"

He turned off Rotten Row abruptly, following a smaller lane toward the Serpentine. He didn't say a word, and while his silence didn't frighten her, Madeleine had enough sense not to provoke him further. While he kept his hands loose on the reins, his shoulders were tense, and he was taut with something he could barely keep in check.

Finally he pulled them to a halt near a small copse of trees. They were still in plain view if anyone happened across them, but not noticeable from the more frequently used paths. Setting the brake, he turned to her — and she nearly recoiled from the blaze of anger in his blue eyes.

"Is that why you won't have me? Because I am turning into my father?"

"You aren't turning into your father," she said, trying to soothe him. "But you must understand how I feel about family. My parents sent me away and stayed in France because they felt they had a duty to their country and their estate. Aunt Augusta and Alex have made it clear that they will also place duty over my happiness if my acting threatens our family. In our class, everything — duty, money, honor, status — trumps love. And I am not prepared to love a duke. Even if you love me, your duties will eventually win."

"No," he said flatly. "Come with me to Scotland. My managers can oversee the duchy, and we can be as free as we please in the Highlands."

She knew that what she wanted was a contradiction even as she said it, but she couldn't stop herself. "You would respect yourself less for leaving your responsibilities again. And if you didn't, I would respect you less, after the pain it caused your sisters before. Perhaps your duty didn't trump your love for them, but something did."

He laughed harshly. "You can't have it both ways, Mad. The only way I can meet this fantasy of yours is if you trust that I can be the duke I am supposed to be without ever leaving you. But it's clear you won't be satisfied with one if I cannot provide the other."

"I'm sorry, Ferguson," she said. "It may be possible — but it seems just as likely you will either become an autocrat or run away again."

His voice turned to chipped ice. "When I was ten, my mother died. I believe my father loved her — I saw him kiss her whenever he could get away with it. I never understood why he turned so cold after she died, why he sent Ellie and me away, why he could never bear to look at me. I thought I must have done something wrong, upset him somehow."

She made a soft sound of distress, but he ignored her. "Now I know how much it must have pained him to see us, when we looked so much like her. I can't forgive him for leaving us — he should have been stronger, should have loved us despite his loss. And I did the same thing to my sisters, leaving them to preserve myself. It's something I can't forgive, and I can't expect you to either. But if I lost you, Mad..."

His voice trailed off. She felt tears gathering in her eyes — not at the thought of her future with or without Ferguson, but of the little boy he must have been, just as confused as she was when she lost her parents.

"If I lost you, I would become the man he was. So I can't let you go," he said, force and despair mingling in his voice — a tone she never thought to hear from him. "I will never run away from you, unless you beg me to. And the only way I will turn into an autocrat is if you disappear from my life."

CHAPTER TWENTY-THREE

She stared at him in shock, her gorgeous green eyes lit up by a sunbeam and shining with unshed tears. He should have been more careful, shouldn't have been so open. She had been a virgin the night before, and he realized too late that she did not know how to cope with the depth of his demands. Hell, even the most experienced Cyprian would have been scared off by how much he claimed to need her.

He clamped his lips shut. He vowed he would not make the moment any worse. After all, he had his answer now — she was afraid of who he might become, and he had as good as confirmed that he was already on that path.

So even though she didn't give him the answer he wanted, he was supremely relieved when she finally spoke. "I cannot trust you yet," she said, the misery in her voice mollifying just a bit of his wounded pride. "But I would not want to lose you either."

She hadn't accepted his proposal — but at least she had not written him off as a lunatic after his last speech. He could live with her answer. And he would use every moment she gave him to win her over.

He raised her gloved hand to his lips, brushing a kiss across her knuckles. He wanted to strip the glove off her hand, kiss each finger with the attention it deserved, nuzzle her wrist before moving up her arm to claim her mouth. But they were still in Hyde Park, and he was with Madeleine, not Marguerite.

So he dropped her hand and said, "I hope you shall trust me someday, and I will prove to you that I am worthy of it. At least we have two more weeks at the theatre — it would kill me to only see you at rout-parties and musicales."

He could surely convince her by the time the play ended. With her passion and his desire to give her pleasure, he did not think she could outlast his efforts to seduce her. But she sighed at his words. "We cannot be alone after the theatre anymore. Alex caught me when I returned to Salford House last night, and he is furious at us."

She shared what had happened in a quick, nearly toneless monologue, as though she could not stand to tell him without stripping the emotion out first. He could not imagine going straight from their bed to an inquisition in front of her relatives. When she finished the retelling, he did not know who he wished to skewer first — Amelia for betraying her, Augusta for planning to exile her to Bermuda, or Salford for threatening to force her into marriage.

"I told you Amelia was a harpy," he said when she finished.

"She did what she thought best. I cannot fault her intentions, even if her actions lacked finesse."

He knew better than to pursue that thread — even if she felt betrayed by her cousin, she would not tolerate someone else's criticism. He also decided to leave the subject of Salford alone. It wasn't a nice thought, but the knowledge that Salford might force an engagement suited Ferguson's desires even if he preferred Madeleine's consent.

Instead, he said, "We have to ensure that you are not forced to move to Bermuda. It would be harder for me to court you there, after all."

She grinned, and he was glad to see she could still be amused. "Moving to Bermuda may have its benefits."

He laughed. "If Bermuda is good enough for Lady Mad, it is good enough for me. Still, I believe we can survive the next two weeks without incident. Unless you decided to end the play early?"

Madeleine hesitated, looking away from him to survey the field beyond. He realized she was hiding something — something that affected them both. "What is it, Mad?"

"I cannot quit," she said, looking back at him with equal parts resignation and determination. "It should have ended the first night you attended, but Madame Legrand threatened to sell my identity to the *Gazette* if I did not agree to extend the run."

"What? I thought you wanted to be on stage."

"I do!" she said. "I've wanted to act since Amelia and I put on our first plays in the nursery."

"Why didn't you tell me? I could have convinced Madame Legrand to reconsider."

"Unless you intend to kill her, I don't see how you can help," Madeleine said. "And regardless — I did not tell Alex, but I wasn't opposed to staying on. I do love the stage. And you and I would not have had so much time together without it."

He felt another rush of desire — no one else had ever risked so much to be with him.

"So you must understand, Ferguson, I'm not sure I would stop now even if I could. As long as Madame Legrand frees me in two weeks as promised, I am enjoying myself too much to retire."

It was risky, and daring, and dangerous — everything that had attracted him to her, even before he recognized her humor and kindness. Every time she stepped on stage, there was a chance someone would recognize her. The risk was small, he knew; no one had identified her yet, and he never would have guessed if he had not followed her coach.

But still, it was a risk — one he could remove, since he owned the theatre.

He stayed quiet, though. Madeleine feared he would turn into an autocrat. If he gave into his urge to shut down the theatre against her wishes to save her, he would prove her right — and lose her forever.

So he merely offered his continued support, ruthlessly suppressed the desire to kiss her, and turned the horses back toward Salford House. He would listen for any hint of danger and pull her out if he sensed trouble — or if Caro made any threats too direct to ignore. Otherwise, he would let her keep acting and ensure that no one else tracked her to the Stauntons.

They drove back in companionable silence, too spent from their conversation to think about pleasantries. He felt the same flutter of peace that he had felt in Madeleine's bed, thought briefly that the haven he had with her was even more attractive than her passion — and promptly ordered himself to stop thinking. He would not erupt in another mooncalf plea for her hand, not when she had just survived his last one.

So when they arrived at her cousin's house, he accompanied her to the door, acted like a perfect gentleman as he took his leave — and promptly fled before he said anything stupid. How he could convince her to say that she loved him, he didn't know. But he wouldn't give up, not until he heard those words.

*   *   *

Madeleine would have run up the stairs to her room if she could do so without drawing attention. She didn't want to see Augusta, or Amelia, or anyone else — she wanted to lock herself in her room and consider all the hope and fear and love and despair swirling within her after her ride with Ferguson.

But Chilton stopped her before she could even reach the staircase. "Lord Salford requests that you please attend him in his study, Lady Madeleine."

She hesitated, tempted to ignore the demand. Chilton saw her pause and said, "His lordship suggested that I emphasize the 'please,' my lady."

He somehow maintained his proper bearing, but his eyes gleamed. She grinned at him despite herself. "Then I couldn't possibly refuse his lordship, right?"

He bowed. "Shall I bring you a cup of tea as well?"

She wouldn't be there long enough to sit, let alone take a convivial beverage with her overbearing cousin. "No need, Chilton, but thank you."

She squared her shoulders as she walked down the hall to Alex's study. She thought it was preferable to walk there under her own power, rather than having Alex drag her as he did the previous night. But this was almost worse — willingly walking toward an interview she knew she didn't want.

It wasn't just that she didn't want to talk to Alex. She would have to talk to him eventually, and his control of the purse strings meant he could force the issue if she waited too long. She wanted time, though — time to consider everything her family had done to her, and the escape Ferguson offered. He seemed genuine in his love, eager to help her at the theatre without planning how to dispose of her when she was caught.

But she didn't have time. She was already at the door to the study, knocking before she could debate it any longer. Alex bade her to enter and she stepped through the door, closing it behind her.

He wasn't behind his desk, where she expected him to be. He stood against the far wall, looking out the French door to the garden beyond. Usually, he was at home in this room, which he had made his own in the decade since his father's death. While the desk was littered with all the papers that buried a man in his position, it wasn't all dedicated to the Salford estate. Some shelves were cleared to display urns, medallions, small statues — the ephemera of the ancient world, which he would have devoted his life to if his inheritance had not come first.

But today, he looked pensive, more like the scholar he used to be than the powerful earl he had become. "Thank you for joining me," he said quietly, turning to greet her as she stood uncertainly by her usual chair.

"Did I have a choice?" she asked. Her tone wasn't meant to wound — it was straightforward, a statement of fact rather than an accusation.

He winced anyway. "Last night I had to be your guardian. I hope today we may talk as cousins?"

She walked across the room to join him, unwilling to give ground by sitting in the chair he had so recently chastised her in. "What do you want to say, Alex? I'll listen, but I cannot stay forever

— I must go to the theatre in a few hours."

He briefly compressed his lips into a thin line, not liking the reminder of where she spent her evenings. But he didn't touch on the subject again. "Shall we take a turn in the gardens while we talk?"

She nodded. It was better than sitting in this room with him. He unlatched the door and escorted her outside. The gardens were small, as most townhouse gardens were, just large enough for a couple of paths around the flowerbeds and a fountain in the center, gurgling happily in the spring sunshine. The door she used to sneak between this house and Marguerite's house was cut into the back wall, surrounded by climbing vines just beginning to bud. It was a peaceful, serene retreat in the heart of London, but she found no peace in it today.

They walked slowly around the perimeter, Madeleine not wanting to say anything and Alex choking back his words before they could leave his mouth. On their second circuit, he finally cleared his throat. "I owe you an apology for what I said last night."

She waited, but he didn't say anything else. "Is that the apology?" she asked.

He laughed, a startled sound so at odds with their usual comfort together. "I am sorry, Maddie. I've wished for years that you would do something more than what was expected of you, and now that you've finally done it, I threatened to turn you into a pariah. Please know that I won't send you away unless there is no other option left — I'll do anything to help you now that I know what you're doing."

They paused near the fountain. Madeleine sat on the lip of the marble structure, staring down at the floating twigs that had fallen during an earlier spring gale. "Why would you wish for me to do something else? Shouldn't you want me to be a proper spinster?"

He stood beside her, refusing her gestured offer of a seat next to her. "You've always had a spark of rebellion, something more than the proper miss you forced yourself to be. Amelia excels at doing whatever she wishes, but you were always so cautious that I feared you might never do anything interesting. The only shame is that your rebellion might ruin you — but part of me is glad you've finally done something."

She scowled at Amelia's name. "If you would have me follow Amelia's lead, you are mistaken."

"I didn't say you should follow her lead — if anything, you've followed it too much in the past, ignoring society like she did even though your personality is more suited to people than to pen and paper."

Madeleine stood abruptly. She didn't want to hear his comparisons, not when he had made it all too clear the night before that he would sacrifice her to save his sister. "There's no need to apologize now, Alex. You can apologize later, after you send me to Bermuda or force me to marry Ferguson."

She tried to sweep past him, her temper high. He caught her arm, gentler than he was the previous night but still unavoidable. "Do you know why I was so angry last night?"

"I put your reputation at risk."

"No. If it weren't for all the people who depend upon me, my reputation could go hang. I was angry because you lied to me. After all these years, you still felt you couldn't take me into your confidences."

She closed her eyes. The lying had been the worst part of the whole ordeal. It wasn't that she hadn't trusted them — but she thought they would try to stop her, and she had put her desires ahead of propriety. "I am sorry, Alex."

"I'm sorry, too," he said, dropping his hand from her arm. "I just want you to know that your lies were what angered me, not your acting. You really were superb when I saw you onstage last night, you know."

She nodded stiffly at the compliment, but there was nothing else she wanted to say. She walked away, slowly weaving her way back to the house. He let her go, not saying another word.

She took the servants' stairs to avoid walking past the sitting rooms where Amelia might be waiting for her. By the time she reached her chamber, her thoughts were a maelstrom again, the longing and indecisiveness about Ferguson's proposal mingling with her sadness over the breach with the Stauntons. She would have to talk to them again, just as she would have to answer Ferguson's next proposal, but she couldn't face either of them yet.

In that moment, torn between the betrayal she had already experienced and the fear of future heartbreak, she didn't know which direction to turn.

All she could hope for was the clarity she currently lacked — and some insight into the heart she had kept closed for so long.

CHAPTER TWENTY-FOUR

Ferguson didn't want to go back to Rothwell House. For once, he would be happy if his sisters ignored him. He needed to think, and he preferred the solitude of his study to the snakepit of his club. When he arrived, though, the butler said that all three of his sisters were in one of the innumerable sitting rooms and desired an audience.

He was surprised that Ellie, in particular, wanted to see him; the twins avoided him too, but she had more cause. He ordered the butler to send tea to his study and invite them to join him there. It was impolite to ask them to relocate for him — but if his day got any worse, he might be glad to have his decanters close at hand.

When he reached the room, he settled in behind his father's massive desk — his desk now, although it might take years to grow accustomed to sitting behind it rather than standing unrepentant before it. Running his hands over the cool oak, he wondered where it had originated. The fixture fascinated him when he was small, before his mother's death, when his father used to sit him on his lap so Ferguson could practice his letters. Did the duke have it made especially to fit his status?

Or did he inherit it from his own father and become the type of man who would own such a desk?

It was a dangerous question, one he did not want to consider. He could think of better uses for the desk, uses that would turn his father apoplectic with rage. What would Madeleine look like if she were splayed across it? Perhaps in a lush silk dress, her bodice pushed down and her hair falling about her shoulders? Or kneeling on the floor, taking him into her mouth...

He couldn't think of that now. He would win in the end, but he was far from claiming her in this house, as his wife. It would all happen in good time, if he stayed patient and didn't frighten her off.

Now, though, he needed to settle affairs with his sisters, or at least come to some sort of truce. He didn't expect them to forgive him — but it would be nice if they would be civil, and not leave him alone in the enormous dining room every night like some sort of leper.

A footman brought the teacart before his sisters arrived, taking a circuitous route along the side of the room to place it by the chair near his desk. The carpets looked new — they weren't the same pattern Ferguson had traced with his boot during any of the interminable lectures from his father. It was a shame the carpet had been replaced; perhaps it held too many memories for his father as well. Or it may have started to fray, and his father thought it was no longer suitably opulent for his station. Either way, he found it amusing that the footman avoided trundling the teacart across the carpet — Ferguson could afford to buy a hundred replacements on a whim.

He bowed and left hurriedly, just as most of the servants did when they waited on him in his study. Did they think he did not deserve to be there? Were they afraid he might be the same tyrant as his old man? Or were they simply so cowed from years of service to the previous duke that they did not know how to be at ease in his company? At least Berrings was comfortable with him now, although even he had kept glancing at Ferguson's chair at first as though he expected the old duke to reappear.

He drummed his fingers on the desk. It was a vexing issue — one he would have to get to the bottom of if he stayed in London, if only so he did not feel like a cur in his own house.

His sisters entered shortly after the footman left — Maria and Catherine, still shrouded in black, with Ellie bringing up the rear. She was certainly not in mourning, not with that blue walking dress and her messy red curls unconstrained by a widow's cap. Ferguson was struck by how much she looked like her mother in the one portrait that still survived, the portrait his grandfather had staunchly refused to destroy despite his father's best efforts to wipe all physical remnants of her from the earth.

No wonder his father had been so cold to Ellie. If he could not bear to keep a portrait of his wife, how could he stand to see a woman who looked just like her?

The twins stayed rooted at the door, holding hands like petitioners for a great lord's favor. He thought he could tell them apart now; Kate wore a fiercer look, while Maria closed her eyes and trembled. She coughed, a sound that turned into a strangled gasp, and Kate squeezed her hand.

"Do you think we might move to the drawing room, your grace, if it would not inconvenience you?"

Kate still called him "your grace" — as though he was firmly the duke in their minds, with no blood at all between them. "I like to think the old man would hate to see someone else take his place.

There is some justice in discussing the future here, don't you think?"

It was the wrong thing to say. They both turned ashen, and Maria looked ready to cry. But it was Ellie who broke the silence. "Forcing us to meet in this room is positively barbaric, even for you," she declared, skirting the center of the room to accost him at the side of his desk.

"Lovely to see you again too, Ellie," Ferguson murmured. "But I see no harm in meeting here, even if we all have unpleasant memories of him calling us out on the carpet."

Ellie frowned at him, some of the anger leaching out of her blue eyes. "Then you didn't choose to meet here because of what happened in this room?"

"I've no idea what you are going on about, Ellie. What happened?"

"This is where Richard shot Father, you dolt," she said, not sparing anyone the blow. "Father died behind the desk, and then Richard turned his pistol on himself. And poor Maria was the one who found them — Richard's pistol was still smoking when she rushed in."

Ferguson felt sick. That explained the new carpets — and why no one but him ever crossed the middle of the room. And if his father had died behind this desk...

He stood abruptly, knocking the chair over, and Maria started crying in earnest. "Perhaps the drawing room would be better after all."

Ellie gave him a scathing look, then turned on her heel and marched toward the door. She tried to comfort Maria, but the twins scorned her just as they snubbed Ferguson, preferring to keep to their own company. Ellie shrugged her shoulders and walked on without them — but her spine was so stiff that Ferguson saw through her disinterest.

They repaired to one of the drawing rooms across the passageway, a room decorated in the creams and reds of the Rothwell coat of arms. The twins sat with perfect posture on a red and cream striped settee, arranging their skirts like shields around them. Ellie flung herself into a nearby armchair, her insouciance a remarkable departure from her attitude ten years earlier, when she had been so desperate to please their father.

In the ten years of Ferguson's Scottish exile, and in the long, lonely years at Cambridge and Eton before that, he had often wished for a real family.

But with the remnants of his family arrayed before him, he remembered that family brought its own set of demons.

They had abandoned the teacart in their haste, but he suspected this would be an unpleasant business discussion rather than a social call. He leaned against the mantel, arms crossed, and looked at Ellie. "What do you wish to speak to me about?"

Ellie gestured at the twins. "You should ask them, since they do not seem to want my assistance."

Kate glared at her. "I do not see how you could help with our ambitions. We want time to explore society before being forced to marry, not time to disgrace ourselves as you have done."

She may have been right, but it didn't stop Ferguson's need to defend his sister. He barely knew the twins, but he had grown up with Ellie, and he refused to see her shamed by her own family.

"Ellie is not a disgrace. You would do well to remember that, Catherine. She could teach you many things if you let her."

"Father said he did not know which of you was a worse

influence," Kate retorted. "But it was because of both of you that he kept us penned up. He said he would have cloistered us if he could to keep us from becoming like the rest of his children, but he wouldn't turn into a Papist to protect us."

Ellie laughed, a dark sound without a trace of humor. "Father would have cloistered you regardless of his religious beliefs if he could have seen an advantage to it. I'm sure he intended for you to come out when it convenienced him. Perhaps he was waiting for some property he wanted to come up on the marriage mart, since God knows he didn't need the money."

"Regardless, it would have been nice if you had tried to be real siblings, rather than leaving us alone," Kate said. "We never did care for Henry and Richard, and they were too old besides, but both of you..."

She trailed off. Ellie caught Ferguson's eye for just a moment, recognizing their old alliance before remembering what Ferguson had done to end it. She looked as guilty as Ferguson felt, though. Until Ferguson had escaped to Scotland, they had always watched out for each other, avoiding their older brothers and ignoring the babes who were born after their mother was replaced.

Ferguson cleared his throat. "What's done is done. Besides, when I left, you still had your mother to look after you."

Maria's eyes filled with tears again. "Mama was nearly as indifferent as Father was, in her own way. She was always going off to Bath to take the waters, since she was too fragile to bear Father's remarks about how she failed to do her duty."

The last duchess barely survived giving birth to the twins, and she had not had any pregnancies after that. Demanding more heirs when he already had three sons seemed unnecessary — but the duke knew even then that Henry and Richard were unstable, and he would not wish to have Ferguson as his only insurance policy.

Still, from what Ferguson had seen before he left, it was the older children, particularly the sons, who were lightning rods for their father's temper. Even Ellie had not suffered too much when she was younger, although he suspected that his father became harder with her as she grew to look more like their mother — and especially after her husband died and she refused to return to his household.

So he snapped impatiently, "We can either all go on like this forever, despising each other for what happened a decade ago, or we can overcome it. I would prefer to forgive each other, if only because I think the old man would hate to see us unite."

"'Forgive each other'?" Ellie asked, with another bitter laugh. "What, precisely, do you have to forgive us for?"

Ferguson shifted his weight to his other booted foot. "I've nothing to forgive you for directly — but I must find it within me to forgive you for living your entire life in reaction to the old man if we are to have a real relationship now."

"How dare you," Ellie spat. "As though running off to Scotland was not a reaction to our dear father."

"I did not say it wasn't," Ferguson said. "But I think we all need to stop running away — unless you like the life you have?"

She looked down at her hands, twisting one of her rings around her finger. The twins looked back and forth between them as though watching a prizefight, mouths gaping in shock.

Finally, Kate said, "If you aren't returning to Scotland, it surely doesn't matter to you whether we marry quickly. Will you give me and Maria time to find the right matches, and not pressure us to marry so you can leave?"

He had forgotten the question that started the whole conversation, but perhaps it was good that they had spoken of other issues first. He might have answered differently had he not just told Ellie to stop running. He sighed. "I can't say I will stay in London forever, but I will not push you to marry before you are ready."

"You've had quite the change of heart in the last two weeks, brother," Ellie said, flexing her fingers out in front of her as though to deny the temptation of toying with her ring. "Do either of your lady loves have anything to do with this?"

He shot her a warning glance. She knew about Madeleine's secret, but the twins did not. It was too late, though. "You're courting two women at once?" Kate asked.

"'Courting' isn't the right word for a mistress, dear," Ellie said. "That term only applies to Lady Madeleine, does it not?"

"If you do anything to harm her, Ellie..."

"I won't do a thing," Ellie said. "If you had been here the past ten years, you would realize my reputation for indiscretions is just as inaccurate as your reputation for seduction. But I do find it suspicious that you are suddenly considering staying in London for any length of time."

He could not explain himself without saying Madeleine had already refused him, and that was as much her secret as it was his. All he divulged was, "I do have to marry someday, if only so you don't all end up with our odious cousin Charles as the head of the family. London seems as good a place as any to find a duchess."

Kate's eyes sparkled with the first real humor he had seen from her since his return. "So you need matchmaking just as much as we do? Can we help?"

"Will you at least agree to come out if I say yes?"

Kate and Maria looked at each other. He hadn't realized how much he had wanted to see them happy until that moment, and he felt a little twist of emotion as they both grinned at him.

"That is a fair trade," Maria said. "After all, we should investigate to make sure Lady Madeleine is the right woman for you, and not just the first one you saw after coming back to London."

He didn't need their help, even though Madeleine was, in fact, the first woman he had seen in London — but if it led to an easier bond with the twins, he would play along. He turned his attention to Ellie. "Do you care to have a hand in bringing them out, or do you prefer to stay away from this muddle?"

Ellie still lounged in her chair with a relaxed air, but he saw her frown. "It is their decision, not mine. I will help to the extent that they do not think my reputation is a burden."

Kate's grin widened. "If the plan is to live without reacting to Father, then I think it's only fitting you should be at our debut. We may as well show the ton that we all stand together despite what they think of both of you."

With her carefree air and the rumors still swirling about their father's death, Ferguson suspected the ton would soon see Kate in the same light if she was not careful, but he kept the thought to himself. He was too relieved that they would come out and move on with their lives without continuing to argue — and that they had thawed slightly to Ellie, even if the four of them were far from being friends.

Ellie stood abruptly, her eyes moist. She looked at Ferguson for a long moment; if there were tears there, they were just a sheen over a pool of resolve.

"Don't disappoint me, Will," she said, using the name he had abandoned when he left for Eton. "I couldn't bear it if you left me behind again."

He didn't say anything as she departed. He wondered how long it would take for her to believe that he would not abandon her — it was rather similar to Madeleine's distrust of him. But where Madeleine's concern was based on hearsay, Ellie had spent the last decade angry at him.

She might think he would turn into their father — but she had inherited the old man's bitterness. He just had to convince Madeleine, his sisters, and everyone else that he wasn't the man they thought he was before they gave up on him entirely.

Or before the temptation to hang it all and go back to Scotland grew any stronger.

CHAPTER TWENTY-FIVE

That night, Madeleine sat in silence in Ferguson's coach. Josephine rode with them, on Alex's orders, and there was nothing they wished to talk about with an audience.

But despite her maid's presence, it felt like she and Ferguson inhabited a special world, created just for the two of them. The thought consumed her, made her wish that they never had to rejoin the world that would someday pull them apart. She felt it just watching him stride into a room, whether it was the theatre or a crowded ballroom in Mayfair, and it was all she could think of when she fell into his arms. In those moments, she forgot her reasons for refusing him — and never wanted to let him go.

But could those feelings last when her time at the theatre ended? Or did she feel so special with him because they were in extraordinary circumstances, magical only because they could never be repeated?

She looked across the coach. His face was inscrutable in the shadows. If they could talk, she knew what he would say about her thoughts — that what they had was unique, and that she should become his duchess.

But she had seen love matches flare out, leaving two unhappy people trapped in the wreckage. Ferguson had seen his own father destroyed by love — it could be a poison as much as a pleasure. Could this bond they shared turn into something lasting?

Or would it grow darker, twist around into loathing as the pressures of society overtook them?

Perhaps the pensive look on her face was what convinced Josephine that it was safe to leave her alone with Ferguson when they arrived. The maid left her in the foyer, telling her to dress while she cleared the path into Salford House.

Madeleine did not feel confident loving anyone. But she didn't feel like letting go either. So as soon as Josephine was out of sight, she took Ferguson's hand and pulled him up the stairs.

His lips were on her before he even shut the door. He had been unreadable in the coach, but now his desire for her was unmistakable. Their mouths locked against each other, his hands skimming over her derriere, her fingers burying themselves in his hair. The heat, the hunger, all the swirling need and frustration and desire and fear — the strength of it all scared her, even as it added a fierce edge to their kiss.

He untied her cravat and pulled her shirt over her head, dumping it on the floor before claiming her lips again. She tried to do the same to him, but he caught her hands and pulled away.

"You must return to Salford House too soon, love," he said. "We have to dress you, not undress me."

He used the endearment like it was easy for him, like he had already come to terms with what was between them. She loved it and hated it, just as undecided about the word as she was about what he wanted from her. So she kissed him, not wanting to think about the question he would undoubtedly ask her again.

He stopped her after one last kiss and turned her bodily toward the mirror. "No more, Mad, if we're going to get you ready again."

He disappeared into her dressing room. She stared at herself in the mirror while he rummaged through her clothes. She still wore her powdered wig from the theatre, disheveled from Hamlet's final madness, which heightened the pallor of her skin — and the blush spreading across her cheeks. Her breasts were bound, but she was bare from the waist up, and her belly narrowed under her ribs before her hips flared out to fill her breeches.

Ferguson returned, dumping a dress and underthings on the chair beside her. Then he stood behind her, placing a kiss on the nape of her neck as he started to pull hairpins out of her wig.

"Do you intend to be my lady's maid, then?" she asked, her voice coming out in a breathy thread.

"If you are willing to submit to my ministrations," he said. "Or I could ring for Lizzie, but I would have to leave..."

He removed her wig and set it on the dressing table. Instead of attacking the pins that held her own hair to her head, he dropped his fingers down to graze across her shoulders, pulling her closer against his chest as he kissed the side of her neck.

She tilted her head to improve his access. "I will require a demonstration of your talents before I agree to keep you as my dresser."

He chuckled, and she felt his laughter rumble through her. "Just a short demonstration, my lady. I do not usually work without a guarantee of payment."

Madeleine tried to turn around toward him, eager for another kiss, but he pinned her in place. "I want you to watch in the mirror as I dress you."

His voice dropped, and she shivered in response. She glanced at him in the mirror. The controlled look was back in his eyes — he intended to do more than help her with her clothes.

Thank goodness, she thought. She should have been ashamed, should have denied wanting something so wanton — her morals were appalling. But there was no mockery in his gaze, no judgment to chide her for her bad behavior.

He wanted this just as much as she did.

So when his hands came around her sides to untie the knot holding her bindings in place, she stayed still, watching as he had asked her to. She leaned against him, her back against his muscled chest, the hard ridge of his erection pressing insistently above the curve of her derriere. He only released her to unwind the linen, not slow and sensual like the last time, but fast and impatient, eager to see his prize. He twisted it around his fist as he moved his arm around her body, leaving her standing in place as he pulled the cloth away. Then he dropped it to the floor, bringing his hands back up to cup her.

She watched as her breasts filled his palms, shuddered as he massaged his fingers into her flesh. The angry red marks of the bindings crisscrossed her skin, and he traced one with his thumb. "When we are married, you must not abuse yourself like this again."

He said it lightly, the same offhanded tone that said he already accepted her as his fate — and believed she would accept him as well.

"So you would have me stop acting?" she asked, her voice frigid even in its breathlessness.

He flicked his thumb across her nipple, and she gasped at the sensation after so many hours bound up in linen. She saw him smile in the mirror as he repeated the motion with her other nipple, and she sensed that he wanted to distract her.

But he answered her question. "I think it's dangerous, foolish, and risky. But even though I should order you away from the theatre," and here he paused to place a long, aching kiss at the base of her neck, "I wouldn't ask you to give it up."

His answer shocked her. No one, not even her own family, would think that a duchess could sneak off to the theatre on a whim.

However, he wasn't finished. "If I thought you were on the verge of ruin, I would have to stop you — for your sake, though, not mine."

"This all supposes that I agree to marry you, of course. If I recall correctly, I refused you."

His gaze in the mirror hardened; he now directed his control at his temper as well as his lust. He renewed his onslaught, his palms pressing against the sides of her breasts, kneading into her with a feeling that was half pleasure, half almost pain. With his fingers massaging from the other side, he quickly built her to the point where her nipples were hardened nubs, the small pink tips aching to be sucked.

He still didn't let her turn — still kept her facing the mirror. "There isn't time tonight to take what I want," he whispered in her ear, his breath caressing her skin with its heat. "But I will certainly give you what you want."

She should have denied his body just as she denied his proposal — but the temptation was too high and her blood was too hot to make him stop. So she watched as his tanned, deliciously rough hand skimmed down over her belly, lingered briefly to run a thumb across her navel, and then slowly, slowly began to unbutton the placket of her breeches.

She squirmed against him and he pulled her closer, wrapping

his left arm around her chest and letting the hand rest lazily on her right breast. His other hand continued its work, button after button, until her breeches were open and ready for him.

She closed her eyes as his hand slid underneath her clothing, whimpered as he found the nub of pleasure he had driven her wild with on their first night together. She was already wet for him, and he ran a finger deeper into her folds, using her own moisture to enhance the torment.

With every stroke, she writhed against him, and the building pleasure only increased her sensitivity. She felt the brocade of his waistcoat abrading her back, the buttons like cold little stars in the heat that had become her world. His arm, still encased in his jacket, rubbed against her breasts as he held her against him, and she realized that her own movements against him were causing her pleasure to spiral upward.

She couldn't get purchase on anything, balanced precariously on her high heels. She tried to reach the table, but Ferguson was unyielding. He kept her flush against him, increasing the pace, his fingers teasing her with a pleasure that was just out of reach. Finally, she reached over her head, digging her nails into his shoulder — wanting him even closer, using his body for leverage to reach the pinnacle he drove her toward.

That last little movement, thrusting herself up into his hand, was her undoing. She would have screamed his name as she fell over the edge, but he clamped a hand over her mouth. His fingers kept their pace, though, stringing the pleasure out in a series of intense waves, each peak devastating in its power.

As the onslaught slowly subsided, Madeleine was glad Ferguson had kept her so close; her legs quivered under her, and she thought she might collapse if she was not still pressed against him. He removed his hand from her mouth, brushing a knuckle across her chin to tilt it up.

She opened her eyes. By all conventional mores, the tableau in the mirror should have shamed her. Instead, she looked... sensual, more erotic than any drawing or painting she had ever seen. The look in his eyes said he desired her; his member still jutting into her back confirmed it. She had never thought of herself as desirable, with her very un-English complexion and curves. But with his arm wrapped around her shoulders and his other hand slowly withdrawing from her breeches, she looked like the most desired woman in the world.

She also looked like she belonged in that role. It was the same kick of pleasure she got at the theatre — this was a man who adored her, who might worship the ground she walked on where so many others had failed to even notice her, even if he worshipped nothing and no one else.

But if she knew anything from the theatre, it was that adoration was a fickle thing. The same audience that wanted her tonight might throw shoes at her the next. And worship was not the same as love — and not the type of behavior a rake like Ferguson would sustain forever.

Even as she had the thought, Ferguson's arm tightened around her. "You may miss the theatre, but I can assure you that you'll miss this if you don't say yes. None of your other options are more appealing."

He was right. No woman would ever willingly trade an aristocratic life for the hand-to-mouth — or stage-to-bed — existence of the theatre. And spending the rest of her life in Ferguson's arms would be preferable to an endlessly dull round of at-homes with

Aunt Augusta.

Still, her entire rebellion was based on the desire to choose what to do with her life. Ferguson's arms, draped possessively around her, said he thought the choice — his choice — was already made. How many more choices would he make for her if they were married?

So Madeleine lifted her chin and said in her coolest tones, "Your demonstration was quite sufficient. If you will help me to finish dressing, I should return to Salford House."

She saw his jaw clench, but he didn't say anything else. He ruthlessly stripped her out of her breeches, hose, and heels, still gentle, but without a single lingering caress. She raised her arms and he dropped the chemise over her head, fastened her stays around her, and quickly smoothed the evening gown down on top of it all.

He had all the efficiency of a lady's maid, treating her like a chore instead of a prize. She couldn't fault him. She had pushed him to the limit of his patience, and he was probably eager to see her leave.

She tried to make a joke, hoping humor would ease the tension. "I never thought to be thankful for all the other mistresses you've had, but you are much more skilled at this than I assumed."

He didn't laugh. "Don't test me. You shall not put yourself in the same category as my former mistresses."

He turned her toward him as he spoke, and he glared down at her until she shifted uncomfortably under his gaze. "Do you know what truly surprises me about you, Mad? It's not the theatre, or your talent, or all the passion you've kept hidden away. It's that you can be so brave when it comes to the stage..."

He broke off, sweeping his gaze over her face again like he was searching for the last clue to a puzzle. Then he kissed her, slowly, with the caressing tenderness that was missing from their earlier inferno.

He finally pulled away, leaving her dazed — and all the more vulnerable to his next words. "So brave — and yet with love, you are such a coward."

She gasped. His face was hard again, his temper high. "I won't force you to acknowledge how you feel, even though I want to — even though I think *you* want me to. It would be easier for you to accept me if you didn't have to choose, if you didn't have to believe in me the way I believe in you."

"Ferguson," she started, but he cut her off.

"Don't say a word," he said, somehow gentle despite his anger. "I won't ask again until the play is over. But I must warn you that 'yes' won't be enough for me anymore — I want your heart, in exchange for the one you've already captured from me. And if you are too afraid to say it" — and here he broke off for one last, all-consuming kiss — "you aren't the woman I thought you were."

He left then, not waiting for her to speak, merely saying he would send Lizzie to fix her hair. As she waited, she stared in the mirror, shocked by what had just transpired. Their whole conversation — both the delightful interlude and the devastating aftermath — had taken only fifteen minutes, and yet it felt like fifteen years.

Was she really a coward? She had felt so daring, standing up on stage, sleeping with Ferguson. But all those risks felt like they were a dream, and what she ran from now was the reality of the rest of her life.

She touched her lips, still sensitive after his onslaught. What would she say when he asked his question again? And what was worse — giving in to her love despite her fears and misgivings, or denying it because she was just as much of a coward as Ferguson accused her of being?

CHAPTER TWENTY-SIX

Two weeks later, Madeleine sprawled on the worn floorboards of the stage, remaining motionless as the final scene played out around her. She always loved the moment when she died. This audience wept — she had brought them to their knees again.

Tonight, waiting for the play to end felt even more intense. If Madame Legrand kept her promise, this was her last public performance. Not just her last performance — the last time she would use a sword, the last time she would raise her voice and let it soar over the room, the last time she could wear breeches — the last time anyone noticed her talent rather than her title.

And the last time Ferguson escorted her as his mistress.

She heard the chorus rise behind her, the final bits of dialogue beginning as Fortinbras proclaimed the tragedy he had stumbled upon in the Danish court. The floorboards pulsed as her fellow actors moved around her body, and she realized she was trembling. Unless he had changed his mind, Ferguson would expect an answer to his proposal tonight.

He wouldn't change his mind. He made his desire clear in every moment he could steal with her, as though seducing her was the answer to winning her heart. It wasn't his sexual prowess that she needed assured of — although she was happy to let him try to win her that way. The issue was her heart — and the knowledge that she was just as cowardly as Ferguson had accused her of being.

Tonight, he would want words, not kisses. But was she ready to answer him?

The music stopped and the curtain dropped. She heard the audience screaming Marguerite's name, felt their clapping and stomping in her bones. The man who played Fortinbras helped her up and she dusted off her jacket, trying to calm herself so that she could greet their applause with nonchalant grace. But when the curtain rose again and she prepared to take her bow, there was only one man she could see.

Ferguson sat in the front row, directly in her line of vision, his gaze roving over her just as she knew his hands would when he had her alone. He had sat there through the whole play, and on this final night, he was the only person she wanted to see. She did not know if he could sense her thoughts, but when she had walked onto the stage at the beginning of this final play, she realized her last performance was for him.

The sound of the crowd was an indistinct roar. She bowed, then bowed again, but the general adoration of the audience, which had thrilled her for weeks, was no longer enough. It was Ferguson's attention that filled her, his applause that warmed her and made her feel like she had done something worth commending.

Madame Legrand bustled out, ready to address her patrons. Madeleine froze, still watching Ferguson. He seemed poised to tackle Madame at the first hint of betrayal. Madeleine thought the woman's word was good — but greed often overcame good intentions.

"Ladies and gentleman…" Madame Legrand began. While her

French accent was still laughable compared to Madeleine's, her words were appropriate, thanking them for their attendance and asking them to return for the staging of *Richard III* that would begin the following week.

After acknowledging the polite smattering of applause, she turned to Madeleine. "And now, if you would all be so kind, please join me in wishing Madame Guerrier much joy on her retirement from the stage."

Madeleine exhaled a breath she hadn't intended to hold. The two women smiled briefly at each other, and Madeleine realized she had survived her act unscathed. She looked down at Ferguson, who still watched her, and he grinned at her triumph.

But then she curtseyed to the audience and noticed their reaction. People streamed out in droves as soon as the play ended, but those near the doors turned back as though they couldn't believe their ears, blocking the exits. Those prone to tears wept again in earnest; others stared at her in shock. Actresses who achieved Madeleine's early success simply did not retire after their first engagement. The news would take everyone by surprise.

She finally looked more closely at the people surrounding Ferguson. The aristocrats had claimed the best seats, and the people she recognized from the ton — an even mix of rakish men and daring matrons — stared at Ferguson, their gloved hands covering their mouths as they whispered into their companions' ears.

She curtseyed again, taking care not to look at Ferguson as she came up from her bow. The audience would think what it wished to think. With Marguerite Guerrier absent from London, the gossips would soon move on to other topics. She would not let their reaction stop her from taking joy in the sweetness of this moment. After all, it was a compliment that no one wanted her to quit.

She had done the impossible — put aside her proper life, conquered the stage, and survived to take up whatever life she wished to choose next. No one had discovered her. Both Augusta and Alex had assured her that they would neither send her to Bermuda nor force her to marry Ferguson if she came home unscathed tonight. She still wasn't speaking to Amelia, but she and the others had formed the rocky beginning of a truce.

She was free to give Ferguson an answer from her heart — if her heart and tongue could finally cooperate.

The curtain dropped between them for the final time, but she saw him turn toward the door before the heavy velvet blocked her view. He would come for her — and she needed to be ready for him.

*   *   *

From the look on Madeleine's face when he entered her tiny dressing room, Ferguson knew she expected him. Throughout her final performance, it felt like her attention was fixed on him, and he was glad she thought of him rather than the career she was leaving behind.

Even better, she had become increasingly unguarded with him over the past two weeks. Whether conversing in a ballroom during a party only made bearable by each other's presence, or burning together through the fast, stolen moments they found at the house on Dover Street, Ferguson sensed she was beginning to open to him, slowly willing to divulge feelings she'd never admitted to anyone else.

She was different tonight, though. Her cheeks were flushed and her green eyes sparkled — an artist in her moment of triumph. But as she watched him watching her, her eyes widened and he heard her suck in a breath. He had seen her like this before — on the verge of panic, unable to declare her feelings.

He knew the smart thing would be to soothe her, to wait a week — or at least until morning — before renewing his proposal. But the same madness that came over him in Hyde Park claimed him again. He loved her, needed her, couldn't imagine losing her, and he didn't want to wait another minute to possess her.

It took all his resolve to approach her slowly, like the gentleman he should be rather than the beast he knew he was. He would wait until they returned to their house, as much as it killed him to stay silent. After all, most women would not enjoy entertaining a marriage proposal in a cramped, dusty closet in Seven Dials.

And depending on her answer, he might appreciate a nearby bed — or the ability to leave without having to see her home first.

So he was gentle as he pulled her into his arms, restrained as he placed a slow, grazing kiss on her lips. "You were magnificent, Marguerite."

He caught himself just in time, calling her by her pseudonym in case anyone was in hearing range. She quirked her lips in a quick grin and he was pleased to see her fear ebb. "The audience will miss me, will they not?"

He threaded his fingers through hers, a simple intimacy his life had lacked for so long. "Better to leave them wanting more of you, darling."

She pulled him toward her, kissing him herself. He let her take the lead, enjoying the light touch of her lips against his, turning ravenous as she deepened the kiss. She still had a reputation for shyness in the ton, but she was no longer reserved with him — and no longer waited for him to move first.

By the time she broke off the kiss, he was hard for her, the blood rushing out of his head and taking all his good intentions with it. He tried to pull her back into the kiss, but she sidestepped him with a wicked grin. "I thought you advised me to 'leave them wanting more'?"

He laughed. "You don't need any lessons in how to frustrate me. If you only knew how I've wanted you these past weeks..."

He bit off the words before he could say anything else. It was disconcerting, how he could not control his impulses with her. He wouldn't let his tongue run away with him tonight. She deserved a silvery proposal, not a bumbling outpouring of affection.

And if she did intend to reject him, he refused to sound like he was begging.

Thankfully, she wasn't put off by the need in his voice. She whispered, "I've wanted you too, Ferguson."

His trousers became uncomfortable at the thought of her dreaming of him. From her downward glance and slow, blooming smile, she knew how she affected him. He cleared his throat, but his voice still rasped as he said, "Shall we return to your house?"

She edged past him to open the door and peek outside. "Josephine said to wait here. She did not like how the crowd sounded and wished to check the alleyway first."

Ferguson should have thought of that. In his desire to reach Madeleine, he had used the hidden door beside the stage rather than circling to the alley entrance. But before he could go outside, Josephine returned with Madame Legrand.

"The door guard says there are many people waiting to see you, ma petite," Josephine said, her eyes narrowed and her voice full of concern. "They are in an uproar that you will no longer act."

Madeleine didn't panic. "It is nothing to be concerned about, Josephine. I will simply stay in costume and Ferguson can keep me safe."

She sounded so confident in his ability to protect her. He found he liked it. And he had no intention of violating her faith.

Josephine wasn't assured, but she agreed to stay behind and take a cab home after the crowd dispersed. She had attended Madeleine's shopping excursions and errands too many times over the years to risk being seen with her tonight. Leaving Madeleine unchaperoned with Ferguson was better than giving such a blatant clue to Madeleine's identity.

Ferguson thought the mob had done him a favor, despite the danger — and he would put their unchaperoned time to good use.

Madeleine draped her cloak over her arm. With her wig in place and no dresslike fabric to obscure her masculine attire, she still looked like Marguerite. If they hurried through the crowd, the dimness of the alley would conceal her. Then she squared her shoulders and turned to Madame Legrand. "Thank you for holding to your word, Madame. I enjoyed every moment of the stage, but I must take up my other responsibilities."

"It was an honor to have you on my stage, Madame Guerrier," she said, maintaining the pretense. "If you ever wish to return, you will be most welcome."

The woman turned and curtsied to Ferguson. "Thank you for your patronage, your grace. I've no doubt next season's plays will benefit from the renovations you are funding."

Ferguson shook his head warningly, but she misinterpreted it as modesty. "Don't say that it is nothing, your grace! You could have evicted me entirely, and you've promised to turn the place into a theatre any respectable woman would be pleased to attend. I shall not forget your generosity."

Madeleine rounded on Ferguson, the previous warmth in her eyes turning to sparks. "Did you bribe Madame to keep her word?"

He sighed. "She would have kept her word regardless. The gesture was made out of gratitude, not as a threat."

Madeleine gave him a coolly assessing look — one so many women excelled at, promising she would return to the subject when she had a chance to rail at him properly. She turned briefly to shake hands with Madame Legrand, saying she looked forward to attending the new theatre as a member of the audience.

Then she returned her gaze to Ferguson. "Shall we brave the mob, your grace?" she asked.

He offered his arm and swept her out of the dressing room. "You seem annoyed," he observed as they slipped between the discarded sets that lined the passage to the alley entrance.

"Whyever do you think I am annoyed, your grace?" she asked, navigating around a wooden tree and nearly steering him into the wicked-looking rack of theatrical spears on the opposite wall.

"You've called me 'your grace' twice in a minute. Unless you've become a toad-eater, I might almost think you are insulting me."

She drew herself up into her masculine walk as they reached the door, slipping her hand off his arm. "We can address how you bribed Madame in the carriage, your grace," she said insolently. "But I must not be distracted now. We are only moments away from my permanent retirement, and I shan't be found out now."

Madeleine was right. They could not be unguarded in the moments it would take to reach his coach. The doorkeeper held a cudgel in one of his large fists, and Ferguson recognized the actors who played Rosencrantz and Guildenstern loitering to the side, ready to assist.

"The crowd is like to press against you when you leave, your grace," the guard warned.

"Should we try the front?" Madeleine asked.

"'Tis worse," Madame Legrand said, coming up from behind to watch their departure. "And there are more men outside to protect you here. I asked several actors and stagehands to cordon the path to your carriage. Do not hesitate, though. They will not be able to hold the crowd for long."

Ferguson felt all the instincts from a long line of dukes and lairds rise up within him. "Very well," he said, changing his grip on his walking stick so he could use it as a club. He trapped Madeleine's arm against him again, warning her to stay close and ignoring her brief attempt to pull away. He nodded at the guard, and the man threw the door open into the alleyway.

Outside, it was chaos — like a crowd at a prizefight, although there were more women in the alleyway than one would ever see around a ring. The crowd turned toward the door and roared, and he saw instantly how dangerous they could be. Several of the men held bottles, and Ferguson could smell how desperate they were to see Marguerite one final time — the mingling odors of unwashed flesh, expensive perfumes, and gin were an explosive combination.

Madeleine instinctively stepped closer to him, barely evading the grasping fingers coming at her over the arms of the guards. The line of men Madame had stationed there protected a bare three feet of space between the mob and the back wall of the theatre. It was just enough for Madeleine and Ferguson to slip through to the coach at the end of the line — if the line could hold, and if the coachman could keep the horses from bolting in the melee.

The line already threatened to collapse, and he couldn't regroup them if they fell. He didn't wait to see if Madeleine was ready. He dashed for the carriage, half dragging her beside him and swatting away the proffered bouquets and outstretched arms as they passed. He kept her between him and the wall, safe from others' hands even if he couldn't protect her from the noise or smell.

At the pace he set, it took only a few moments to reach the coach. One moment more, and a guard had flung open the door so Ferguson could hand her up onto the step. She turned before sliding through the door, however, wavering on one high-heeled shoe as she surveyed the crowd.

In the dim torchlight, Ferguson saw her tears. He swore under his breath. He never should have let her come this close to such a frightening crowd.

But then she grasped his shoulder, resting on it to lean over him and take the nearest posy from someone's outstretched hand. The devotee, a young aristocrat who looked no more than twenty, gasped and stuttered his compliments, as red as the flowers she took from him. The crowd hushed abruptly as they watched her bring the flowers to her face, and Ferguson realized she wasn't afraid.

She was sad to leave all of this behind.

And he was undeniably jealous that she stopped to wave them all farewell.

So it was with more force than usual that he said, "Get into the carriage." She looked down at him, tears still on her cheeks, and nodded once. Then she saluted the crowd, a final masculine bow before she disappeared into the coach.

The crowd started yelling again, this time hurling insults at him. Ferguson didn't linger. He flung himself into the coach beside Madeleine and pulled the door shut behind him. As the coachman attempted to steer them out of the alley, he flicked the curtain aside to survey the crowd. Now that he could see across the mob, it was apparent that those who worshipped at the actress's altar included every class that could afford the price of a ticket. They were just as sad about Madeleine's retirement as she appeared to be.

The haze of jealousy ebbed, and a strange emotion took its place — pride. Others would condemn her if they knew what she had done, but Madeleine was truly impressive on the stage. She had also been steadfast in her determination to tread the boards despite the dangers. She couldn't articulate her feelings the way he would like, but her courage in this matter awed him.

He closed the curtain and pulled her hand into his, still clutching the boy's flowers. "Are you angry with me?" she asked, sounding uncertain with him for the first time in weeks.

He brought her hand to his lips and kissed the tip of each finger, the heat of her skin mingling with the scent of the flowers. "No. I am sorry I was so abrupt with you — I needed to see you safe."

She brought her other hand up to remove the flowers so she could twine her fingers around his, and she rested her head against his shoulder. He wanted to kiss her there, but she still wore her powdered wig. He tightened his grip on her hand and said, "Are you truly ready to give up the stage?"

Her fingers stilled within his, and her pause was ugly in contrast to the boisterous noises of the theatre district at night. Finally, she whispered, "That was not the question I expected of you, Ferguson."

He watched her bowed profile in the dim lamplight. "This is

related, is it not?"

She edged away from him, into the corner, his hand trailing after her like a ship's mooring not yet cut. "I don't know how to say what I need to say."

She was going to say no. He snatched his hand away, stiffening his spine against his sudden panic. She was going to say no, and her family hated him, so there would be no help from that quarter. And she hadn't been publicly ruined after all, so she didn't need him, not really. Unless she found herself with child, she could pretend they had never even met.

His thoughts spiraled down into some dark, ugly place, wondering how he could change her mind. But then Madeleine stroked his face, and her voice pulled him back to the surface.

"What did you do to Madame Legrand?" she asked.

The question disoriented him. He had forgotten all about Legrand. He was waiting for Madeleine's denial, not a reference to his bribery. "She claimed she would let you go, but I wanted to make sure she knew that I could destroy her if she gave your name to the press. Refurbishing the building was an inducement, but if she needs a stronger method of encouragement, she knows I will tear it down."

"But surely you can't raze a theatre you don't own?"

"I do own it," he said, not attempting to prevaricate. "That was why I attended the first night. My steward suggesting raising the rents and thought I might like to see your performance."

She looked stunned. She would take this as yet another sign of his autocratic nature. But before he could muster a defense, she said, "So you could have demanded that Madame Legrand release me at any time?"

He nodded warily. "The thought crossed my mind when you said she had forced you, but since you didn't seem eager to quit, I didn't do anything about it."

Of course, he had gotten something by leaving Madame Legrand alone — two weeks with Madeleine in their private charade. But she looked at him like he had just showered her in diamonds.

"Do you know what I will always remember from tonight's performance?" she asked.

"The mob?" he guessed, surprised again as the conversation took another unexpected turn.

"No. I will remember you applauding as I took my final bow. I was sure then about the answer to your question, but I am even more sure now."

"What did I do to make you sure?" he asked, phrasing his question carefully in case he needed to learn what he would have to do to win her over.

"You were there for me. You were there through everything, even though every other man would have fled — or worse, ruined me."

"I did ruin you," he pointed out.

She grinned. "Yes, but I must confess I enjoyed it."

Her smile kindled a glimmer of hope. "But won't you miss this life?"

Madeleine looked down at the small bouquet in her lap. "I may always miss it. I imagine it is like a sailor who retires to the countryside — he is safe, but I suspect some part of him always longs for the sea. But surely you knew that — you must feel the same about leaving Scotland?"

"Not precisely," he said. Scotland had been an escape, not a desired destination in its own right. "My life there is not so different

SARA RAMSEY

than what I may have had on any English estate, after all."

"Then you no longer wish to return there?"

Ferguson sensed the trap in the question, knew better than to commit — or to falsely deny. "If I have reason to stay in England, I shall."

He wasn't purposefully dishonest. After all, how could he answer that question when he was so far from knowing his own mind on the matter? It satisfied Madeleine, though, and she smiled at him with all the certainty she had lacked when they left the theatre.

"So you really shan't miss the theatre?"

"I had my adventure. It ended as all adventures must, and it's not the theatre I will miss. I believe I shall miss a certain house on Dover Street, and the man who paid to keep me there."

"Is it just his riches you care about?" he asked with mock severity. He felt himself grinning like a fool, though. Surely she wouldn't jest like this if she meant to deny him.

She pretended to consider. "He does have a title, of course."

He pulled her back toward him, dropped his hand to caress the juncture of her thighs, and she squealed at his sudden touch. "He is also... rather accomplished."

She was breathless already, and the curl of her fingers into his jacket made him ache to give her everything her body already clamored for. But she somehow managed to resist him, just enough to look into his eyes.

"Are you not going to ask your question, Ferguson?"

They were in a carriage, with her in breeches and his jacket covered in powder from her wig. It was an absurd location for a proposal — but they were an absurd couple.

So he picked up her hands and cradled them in his. "Madeleine, you are everything I've dreamed of and nothing I deserve. Say you'll redeem my faults and marry me?"

It wasn't the speech he had memorized, but he couldn't remember a word of it with her eyes shining up at him. He couldn't say it again, though — he just had to hope she would finally give them the answer they both needed.

CHAPTER TWENTY-SEVEN

She had expected the question — had practically begged him to ask it — but she was still surprised at the depth of the joy that filled her. He was sincere in his love for her.

And over the past two weeks, she finally believed him. He had seen all her secrets and loved her for them, not despite them. Tonight only confirmed it. He had watched her like he enjoyed seeing her on stage, not like he wanted to change or control her.

With that realization, her panic died. Neither of them was blessed with the family they wanted, although hers was infinitely preferable to his. Her past scared her, scarred her, taught her that love was a fleeting thing that couldn't stand up to duty. But if Ferguson could love the part of her that contradicted every virtue of a straitlaced duchess — how could the family they created together go wrong if he loved her like that?

Madeleine lingered briefly on her joy, trying to commit the picture of him, and this moment, to memory, but his fingers tightened on hers and she realized he was more nervous than he sounded.

"Ferguson," she said, wrapping her arms around his neck. "I never thought I would find a love worth the risk, but you've proved me wrong. Regardless of what we face, I cannot imagine anything I would rather do than spend my life with you."

He cupped her face with his hands. She saw the emotions rioting in his blue eyes — all the elation and eagerness she knew she mirrored. "Then is that a yes?"

The sweetness of the moment brought unexpected tears to her eyes. "Yes. I love you, Ferguson. I don't know why it took me so long to realize it, but thank you for waiting."

He grinned, and she brought a hand around to brush a piece of dark auburn hair off his forehead. "Do you know how I survived the wait?" he asked, running his thumb across her lips.

She shook her head against the constraint of his hands and his grin turned wicked. "I imagined all the ways I could pleasure you when you finally agreed to be mine. I think you will discover that my imagination is quite wild."

Her cheeks heated under his hand. "You will have many nights to show me, love."

It was the first time she had called him that, and he rewarded her with a kiss — a deep, claiming kiss, one she could sink into, one that sent tendrils of heat weaving through every hidden chamber of her soul. She stroked his cheek, felt the smoothness of his skin, and knew he had shaved for her — as though he did not want a single problem to mar this evening.

He kept up his assault on her mouth, driving her to the point where she was desperate for something beyond their kiss, lovely as it was. She reached down between them, searching for the bulge in his breeches, hoping to urge him on. He captured her hand in one of his, breaking away from the kiss long enough to speak. "Not yet, Mad — taking you in a carriage is on the list, but I'd rather save it for a night when we've more than five minutes to devote to it."

She laughed, and he captured the sound with another kiss. The man was just as mad as she was — and they were perfect for each other.

By the time the carriage stopped, she couldn't wait to leave it, had already shoved the door open before the coachman could descend from the box. Ferguson outmaneuvered her, though, stepping down first and then turning to take her in his arms. This time, he didn't set her on the pavement — he kept her cradled against him, carrying her in impatient, ground-eating strides to the door of Marguerite's house.

Bristow could barely open the door in time for Ferguson to stride through it. She heard the butler greet them with an equal mix of deference and amusement, but neither of them acknowledged him. Ferguson was already halfway up the stairs before the front door closed behind them, and into her chamber a few moments later.

He shut the door with his shoulder. The arm under her knees shifted as he turned the key in the lock. Then his mouth was on her again, as though he couldn't waste the precious seconds it would take to settle her onto the bed.

She couldn't waste them either. Telling him she loved him was like removing the last boulder between her heart and the world. A torrent of emotion flooded through her, washing away every trace of restraint, every bit of conscious thought. She clung to him, the one constant in her shifting internal landscape, a need and a fulfillment wrapped up together. He offered it to her freely, demand and devotion both, an unbreakable cycle she would have an entire lifetime to explore.

Tonight, the devotion was in his eyes, sparking blue in the low light of her bedroom. But the demand was in the way his tongue plundered her mouth, his hands roving over her as he sat on the chaise-longue and adjusted her position in his arms. He was too hungry for gentleness, and she was too eager to care.

He broke away, attacking the hairpins holding her wig in place. "I've dreamed of this, Mad," he said, his rough voice thrilling her as her hair cascaded down her back. "I've dreamed of you taking me in your mouth, those wet lips wrapping around my cock. I've dreamed of you straddling me here, riding me so slowly that every move was a torture neither of us could get enough of."

His hands ran through her hair, sifting it out across her skin, and she arched against him. All he did was tell her his fantasies — but his voice was so wicked, and the caresses moving down her back so tantalizing, that she was already growing moist for him. The pictures he painted were darkly erotic, the kind of dreams she'd begun to have but could never put into words. He still cradled her, and one hand continued to stroke her spine — but the other came around to curve over her sex, his thumb making slow, lazy circles against her breeches.

She whimpered, but while he purposefully stayed away from the nub that already begged for his touch, his words only drove her higher. "I've dreamed of taking you hard and fast outside a ballroom, muffling your screams, then escorting you inside and dancing with you as though you were the most proper woman in the world. I've dreamed of bending you over my desk, of you scattering every paper and ledger in your desperate need to come."

His thumb flicked across her clitoris, just once, but it was enough to make her moan. His voice softened. "I've dreamed of making love to you — slow and sweet, in my bed in Scotland, knowing we have years ahead of us for everything. I've dreamed of you on your side, of slipping into you from behind while your belly grows with our child."

The last image broke her. The flood of emotion and the cascade of need collided. She slammed up into his hand, his name on her lips. He gave her what she demanded, his fingers rough and insistent against her, stroking fast and hard. She screamed as she came, as all the visions and dreams melted into one perfect moment of clarity.

Her orgasm didn't last long — just long enough to temporarily sate her, but not long enough to exhaust her. But in that moment, she saw the decades stretch before them, and dreamed the same dream that Ferguson did — of having him, surrendering to him, conquering him, wherever they could and however they wished.

She wrapped her arms around him, no longer desperate but guessing that he was. "Let's make one of those dreams come true."

He was still in enough control to shake his head. "You still have to return to Salford House, love, much as I would like to keep you here."

She tugged on his cravat, loosening the fabric before scraping her nails down the skin she revealed. He shuddered at her touch, closer to the edge than he would admit. "But this is the last night we'll have this chair." She pulled the shirt out of his breeches, reaching up under the layers of jacket and shirt to stroke the hard muscles of his stomach, letting her arm just barely graze his shaft in the same teasing way that had driven her mad only a few moments earlier.

He groaned in response, tried to push her hand away. He only succeeded in pushing her hand closer to his cock, and she felt the way it strained toward her, imprisoned in his breeches. "I've dreamed of this chair too, Ferguson," she whispered. "Unless you aren't ready...?"

She smiled as she trailed off, stroking him again, and he growled in response. "Take off your breeches," he demanded, the last bit of his control snapping.

She stood, still touching him as her legs straddled his knees. She put first one foot, then the other, on the chaise next to him, letting him pull off her high-heeled shoes and silk stockings. She unfastened her breeches slowly, knowing it was the last time, and each button slipping through its hole was like a clock ticking down to the moment when she could have him inside her. The crotch was soaked through, and she blushed at the feel of her moisture as she shimmied out of her breeches — she couldn't have worn them again even if she wanted to.

They pooled at her feet and he lifted her out of them before she could kick them aside. Turning to recline against the arm, he made her kneel over him, and he stretched out beneath her like a pagan offering. He made quicker work of his buttons than she had, and his cock sprang forth, as hard as she knew it would be.

His hand reached for her sex again, but he didn't linger — he just smiled wickedly as he felt how wet she was for him. She wasn't sure what he wanted from her, even though she had a fair guess, but he didn't leave her in the dark. Grasping her hips, he pulled her forward, then nudged her down, slowly, until the tip of his shaft brushed against her opening.

In the past two weeks, he'd given her more orgasms than she could count, but he hadn't penetrated her since their first night in this room. She braced herself for the pain, ready to bear that moment for the pleasure that would follow. But when he surged into her, she only felt heat — and his cock rubbing against something deep inside her that had her aching to come again.

His hands at her hips guided her down until she was fully impaled, her legs deliciously strained as she straddled him. She gasped as he filled her, gasped again as his hands urged her upward, then pulled her down again. It took only a few strokes for her to realize she could control the tempo, and she threaded her fingers through his so he no longer set the pace. He smiled at her, almost a grimace as he tried to control herself.

She rose up and came down, over and over. The only points of contact were his manhood in her passage and his fingers wrapped in hers. Her breasts were still bound, aching for stimulation, but she was too impatient to give in to that desire. She quickly approached that pinnacle again, and she moved faster, her strokes shorter and harder as her need overtook her.

The climax exploded on her and she screamed again, her legs collapsing as she went over the cliff. He grabbed her hips, slammed up into her one more time before his own release overtook him. She felt his seed spill inside her as he fell back against the chaise, pulling her down to rest against his chest.

She lay against him for endless minutes, rising and falling with his breath, feeling him soften inside her. His hand slid through her hair, stroking her back, and she curled against him, utterly content.

Dreams had never come true so easily before — but now she couldn't wait for the next one.

She smiled at the thought, and he roused himself to kiss her. "Thank you, Mad."

"What are you thanking me for?"

"Besides making me take you against my better judgment?" he asked, quirking a grin at her. She swatted at him, and he caught her hand to place a kiss in her palm. "For believing in me enough to marry me. I won't let you down."

"I know," she said. The fear was still there, but it was almost like she was afraid because she was accustomed to being afraid, not because she really felt it. How could she feel it when Ferguson held her the way he did?

He let her go too soon, reminding her that she needed to get back to Salford House before they brought Alex down upon their heads. He sent Lizzie up to help her, perhaps not trusting himself to keep his hands off her long enough to get her into a dress.

But when she walked out of her room, properly decked out in muslin, with her hair pinned up beneath a cap, he waited for her. "Before you go, Mad — there's one more thing I wish to show you."

He took her arm, escorting her down the stairs to the drawing room. The room had the bare minimum of furniture necessary to make it appear lived in, in case any suitors tried to peer in through the windows, but she had never entered it before. There was a settee, two chairs, a spotless rug, and a small table, with an ornate chest sitting upon it that was out of place in the austerity of a house no one occupied. It was intricately carved, with the Rothwell coat of arms across the top and a chain of Celtic knots around the sides. Several bands of heavy iron crisscrossed the oak, and a large, heart-shaped lock held it shut.

Ferguson pulled a key out of his pocket and opened the chest. As he lifted the lid, two tiers came out with it on clever hinges. The box was two feet long, a foot tall, and a foot wide — and it was brimming with jewels.

"What on earth is this?" she asked, stepping forward to see the contents in the light.

Rubies, sapphires, diamonds, emeralds, ropes of pearls, amber beads — every color, shape and size imaginable, like a queen's ransom spread out before her. "These were my mother's," Ferguson said. "There are other suites of jewels in the Rothwell vault, but I thought we might find a betrothal ring for you here. I haven't looked yet, though — if you don't like any of these rings, we can have Rundell and Bridge make whatever you want."

He sifted through the top tier, pulling out a ring that was more suitable for a man. The band was dark, like tarnished silver or even iron, with a ruby set into it. The band had the same Celtic motif as the chest, and Ferguson winced as he held it.

"That looks too big for me," she said, wondering why it was in a woman's collection.

He twisted it slowly, tracing the knots with his finger. "The stone was my mother's, but my father had it reset for himself."

He slid it onto the ring finger of his right hand. She had never noticed before, but he didn't wear a signet ring. This was a better fit, though — it was a hard ring, meant for a powerful man, not the lily-white hand of a dilettante.

Then he looked up and seemed to catch himself. "She had other rings, though. Shall we look?"

It took several minutes to sort through the pile. The top tiers held loose gems, rings, earrings, and other small baubles, but the lower section of the casket held complete sets, each wrapped separately in flannel. There was a set of emeralds, another of rubies, and a third of diamonds. She expected sapphires as Ferguson unwrapped the last bundle — but instead of the soft click of stones rubbing on stones, she heard the crinkle of old paper.

"What is it?" she asked, leaning over Ferguson's arm. She was draped in several different necklaces, feeling almost obscene as her pearls and diamonds brushed against him.

He fanned the papers out in front of them, and bits of dried sealing wax rained down on the table. "Why on earth would he save these?" Ferguson muttered, more to himself than to her.

She tried to get a closer look. She guessed they were love letters, but she was wrong — the wrappers were all addressed to Ferguson, with the ducal crest as the seal.

She placed her hand on his, and she felt it tremble. "What is it, Ferguson?" she asked again.

He rearranged them slowly, tapping them against the table to line them back up into a neat pile. "Father wrote to me while I was away, but I always returned the letters unopened. I didn't expect him to save them."

He carefully wrapped them back up in the flannel, slipping them into base of the jewel case. "Aren't you going to read them?" she asked.

"Not now," he said shortly, dumping jewels in to cover the letters. She pulled back, suddenly unsure of what he needed. If she discovered letters from her parents... she would have killed someone before she let them be taken away.

He must have sensed her disapproval, because he turned around and pulled her hands into his. "I'll read them someday, Mad. But tonight, I want all my memories to be of you. I know now that my father doesn't own me, and I don't have to become him. The letters will be there when I'm ready."

She hugged him, and the comfort of his arms was just as vital to her now as the other pleasures he gave her. They stood there silently, and her heart ached for him, but she wasn't worried anymore. He seemed at peace with who he was, who he was meant to be.

She left a few minutes later, after selecting a gorgeous emerald ring that he would present her with after making the formal request to Alex in the morning. He kissed her one last time before she slipped through the door to the alleyway. They would soon live together, but she would miss the feeling of wickedness she had in their little house. Luckily, with Ferguson as her husband, she could have wickedness whenever she desired.

She couldn't believe they had escaped the theatre, that everything felt so right — but the dream was real.

And she couldn't wait for the rest of their dreams to come true.

CHAPTER TWENTY-EIGHT

Three nights later, at Lady Andover's ball, Madeleine felt a brief burst of her old panic. Not that her feelings for Ferguson were different — but her position in the ton was.

Outwardly, little had changed — she was still the same Madeleine, safe and dull as ever. But the addition of the enormous emerald on her right hand attracted the scrutiny of everyone in the ton.

It had taken two days before Alex was satisfied with the marriage settlements. Ferguson raised no objections to Alex's demands, and she suspected Alex enjoyed stalling the negotiations more than he should have. But word had spread as Madeleine was seen wearing Ferguson's ring, and by nightfall, everyone was buzzing.

Some were quite happy for her; Lady Jersey, for instance, was very kind in her usual chatty way. And Ferguson's aunt Sophronia, the duchess of Harwich, was thrilled, even if she looked a bit grim about the eyes as she watched Madeleine being accosted by well wishers.

But not all who came to her were pleasant. Oh, they were kind — but almost pitying, too, as though they were sorry that she had been so long on the shelf that she would settle for a man of dubious morals, even if he was a duke.

"I do hope his temper has improved," said one matron doubtfully.

"A splendid match, I'm sure, although I told Lady Sefton that I would not have leapt so soon after his father's unfortunate demise," remarked another.

"You'll be wanting a stout lock on your door in case he goes mad like his brother," a third lady said, no doubt thinking her advanced age excused her bluntness.

The rumors about his brother — and the possibility that Ferguson might also be tainted — surprised her. She knew he wasn't mad, but she didn't expect others to view him with such suspicion. Would it always be like this for her, spending the rest of her life watching the ton scrutinize Ferguson for any hint of encroaching insanity?

But when he emerged from the crowd to stand beside her, her doubts vanished. It might almost be amusing to hear the ton's gossip if he was beside her to enjoy it.

And if it wasn't amusing, at least he could make it up to her when they were alone.

"How are you this evening, my love?" he asked.

As he greeted her, he picked up her hand and kissed the ring he had given her. She smiled at the gesture, feeling warmth spread through all the places tonight's foray into society had frozen. "I shall be better when we are married, I believe."

His thumb slid down to caress the pulse point in her wrist — a gesture she never would have guessed as erotic, but all the more of a tease since she could not kiss him that night, let alone take him into her bed.

"It is only a month away — surely we can survive," he said, not sounding sure at all.

Madeleine would have married him within the week, but her aunt refused to plan a wedding with such unseemly haste. Augusta was thrilled with their match, already shopping for Madeleine's trousseau — but she still insisted on Madeleine being chaperoned when he called, even though the twinkle in her eyes said she knew it was already too late for that. Augusta had never minded the girls' unconventional pursuits as long as they were discreet; now that Madeleine was safe from scandal, she had returned to the calm understanding she always displayed.

So unless some miracle occurred, they would only have stolen moments at parties such as these for the next month — and it felt like being sent to a nunnery, after all she had experienced at Ferguson's hands.

He pulled her onto the dance floor, claiming one of the waltzes she now always saved for him. In the only act that betrayed his autocratic tendencies, Ferguson demanded that she only waltz with him — a promise she kept eagerly, since no other partner would satisfy her.

"The twins said you went on a shopping excursion today?" Ferguson asked as they settled into the rhythm of the dance.

"Yes, and they were eager to bankrupt you," Madeleine said. "Not that I can fault them — they've dressed only in mourning for nearly four years."

"Just remember they will soon be spending you into Fleet Prison too," Ferguson laughed.

She thought the laugh sounded forced. There was a tightness to his jaw that worried her. Perhaps he felt the additional eyes upon him tonight as well — they were being given an oddly wide berth by their fellow dancers.

She didn't remark on it, though. She kept her tone light and fixed a smile on her face.

"I will tire of the shopping long before we are paupered. They could have finished hours earlier, but you should have seen them — like little girls in a sweet shop. I do not believe they had been to a modiste's salon before. Kate said your father had dressmakers come to them."

"Father tried beating Henry and Richard, and verbally flaying me and Ellie. By the time the twins grew older, he must have thought it easier to just keep them penned up."

He said it so matter of factly, still staring slightly over her head to survey the crowd, that her heart broke a little for him. "They are improving, though — they were civil to me today. And they are thrilled that you are marrying and staying in England. It will be good for them to have us to help them navigate the ton."

The sudden frost in his eyes was almost imperceptible, but she heard it in his voice. "Where did they hear that we are staying in England?"

She faltered slightly, but his grip was too tight to let her fall. "I assured them of it. They are so lonely, after all, and you did say you would stay in England."

"You forget that my remaining in England was contingent on finding a reason to stay."

She sucked in a breath. "I thought I was a reason."

His face was impassive, his voice dispassionate, almost bored. "If you wish to stay in London, we shall discuss it. But I'm sure you will love Scotland, given enough time."

The autocrat slipped out from under his mask and stared her in the face. She had expected it to make an appearance someday, though, and she refused to back down. "We most certainly will discuss it. You've never said a pleasant word about your life in Scotland, other than that it is where your father wasn't. Now that he is dead, what are you still running from?"

For the briefest moment, the autocrat looked almost tortured, twisted into a display of guilt and grief, before all of his emotions disappeared again behind a careful, expressionless façade. "This is neither the time nor the place for this conversation, Lady Madeleine," he said, the formal title cutting into her just as it always wounded him. "But I will thank you for not filling my sisters' heads with more promises until we discuss our arrangements."

She couldn't give in to the desire to scream at him, to shake him and demand to know why he had turned so cold. She also couldn't leave him, not when everyone would see and assume the worst. So she forced herself to watch her steps, instead of his eyes, and to count off the minutes until he would release her.

He maintained his silence too, and while his grip on her never wavered, it also never veered into the sensual realm she was used to with him. He conducted their waltz with military precision, like she was an objective to be conquered.

When the waltz finally ended, he ushered her out of the dancers and deposited her at the side of the room. As the last strains of music faded, he stared hard at her, meeting her gaze for the first time. The guilt and grief was back.

He paused, considering her face, and finally leaned in to say, "Avoid the gaming tables tonight, love. Lady Greville is holding court there, and you would not find her conversation pleasant."

She only had time for a startled nod before he stalked away into the crowd. She stood adrift, twisting her ring on her finger as she watched him pass through the crowd. No one stopped to converse with him, and she wondered if he felt just as alone in the ton as she always had.

But why was he considering Scotland? Had Caro finally found a threat that could sway him? The only secret that could ruin him was Madeleine's — and bile rose in her throat as she speculated about what Caro might have learned.

"My dear, are you feeling well?" Lady Harcastle asked. Ferguson had accidentally led her directly to Prudence's mother. Madeleine rarely wished to see her in most circumstances, and she did not want to see her now.

"Perfectly well, Lady Harcastle," Madeleine said, swallowing hard to combat her nausea. "The duke has some business to attend to."

Lady Harcastle raised a skeptical eyebrow. "Did you believe that? Or, worse, do you think I believe that? You are usually more astute, despite your ancestry."

Madeleine bit her tongue. Lady Harcastle's family had been devastated by the Peninsular War, and unlike most of the ton she absolutely loathed the French. It would do no good to mention that her mother was English — and she couldn't have interjected it anyway, since Lady Harcastle continued to speak.

"I must say I am pleased to see you. I've heard something that cannot wait for my next call at your house."

She looked both grim and sympathetic — a look Madeleine had never received from her before. Madeleine felt her stomach drop, the color fleeing her cheeks as dread replaced it.

Caro must have found her out.

It was the only rumor that would cause this reaction. Ferguson's other exploits were all known and tolerated, and Madeleine had no other secrets.

They had been so close — safe, in fact, with the playhouse shuttered and Marguerite's retirement announced to the world. But apparently they weren't safe enough.

"What do you wish to say?" Madeleine asked, feigning innocent curiosity as though it could change whatever Lady Harcastle had heard.

But it wasn't what she expected. "You have heard the rumors about the previous duke's death?"

"The carriage accident?" Madeleine asked blankly, too stunned by the unexpected turn in the conversation to follow Lady Harcastle's thoughts.

"Don't say you believe that too," she said with an ugly, barking laugh. "Everyone knows Richard shot him."

"Why are you telling me this?" Madeleine asked, exhaling as she felt some of her fear evaporate — she wasn't discovered after all.

Lady Harcastle lowered her voice. "They say such madness runs in families."

"Ferguson isn't mad," Madeleine said impatiently.

"Do you know for sure?" Lady Harcastle countered.

"No more than I can be sure of your sanity."

"Don't be pert. It's unbecoming even if you are to be a duchess," Lady Harcastle snapped. "Mind you, I don't say I believe a word of this, but you need to know what the ton is saying, preferably before you are stuck with him. And if no one else will tell you, it is my duty to."

"Tell me what?" Madeleine asked, wanting to shake the woman and see the ridiculous toque she was wearing shed its feathers on the floor.

"You do remember that he took a mistress — that actress in Seven Dials?"

Her stomach dropped again, this time feeling like it had fled entirely. "It isn't proper for me to discuss such things."

"I've never known you to be missish — but it's worse than that. She hasn't been seen anywhere in days."

"I heard she retired," Madeleine said carefully. "Perhaps she left town."

"Likely that's all it is. But with his brother's madness, and witnesses claiming he forced her into his carriage after her last play — people are talking. And the prevailing rumor is that he murdered her."

CHAPTER TWENTY-NINE

She was the most acclaimed actress of the season, but Madeleine could not catch her breath. Lady Harcastle's words punched it out of her. And before Madeleine could think to leave the ballroom, someone asked her to dance.

She had to submit to a quadrille, two reels and a country dance before she could dance with Ferguson again — and while she waited, her body was in open rebellion. The endless dancing snatched away any remaining air in her lungs, leaving her winded and lightheaded, like she had just run a footrace in a too-tight corset. Her stays pressed against her ribs, her heart beat in her throat, and stars flickered at the edges of her vision. And she had never been more thankful for her gloves — she could feel her palms turning slick within the soft kid, but her latest partner, Mr. Frederick Scolfield, appeared unaware of her distress. The man was her least favorite of Augusta's cousins. He was likely accustomed to girls looking unhappy and nauseated in his arms.

She finally saw Ferguson again as she stood at the top waiting to go down to the end of the figure. He leaned against a wall, watching her — but where the move had left her weak-kneed with anticipation when he used to materialize out of the crowd for her alone, now it only worried her more. Had he heard the rumors?

She wished she felt as calm as he looked. The brilliant light of the chandeliers threw no shadows on his face, and his easy smile was bright, not deadly.

How could anyone think he was a killer?

The end of the dance cast her and her odious cousin Frederick out on the side of the ballroom nearest the stairs, far from where she had last seen Ferguson, and she longingly glanced at the exit. Surely Augusta had heard the rumors, but she wouldn't seek Madeleine out — taking her home early would only confirm that the Stauntons were concerned about Ferguson's sanity. She sucked in a breath, ignoring her cousin's conversational gambits as she focused on keeping her lungs filled. If she could lie as still as death on the floor of Legrand's Theatre during the climax of every play, she could surely feign boredom until she could escape.

Frederick's voice turned petulant. He had enough money and connections that people rarely ignored him outright, even if his partners were not always eager to talk to him. He was still young enough to be an eligible match, but with his weak chin and vapid conversation, a woman would have to be desperate for his funds to consider him. "If you are this cold with the duke, cousin, you won't have a hope of keeping him in your bed," he sneered.

Madeleine did not look at him, positioning herself to watch the crowd. "My marriage is no concern of yours," she said with a sneer of her own.

She heard his sharp inhale as he took a pinch of snuff. "I did wonder how you managed to snare a coronet, but 'tis no surprise now that the truth about his sanity is coming out."

She did turn on him then, the fast whip of her shawl as she

came around brushing half the snuff out of his box. He started to protest, but he took a single look at her face and shut his mouth.

"Ferguson is the sanest man I know," she snapped, in a low voice with a hint of menace she had never known she possessed. "I will thank you for not spreading rumors that have no basis in fact."

He held up a hand in mocking surrender. "As you wish, cousin. But when he abandons you for another prize, do not look to me to dance with you."

Frederick flounced off then, all wounded vanity and pricked ego. Madeleine's thoughts were dark. If Frederick, who rarely knew any news beyond the latest fashion in waistcoats, had heard the rumors, then they were all over London.

She wanted to kill Caro. The rumors must have started with her — the woman was determined to keep Ferguson from finding happiness. But she couldn't seek the woman out in public — and imagine the scandal if she and Ferguson were tried for different murders at the same time?

Ferguson emerged from the crowd, his blue eyes sparking with temper. He had seemed calm from a distance, but perhaps it was the same façade she was trying to maintain. "Please tell me that when we are married, we may refrain from parties for at least a decade," Ferguson said, lifting her hand to kiss it as he greeted her. He didn't acknowledge the way he had left her earlier, and she didn't mention it; their problems were much bigger than she had thought.

On any other night she would have laughed, agreed with him even though his title and the responsibilities he should take up in the Lords would make parties a necessity. But she froze, her fingers wrapping around his.

If the rumors continued, there might not be any hostesses left who would receive them.

"What is it, Mad?" he asked. "Are you unwell?"

Another crest of nausea rose in her throat. Without the distraction of her argument with Frederick, all the nerves came rushing back. "Do you mind if we do not dance? I would far rather talk if it were only possible to be alone."

He took her hand and led her to an alcove, where a bay window overlooked Lady Andover's garden. They were still in sight of the ballroom, but no one would overhear them unless they approached — and from the way the path cleared before them, she guessed no one would dare to interrupt.

As he settled her on the alcove bench and leaned against the wall to protect them from intruders, she saw the shadows he had hidden while dancing — he didn't look like the devil-may-care rake he played for the masses. He looked like a great duke of old, one prepared to do battle to keep his claims.

She shivered, her thin silk dress no match for the chill stealing through her. The intensity in his eyes reminded her of the night he had saved her from Westbrook in the theatre. The warrior was back.

And she was the prize he would battle for.

He stripped off her gloves in an efficient gesture that said nothing of seduction, even if it was vastly improper. As he chafed her hands in his, he said, "What happened, Mad? If I had not been in the same room as you for the last hour, I would have guessed someone died at your feet."

"Why do you say that?"

"Your breath is ragged, your eyes are wide, your skin is chilled — you show every sign of having received a great shock."

He looked so concerned for her that she felt tears start to

gather in her eyes. It was so absurd that anyone could think him a murderer — but now that the rumor had spread, she felt incapable of swaying opinion.

"Tell me," he commanded softly.

The panic rose again. She couldn't remember any other time in her life when things had been so unmanageable — perhaps when her parents died, but she was too young then to strive for control. She closed her eyes, unable to look at him as she said, "I heard the most awful rumor — people are saying that you killed Marguerite."

She swallowed convulsively, willing herself not to cry. He cursed under his breath and dropped her hands. She retrieved her gloves and slowly pulled them on again. His touch was all she wanted, but it was out of place in the ballroom. "I thought the old tabbies would have more discretion than to tell you directly," Ferguson said.

"You knew and didn't say anything?" she asked, annoyance clearing away just enough of her panic that her hands stopped shaking.

"I saw no reason to worry you yet." His voice was soft, with an underbelly of iron. "If the rumor had died on its own, you need never have heard it."

There was no apology in those words. She bristled as she said, "This affects both of us now. I realize you may not have shared such things with the scores of women who have come before, but I deserve more."

"Is that what this is about? How many women I've bedded? I thought you might throw it in my face eventually, but not now."

"There are bigger issues than that," Madeleine said, "although I can't help but wonder if this rumor would have gained legs if you hadn't made so many enemies in the ton. Lady Greville, for one, plans to make your life a misery."

"I cannot undo what happened, just as I couldn't stop Richard from killing my father and making my entire family seem murderous."

"Could you have done so if you had been here?" she asked, looking for blood after his comment about his mistresses.

He froze, the planes of his face hardening, and she instantly regretted her words. "So you think it was wrong of me to go to Scotland?"

She paused, wanting to be sure of her words — and the sentiments behind them. Finally, she said, "I do not think you were wrong. I did much the same, putting my desire to act above my family's needs. I won't say I was wrong either — but we still must live with the consequences."

He raked a hand through his hair, and the strands glowed like embers in the candlelight as they settled back into place. "I don't know if I could have saved Richard," Ferguson said quietly. "Just as I don't know if I can fix how the ton sees me."

It was her turn to comfort him. She didn't like that he hadn't told her, but they needed to move forward rather than dwell on rights and wrongs. "The ton will come around — rakes can be rehabilitated, after all."

He stared down at her, his eyes wide with the desire to believe her. The pause lengthened and turned almost painfully sweet after the heat of their argument. But his eyes finally narrowed, and his next words shattered the peace. "Rakes, yes, but not murderers."

She felt her face fall. He instinctively stepped toward her, caught himself, and returned to his proper stance against the wall. "It will all come out all right," he said soothingly. "I've procured a special license — we can marry and leave for Scotland as soon as you have packed."

"Scotland?" she asked, not understanding.

"Without a body, the rumors will die someday," he said, with a bright certainty she didn't believe. "And you really will love my estate there — beautiful, but not so remote that you cannot go to Edinburgh when it suits you."

"Is that why you were angry earlier about what I said to the twins about England? You've been planning this, haven't you?"

He clenched his jaw, and his hand made a fist against the wall. "What else would you have me do, Mad? I refuse to see the ton cut you. And if there is an investigation, I want you as far away as possible."

"But what of your sisters? My family? Everything I know is here!"

"You are my priority now, not them. Sophronia will bring out the twins alone — I'm sure she'll understand if she's heard the gossip. And you are welcome to have Josephine accompany you if you wish."

He had already decided. His face said even more clearly than his tone that he would not be swayed.

More, he seemed to think she should be comforted by his decisiveness — even though leaving London would mean abandoning her whole life.

Her hands made fists of her own. "You may be accustomed to running away," she said, and he flinched at the words. "But I do not wish to go until we have no other choice."

"Do not dare call me a coward," he bit out. "The ton can go hang, but I'm leaving to protect you, not myself."

"How is this protection?" she cried, before remembering where she was and dropping back into a whisper. "If we leave now, everyone will know you are guilty. If you won't consider what that does to your sisters' prospects, think of the children we may have. What marriages will they be able to make if people believe their father is criminally insane?"

It was a version of the argument Alex had used against her, but Ferguson's face softened at the mention of their possible babes. "If there were another way... but I cannot see it."

"There is another possibility," she said slowly. "If Marguerite appeared regularly..."

The softness disappeared. "Out of the question."

She met his unrelenting glare with a steely one of her own. "But it would put all the rumors to rest. We could live a normal life."

"And constantly worry about you being caught," he retorted. "Better for the ton to think I'm a murderer than to know what you've done."

"Why better? We could ensure that no one thinks you are criminally insane, and I've yet to be caught — it seems like better odds than your reputation faces without me. And if, Heaven forbid, there were to be a trial, how could I watch you hang for killing a woman who would not even exist if not for me?"

He grinned for the first time since they had entered the alcove. "They would take my head off with a sword — I am too wellborn for a commoner's noose. But it won't come to a trial. The House of Lords would have to set the trial, and they won't indict a duke for the death of an actress without any evidence that a crime was committed."

"You do have a lot of enemies," she pointed out. "It only takes a handful of peers wanting revenge for the wives you stole to press for a trial."

He looked out at the crowd. From Madeleine's vantage point, it felt like they were already in a cell. His peers circled, waiting to slam the door. But if he saw the same scene, it hardened his resolve. "I won't have you endanger yourself for me."

"And I won't have you run away for me!" she said, her temper reaching the breaking point. "You may not have intended this, but you are a duke now. From all I've seen, you will make an excellent one. But you cannot go to Scotland every time you wish to escape. And I cannot be your wife if I must always wonder when you will run away from me."

The words, quiet though they were, shattered between them, the shards cutting them both. He stiffened against the wall as though absorbing the blow. "I can't lose you, Mad," he said, his voice raw.

She bowed her head, heard his breath rasp in his throat. "We must stay and fight, Ferguson. I lost one family to the whims of the public — I cannot bear to lose you too."

Their situation in no way resembled the Revolution, but she saw him plant his feet before levering himself away from the wall. His eyes flashed. "You won't lose me if you come with me. But if you won't come to Scotland, then I will face the gossip alone. I would rather see you safe without me than ruined in my arms."

She gasped. Would he really leave her, break off their engagement, to protect her from something that was as much her fault as it was his?

"You can't do that, Ferguson. I'll reveal myself before I let you face a murder charge."

He glanced again at the ballroom, then held up a hand, cutting off her bravado. "Your aunt is bearing down on us. I'll call on you tomorrow morning, and we can settle this then. Until then, please do not do anything to endanger yourself."

Ferguson stalked off, his bearing sleek and predatory. She sighed. If anyone watched him now, he did look capable of murder. He walked directly across the dance floor to the exit, so furious that he didn't care which dancers he interrupted in his haste to leave.

She thanked heavens for her acting talent — when the people who watched Ferguson's progress across the dance floor swiveled toward her, she knew she looked perfectly serene. Disappointed, none stared for long; if she wouldn't give them a dramatic addition to Ferguson's disappearance, they quickly lost interest.

Aunt Augusta didn't ignore her, though. She stepped into the alcove only a few moments after Ferguson left, blocking Madeleine's view just as he reached the door. "Is something wrong, my dear?" she asked as she took a seat beside Madeleine.

Madeleine nearly laughed at the question. Everything was wrong — the rumors, Ferguson's threat to leave her, his belief that they could not stay in London. Where could she possibly begin?

Noting Madeleine's hesitation, Augusta squeezed her hand. "Lady Harcastle told me she spoke to you. I would have waited for morning, but what's done is done."

Her aunt looked at her with so much sympathy that Madeleine felt like crying. Augusta was usually faultless in her control at these events, never betraying a negative emotion. Seeing her concern for Madeleine trump her sense of propriety made Madeleine want to bury her head against her aunt's shoulder and sob like she was a little girl again.

Despite what had happened when they all discovered her acting, Aunt Augusta still loved her, had already forgiven her for the theatre now that she was safe. Like Alex, she had been upset with Madeleine's lies, but after the first flare of anger faded, she was ready to do whatever she could to assist her.

Wasn't that the support she had always wanted from a mother?

"Ferguson wants to take me to Scotland to avoid the rumors," she whispered.

Augusta's blue eyes turned bleak. "If you go to Scotland, it will be difficult to come back. The ton will see it as proof of his guilt."

"I told him that, but he would rather protect me than save himself."

"And what do you want?"

Madeleine paused, not sure how to tell the aunt who had always protected her that she was prepared to take yet another risk. Finally, she said, "I cannot see him punished when it would be easy to have Marguerite return."

Aunt Augusta looked away, glancing out across the crowds. No one could hear what they said, even though their conversation was circumspect enough to avoid betraying Madeleine's secret. "I would rather see you fight than run away, my dear. I've often wondered if your mother might have survived if she had stood up to her husband."

Augusta rarely surprised her, but this time, Madeleine was shocked. "I thought you believed that wives should obey their husbands."

Her aunt snorted. "In most things, it's easier to let them think you are obeying. But Arabella never once asked Loubressac to let her visit England after she married him — or if she did, she let him overrule her. I never saw her again after their wedding. The marquis was too patriotic for his own good, which is not Ferguson's shortcoming. Still, I couldn't bear to see you move so far away without so much as an attempt to make a life here."

"I thought you were willing to send me to Bermuda?" Madeleine asked, letting herself lapse into sarcasm because it was easier than considering what she had just heard about her mother.

Augusta silenced her with a look. "I didn't want to send you to Bermuda, and I still don't. Some scandals require drastic measures, though."

She looked at the crowd again, and Madeleine realized she was watching Amelia. Augusta frowned as she looked at her daughter. "One never knows what Amelia will get up to — so if she's the one I'll have to send away someday, I would just as soon keep you here."

"I won't go to Scotland without a fight," Madeleine said. "But I'm not sure I could give him up if that's the only choice."

Her aunt squeezed her hand. "Then he's the right man for you. If you lose the fight, we'll all survive it somehow. At least Scotland is within carriage range — I do hope that whatever estate he has up there is prepared to accommodate guests."

Madeleine smiled weakly. Augusta stood, reaching down to pull Madeleine up with her. "No more hiding in alcoves tonight. If you can pretend for the next hour that you are at the most amusing party you've ever attended, it will at least make the gossips wonder whether you know something they don't."

Her aunt smiled like the battle-hardened society matron she was, and Madeleine followed her out into the crowd. Their conversation gave Madeleine just enough strength to survive the evening.

But she was going to have to find her own strength if she had any hope of convincing Ferguson to listen to reason.

CHAPTER THIRTY

In the morning, long after he should have been out attending to business, Ferguson walked soundlessly down the carpeted hall outside his bedroom toward the front stairs. It was a technique he had perfected years earlier to escape the house without being harangued by his father, and the creaks in the floorboards were mercifully unchanged. His odd, swerving dance attracted a shocked stare from a passing chambermaid who momentarily forgot her place (and then blushed crimson as she bobbed a curtsy), but at least none of his sisters emerged from their rooms to accost him.

It was actually nice to spend time with them. After he promised not to force them into matches they didn't want, the twins regularly joined him for meals. Even Ellie dropped by occasionally, still brittle and guarded, but showing signs that she might someday forgive him.

But he didn't want to see them this morning, and he exhaled in relief as he reached the top of the steps unnoticed. The previous night had been dark and endless, as he lay in the bed he had never wanted to inherit and thought about the ruin that threatened to come down on all of them. He did not see a way to put the rumors to rest — other than the obvious solution Madeleine proposed. He didn't want to consider it, didn't want her to endanger herself when she was so close to being safe.

What was worse, though — her obvious panic when she first heard that Ferguson was suspected of murder? Or the slow condemnation that settled in her eyes when she thought he might abandon London? That condemnation had turned to anger when he offered to protect her by breaking the engagement — not that he could really bear the idea, and had already discarded it as he said the words. Besides, he suspected she would reveal herself if it came to that, whether he wanted her to or not.

He was so engrossed in thought, so focused on his feet, that he didn't realize he was being watched until he hopped over the last three steps of the main staircase and landed with a soft thud on the marble floor of the foyer. He looked up, expecting his butler. Ellie stood just inside the doorway, her arms crossed as she surveyed him with a knowing gleam in her blue eyes. Kate and Maria sat on a bench beside her, their soft lavender morning gowns an odd contrast to the lush royal blue of Ellie's riding habit. The twins each clutched a valise, and a neat pile of bandboxes sat on the floor beside them. From the way they both gaped at him, they had seen every step of his erratic descent.

"The servants will be sure of your madness if you always take the stairs like that," Ellie drawled.

He bowed, only slightly ironically. "I did not expect the pleasure of your company this morning, or I would have put away my madness for another day."

She smiled swiftly, and just as swiftly lapsed into a frown. "It isn't funny in the slightest. What I am hearing from the people who are brave or stupid enough to tell me will have us all cast out within a fortnight if you cannot sway public opinion."

"Is that why you're collecting the twins?" he asked, gesturing at their luggage. "They are safer with your reputation than mine?"

Ellie laughed. "You will have to do far worse than murder to saddle me with their guardianship." The twins both grinned; their relationship with Ellie had improved over the last few weeks as well, and they took no offense at Ellie's jest.

"Ellie said you will disappear again if the scandal grows," Kate said, sounding determined. "Maria and I have already packed what we care to bring in case you try to sneak away without us. We do not intend to let you go into exile alone."

He could tell them apart now — Kate had a slight quirk to her mouth when she smiled, and Maria had a small scar on her chin where she had accidentally banged it against her harp. Knowing who spoke did not comfort him, but knowing who they were made the words more personal. "So Ellie believes I shall run away?"

"Sneaking down those infernal steps was not an attempt to leave the house without alerting anyone?" Ellie asked.

"It is my house now. Surely I can leave however I wish."

"You could also have the steps fixed, but it doesn't signify. What matters is whether you are indeed running off to Scotland without so much as a farewell."

Ellie was no longer in good humor. Now that he saw the tension in her shoulders, the stiff way she crossed her arms as though trying to keep herself from falling apart, he realized that she expected him to abandon them again. "I am not leaving. Even at my most desperate, I wouldn't run off in a morning coat without a change of clothes," he pointed out. "And if I leave, I will invite you to come along, just as I did last time."

Her eyes turned cold. "There is no need to say your farewells in person. I'm sure a note shall suffice if you can spare a moment to write one."

"What else would you have me do?" he asked, impatient despite her pain. "I cannot disprove a rumor without any evidence for or against it."

"Will you at least take us to Scotland with you?" Maria pleaded. "London will not be the same with only Sophronia to chaperone us."

He looked at the twins. They were eager for an adventure — more excited than he had ever seen them while discussing their debuts. But they were also young, and beautiful, and long overdue for the social whirl. With his fortune, he could give them dowries large enough to buy out at least some suitors' concerns about his family's sanity.

"You would be bored to bits in Scotland," he said. "The nearest neighbor is miles away. There is barely any light in the winter, and far too much in the summer, particularly when you have nothing to do to occupy the days. And the clan tolerates me for my mother's sake and because my grandfather had no sons, but as a rule they do not like the English. You'd be begging to come back to London before the horses even cooled."

Kate and Maria exchanged one of their glances that encompassed an entire silent conversation. "Sounds rather like how we've lived until now," Kate said. "We would have more fun if you and Lady Madeleine were in residence."

She was so direct about the dim, narrow little lives they had lived that Ferguson's heart ached for them — they had no real idea what they had missed. "It's out of the question, my dears — you have so much more to live for here if you give it a chance."

"And you do not?" Ellie interjected, a hard edge to her voice.

"I had my chance, Ellie. If London has no use for me, I've no use for it."

He brushed past her for the door, needing to leave, to see Madeleine and believe they could muddle through this. A footman came out of his little alcove by the entrance to open the door, but Ellie placed her palm flat against the wood. Her glare sent the footman scurrying back like one who believed the rumors of madness.

"They would have a use for you if they knew you weren't a murderer," Ellie said urgently, refusing to back down even though he tried to give her his most quelling look. "If Marguerite would only return..."

She trailed off, mindful of the servants, and gave a sidelong glance at the twins. They were barely breathing, as though hoping to be taken into their older siblings' confidences but expecting to be sent off at any moment.

Then Ellie whispered, "I have an idea, if you would consider it?"

She held her breath too, but he saw no hope in her eyes — she steeled herself against the likelihood that he would choose to carry on without them.

He stared at the door above her head and remembered walking out of it in disgrace ten years earlier. It hadn't felt like disgrace, of course — it had felt like freedom. He actually whistled as he walked toward the carriage waiting to carry him to Scotland — a merry drinking tune that would have given his father fits if the old man had bothered to see him off.

But freedom wasn't all he imagined it to be. And if the twins would be out of place in Scotland, how would Madeleine — the real Madeleine, the lively, laughing temptress beneath her prim society façade — manage to survive the boredom?

He sighed. Ellie heard something in that sound that made her slump against the door in relief. "Very well. Into the library, all of you. I would rather not spend the whole morning here, if it pleases you."

It did please them — particularly the twins, who looked like they had been told they might accompany him to the moon. As he followed them to the library, he looked at his watch and sighed again. He needed to see Madeleine.

He didn't want to run. But could he let Madeleine risk herself for him when all he had to offer in return was a life she didn't seem to want?

CHAPTER THIRTY-ONE

"I expected Ferguson to arrive by now," Madeleine said, striding back and forth in front of Alex's desk like a councilor urging a lord to war.

"He will come," Alex said. "But if you do not stop pacing, I will think you have turned into Amelia."

She eyed her usual chair with distaste and kept walking. What if Ferguson didn't come? She knew he still loved her, and she didn't doubt his heart. But she did doubt his autocratic tendencies and the fate they might lead him to. If he still thought her safety overwhelmed all other priorities, he could break the engagement and go to Scotland alone.

And she would be "safe" — if it was possible to be safe without a heart.

"You don't have to marry the bounder if you've changed your mind," Alex said in the same mild tone as his observation about her pacing. "I doubt the ton will consider you a jilt. You could hardly be expected to marry a presumed murderer, after all."

That stopped her pacing. She turned on him with a frown, one hand on her hip as the other grasped the back of a chair for support. "You know he's not a murderer. If anything, it is my fault he is in this mess. I cannot abandon him so easily."

Alex drummed his fingers on his desk, his brow furrowed as though confronted with an artifact of dubious provenance. "I don't deny that, Maddie. But if all else fails, you can always come back here."

"I thought I was destined for exile in Bermuda?"

"As long as you don't get caught as Marguerite, you can stay here forever. But even if it comes to that, we could smuggle you back in a few years if you live quietly enough."

"It does not matter," she said, the fire of battle escaping her. She sank into her chair, ready now for whatever bad news might come next. She just hoped it would come quickly — with every moment Ferguson delayed, she grew more uncertain, more afraid that her ultimatum the previous night had driven him away.

By the time Chilton opened the door half an hour later, Madeleine was nearly ready to crawl to Scotland herself if it meant keeping him. It was so unlike her, the mad desire to possess someone at all costs, forgoing pride, intelligence, even self-preservation in order to win them.

If that madness was what drove Ferguson's need to protect her, she finally understood why he would choose to run.

"His grace the duke of Rothwell. Lady Catherine and Lady Maria," Chilton announced, ushering them in and closing the door as he left.

Alex rose when the ladies were announced, and Madeleine stood to exchange kisses with the twins. Ferguson hung back, but when she saw the fierce look in his haggard face, her heart leapt. He had slept just as badly as she had — but he also looked ready to fight.

Kate curtsied to Alex, then turned back to Madeleine. "Ferguson says we must wait elsewhere while you conduct your business. But Maria and I wanted to say we are delighted to have someone with your talents in our family."

Ferguson shrugged when Madeleine turned her incredulous gaze on him. "The twins were present when Ellie offered advice on our problem. It did seem expeditious to prove to them that I am not a murderer."

"Pshaw," Kate declared. "You've never had that look about you that Richard used to have. But your secret is safe. We've no one to tell, after all."

Their brother sighed. "All right, girls — perhaps Lord Salford would be so good as to show you to a salon while Lady Madeleine and I converse?"

Alex joined them by the door, but he raised an eyebrow at Rothwell's suggestion. "Leave you alone with my cousin while you send me off unchaperoned with your sisters? Rather bad form, Rothwell, and you can't force me to marry both of them."

Kate giggled and Maria blushed. Madeleine had never thought of Alex as anything more than a cousin, but he was young, handsome and titled — an easy infatuation for two girls who had been raised like nuns. "No teasing my charges," Madeleine said sternly.

Alex bowed to them, and their blue eyes lit up with identical pleasure. "My apologies, ladies. I shall summon Amelia to entertain you. I must have a word with your brother as well."

The twins looked disappointed, but their smiles quickly returned. While Alex went to find Amelia, Kate and Maria told Madeleine about all the items they still wished to purchase before their debuts. They had not left off their mourning colors yet — most of their new dresses weren't ready, and as Maria said, they didn't want to jinx themselves by ending their mourning before their first ball — but they were excited. Madeleine was exhausted just thinking of all the shopping to be done, and Ferguson drily joked that he would deduct their wardrobes from their dowries. But it was good to see the girls in such high spirits. Now that they smiled at Madeleine rather than wishing her dead, she found them quite charming.

Alex returned with Amelia, who greeted the twins and Ferguson with pleasant grace. She nodded tightly to Madeleine, but neither spoke. Madeleine would have to do something to repair the breach, but the pain of betrayal was still there, and she had more pressing threats to remedy.

Amelia collected the twins and offered to show them Alex's sculpture gallery, which delighted them both. But just as they were leaving, Kate turned to Madeleine. "Ellie says that if Ferguson does not mention the masquerade within five minutes, you are to shake him until he does so."

Ferguson scowled as he ushered them out the door. She heard one of the twins giggle as he closed the door behind them. "Do they wish to have a fancy dress ball?" Madeleine asked.

He shook his head. That haggard look was back on his face, with a tightness about the eyes so unlike his typical sang froid. "Let us hear what Salford has to say before we discuss the masquerade."

Madeleine sat on the settee this time, leaving her usual chair for Ferguson. Alex leaned back in his own chair, his fingers steepled in front of him as he chose his words. The sun beyond the windows was glorious, warming the white marble artifacts and giving the room a serenity she did not feel.

Finally, Alex spoke. "I'm sure you both wish me to the devil so you may have a moment in private, and I'll give it to you whether it's proper or not. But Rothwell, you must know that certain members of the House of Lords are pressing for an inquiry. There is little hope of stopping this unless you are both prepared for drastic action."

"Can you not speak for Ferguson in the Lords?" Madeleine asked.

"They would merely think I was protecting you," Alex said, with the gentle tone of one bringing bad news to an invalid.

"What drastic measures are you suggesting, Salford?" Ferguson demanded. "If you want me to free Madeleine from our engagement..."

"No, of course not — although if I could call you out for it, I would enjoy it," Alex said, relishing the thought. "I will not tell you what to do. But please know that regardless of what either of you must do to prove Rothwell's innocence, you have my support."

"Do you mean that?" Madeleine said, searching his face for conditions and boundaries.

He nodded. "I do hope you will stop seeing me as an overbearing monster, Maddie. I only want what is best for you. And I must admit — I was more than a little envious of the time you spent doing something you loved, even if it was a reckless, stupid risk."

Alex smiled at her, surrounded by the artifacts of places he would never visit as long as he stayed where he was supposed to. Her heart stuttered — it was little wonder Alex reacted so badly when he discovered that she had stepped out of her traditional role.

"Thank you," she whispered. It was impossible to say anything else, not with the evidence of all he had sacrificed staring at her from the walls. Finally, she managed to grate out, "We will not be caught."

"I believe you. Rothwell's name for you isn't so inaccurate, even if I hated it at first. You have the courage to find a path, Mad. And if you do not, I will gut your fiancé."

His bloodthirsty look was back, and Ferguson grinned. "Careful, Salford, or you will have the Lords believing you are a murderer as well."

"No doubt they will assume that anyone I killed deserved it," Alex said. "But enough — I shall leave you be so you may make your decision while I evade our sisters."

His lopsided grin told Madeleine he had planned this, but she couldn't fault him for wanting to avoid the hopeful debutantes. After he left, she counted to ten, waiting for Ferguson to speak. He sat silent, eyes focused somewhere between Alex's chair and the lovely light of the window beyond.

"Will you tell me about the masquerade, or shall I shake you?" she asked.

"I would choose the shaking if I could kiss you afterward."

She laughed. "Perhaps you may kiss me anyway after you tell me your thoughts."

He frowned, shifting his gaze to the shelves above her, and she wondered what was so awful that he could not say it. She whispered, "You aren't leaving me behind, are you?"

Ferguson snorted. "As if I could. I would sooner cut off my arm. And even if I did, you and my sisters would track me down before I ever reached the border."

It wasn't a romantic way of stating his intentions. But her heart blossomed even though his heel tapped a nervous beat against the carpet.

"You must understand, Mad — if I thought any good would come of it, I would toss you in my carriage right now, whether you willed it or not, and beg your forgiveness later."

"I believe you," she said ruefully. "There's no need for a demonstration."

That earned a temporary smile. "There won't be one. I couldn't admit it last night, but I know that going to Scotland won't save us. There's no society there to cut you for marrying me, but if I lost you from boredom, or from anger at the turn I served you by burdening you with my reputation..."

He broke off just as she came off the settee to kneel beside his chair. "You won't lose me for that," she vowed fiercely, clasping his hand. "I knew your reputation from the first, but as long as the man beneath is as honorable as I know you are, you've nothing to fear."

He put his other hand on top of hers, squeezing as though it was a lifeline. "It wouldn't be honorable of me to leave my sisters, would it? Or to set you up in a drafty manor miles from anywhere, when you are meant to light up ballrooms and set the ton on its ear?"

"It's Marguerite who does that, not Madeleine."

"But it could be Madeleine, if you are my duchess and choose to show your real self to the ton. Not as an actress, of course. But you could be the darling of the highest circles if you chose."

It was so foreign to her, so unimaginable — and yet so tantalizing, particularly after her run on the stage. But she brushed the vision aside. "I want to be your darling, not the ton's. But I would like to clear your name so I may have the option."

His foot stopped tapping, and he squeezed her hand again. "You were right last night, Mad. The only way to prove my innocence is for Marguerite to reappear."

She sat back on her heels, not knowing until he said the words how much she had hoped to hear them. "I will send word to Madame Legrand. We can stage an encore performance of *Hamlet*."

He shook his head. "I already spoke to her — it was why I was so late reaching you this morning. That was my preference too, but some of the actors are already gone to other productions, and it would be a week or more before she could find replacements. We must move fast if we've any hope of stopping the rumors before the Lords start looking into Marguerite's identity."

Madeleine gasped. Until that moment, she hadn't thought of what an investigation would really turn up. If Marguerite was found to have never existed, the rumors would only grow — and would consume her whole family if anyone pieced together the clues. "What else can we do? I could go to the Lords, but I've never tested my disguise in daylight before."

"No. It's too dangerous, and they may ask questions you cannot answer. If you are serious about resurrecting Marguerite, though — you could attend Westbrook's masquerade tomorrow night. If your costume is appropriate, people would see enough to believe it is Marguerite without guessing who you really are."

The masquerade wouldn't be safe either. She would have to converse, walk amongst the crowd — stand closer to people than she ever had onstage. Other than Ferguson, Westbrook, and a few admirers in the darkened alley behind the theatre, no one else had gotten close enough to really threaten recognition. A masquerade was the best possible option, but she might see people who knew her as Madeleine too well to be fooled by her disguise.

"Will no one raise an objection to Marguerite's presence?" she asked.

"I've been to similar parties before. When a rake like Westbrook hosts the party, the men will be peers, but the women are usually demimondaines or ladies whose husbands no longer demand fidelity.

None of the patronesses of Almack's will be there, if that's what worries you. I wager you will know some of the guests by reputation, but they will not overlap with your aunt's circles."

"But why Westbrook? Lady Greville is not one I wish to see as either Marguerite or Madeleine."

She had received another note from the woman that morning, offering insincere condolences for the rumors circulating about Ferguson. When she told Ferguson, he swore under his breath. "If we see Caro, I will handle her. Unfortunately, I can't call on her to end this — she's so mad for revenge that she might claim I compromised her just to ensure that I couldn't marry you. We can't wait for a better event, though. Westbrook will have invited every fashionable man and woman in London, so your exposure will be broad. There isn't another masquerade with a similar list of guests for at least a fortnight."

She didn't like the thought of attending a party where Caro would hold court, but she agreed that delay was impossible. The Lords could open an investigation well before another opportunity arose. "Very well, we shall attend. But I haven't the least idea of how to prepare for such an event."

"Ellie offered to help you. I can't say I approve of her attending such parties, but at least she can tell you what you need to know."

"She is old enough to decide her own mind," Madeleine said, amused by the protective tone of Ferguson's voice. "She hasn't gone beyond the line — she could still attend proper events if she chose."

Ferguson stroked her hair, an unconscious gesture that soothed her fears. "Let us see you through this before attempting to rehabilitate my sister. Are you sure you wish to do this?"

"There is no other choice. If nothing else, it will be fascinating to attend a disreputable party before I become your very proper duchess."

"There's nothing proper about you, love," he said, his blue eyes sparking with a sudden need that demanded fulfillment.

He gripped her wrist and pulled her up into his lap. She tumbled into his arms with a muffled laugh, and as he angled in to kiss her, she was ready for him. Now that they had a plan — even if it was dangerous — she felt like they could conquer anything. All the heat and fear and excitement coalesced into hunger — and his kiss set it all ablaze. His lips slanted over hers and she opened for him, reveling in the moment when his tongue claimed hers.

She wasn't satisfied with kisses. It had been several days since she'd last had him inside her, and might be several weeks before she could have him again — the price of feigning propriety before the wedding. He must have felt the same. His hands were already kneading into her derriere, angling her away from him so that he could break off their kiss and nibble at the side of her neck before forging a path toward her bosom.

She inhaled sharply as his hand forced her bodice down and freed a breast from her stays. He smelled just how she loved him to — riding leather, starch, and just a hint of sweat, but missing the usual scent of shaving lather. As she felt the stubble of his day-old beard graze her skin, she smiled — he had been so desperate to see her that he hadn't bothered with niceties.

He wasn't bothering with niceties now either. While his mouth sucked wickedly at her breast, his hand bent one of her legs to improve his access, then delved up under her skirts. He traced her stocking, skimmed lightly over the joint of her knee, and lingered on the ribbon holding her stocking in place. From there, it was just bare skin for him to conquer.

He took his time, and between his lips and his slowly roving fingers, she was already quivering for him by the time he found his prize. She looked down, seeing herself for the first time in a dress as he touched her. Somehow, his strong fingers, the muscular arm around her back holding her tight, and the strength of his jaw prominent over her naked breast were even more shocking in contrast to her white muslin morning gown.

"I love your ass in breeches, but skirts are easier," he said, the rough words simultaneously shocking her and making her want more. He slid a finger inside her, then another, claiming her mouth again at the same moment as his first thrust.

She didn't know how he did it, didn't think she could ever explain it — she'd felt urges before she met him, but had never guessed she would flare up like a Roman candle with just a brush of his fingers against her. But before she could even moan a protest — or a demand — he had her right at the very peak of need, waiting for the touch she needed to push her over the edge.

He held her there, freeing himself from his breeches, settling her on top of him like he had on the chaise a few nights earlier. She knew the movements now, could slide down on him easily, biting her lip in a battle to keep herself from screaming.

He pulled her mouth against him this time, using his tongue to keep her quiet, and she matched her tempo to the intensity of his kiss. He was right there with her, holding her hard against him, and it only took a few more strokes before he broke away. "I can't hold on any longer," he said, shoving a hand up under her skirts to flick at that sensitive bundle of nerves that drove her need.

She had thought she might outlast him this time, but he threw her over the cliff. He kissed her again just before she tried to scream, and the pressure of keeping her pleasure in only heightened her climax. She was still shuddering with her silent moans as he stiffened beneath her, still falling when she felt him come inside her.

They couldn't relax against each other, but the aftermath was still blissful — after the terror of last night and the worry of the morning, their lovemaking somehow grounded her again. She brushed a kiss against his forehead before her pulled out and dug into his pocket for a handkerchief. He pressed it between her legs, cleaning her gently so she could pull her skirts down without risk.

When she had pulled her gown together and he had rearranged his trousers, she grinned at him. "I'm sorry you had to repeat a dream so soon."

He grinned back, but his was infinitely more wicked. "We didn't repeat. I added one to the list. After the endless hours Salford kept me waiting here before agreeing to let you marry me, I couldn't resist taking some pleasure out of this room."

She laughed, knowing she should be horrified but too happy to care. He laughed with her, and she was glad the humor between them was restored, even if they were still in danger.

"I'm also sorry we have to go to the masquerade," she said, her tone turning serious. "But I'm glad we're making the attempt."

His eyes went dark. "I won't be pleased until we're safely away from there. But I'll do it, Mad. And then we'll marry, and we'll have all the time in the world for this."

"I do like the sound of that," she said.

He stood up, taking a last look at her and himself to make sure they were properly clothed. "Ellie will come this afternoon to help you. Don't let her talk you into anything too scandalous."

He smiled like he was teasing her, but his tone was still serious. "We can survive one night of scandal, Ferguson. We might even enjoy it."

"That's what I'm afraid of," he said.

She laughed as she kissed him, then let him go. She needed to change, to prepare for Ellie — to get her emotions in order if she was going to attend a masquerade as Marguerite.

They were so close to being safe — and she wasn't going to let herself be distracted. One more night, and he would be hers forever.

CHAPTER THIRTY-TWO

Ellie had developed a reputation as a reckless hoyden, but when she called at Salford House two hours later, she reminded Madeleine of Boadicea on the eve of battle. Her blue eyes, so similar to Ferguson's, gleamed with pleasure at the ruse they were playing, and her red hair piled on top of her head made her look even more like an ancient Celtic queen. And when she walked in to Madeleine's bedroom, shutting the door in the face of the footman who escorted her, she slapped a sheet of paper down on the writing desk like it was a battle plan.

It wasn't a list of regiments and supplies. It was her idea of the costume Madeleine might wear to Westbrook's masquerade. After wearing breeches at the theatre, Madeleine should have felt no shame wearing what Ellie recommended. It was a dress, after all, even if it was the most revealing dress she had ever seen.

"I cannot wear that," Madeleine said, her face turning bright red. "I am not even sure it... covers everything."

Ellie had taken the seat across from her. She flipped the sheet of paper to look at the drawing again. "I wore something similar as Athena once. It would send Lady Salford into vapors — but it's not the ladies that it is designed for."

She grinned saucily. Madeleine couldn't help but smile in return. "Is it truly necessary, though?"

"My dear, with Marguerite's talent and my brother's notoriety, everyone at the ball will be staring at you. You should want them looking at your body, not your face."

Madeleine took the paper back from Ellie and scanned the drawing again. The costume was white muslin, but nothing a proper debutante would wear. It was pinned at the shoulders in the Grecian style, and then cut so deep across the bosom that Madeleine feared she might fall out of it if she had to curtsy low to another guest. The drape clung to the body, and as it was drawn on the model, there was a dampened chemise — or nothing at all — beneath it.

"I shall die of embarrassment," Madeleine said. "And I don't even like the Greeks. Can I not wear my Hamlet costume and be done with it?"

"Haven't you guessed what the costume is?" Ellie asked. When Madeleine shook her head, she retrieved the sheet and pulled a pencil stub out of her reticule. The model had been headless, but Ellie quickly sketched in a face — nothing that might resemble Madeleine if anyone found the drawing, but enough to add to the picture. Then, she drew a towering pile of hair and festooned it with ropes of small berries — or pomegranate seeds. To the model's wrist, she added a beribboned corsage of poppies. A sheaf of wheat in the woman's hand completed the ensemble.

Madeleine knew the answer before Ellie finished, but was so surprised by her talented sketching that she didn't stop her. When Ellie finally looked up, Madeleine smiled. "Persephone."

"Yes, the Queen of the Underworld, come back from the dead. And Ferguson can dress as Hades. It is perfect, don't you think?"

"Ferguson won't submit to wearing only a sheet around his torso," Madeleine warned.

"I would find that amusing," Ellie said with a laugh. "But he can wear a coat and trousers with a sinister cloak over it. A crown instead of a hat should be enough."

"The ton will think we're laughing at them."

"You are." The smile on Ellie's face was almost evil. "But they will love you all the more for your audacity. If you were not so acclaimed, it might be foolish. If you knew, though, how every man in my circle has clamored to meet you and how they've all cursed Ferguson for keeping you hidden away, you would not be so nervous about this appearance. They will be falling at your feet — especially in that dress."

"Did you draw the dress as well?"

Ellie nodded, slipping her pencil back into her bag. "I cannot sew it, but my modiste works miracles. She can make over my Athena costume for you this afternoon. You can trust her to do the final fitting — she owes me a great debt and won't betray you."

Madeleine wondered how Ellie had so many people in her service whose loyalty was so assured, but it was not her business to ask. She said, "Your talent with drawing is astounding. Do you draw often?"

"I prefer painting, but I haven't painted in an age. Too many parties, don't you know."

Her light tone sounded forced. "If you care to join us, Amelia, Miss Prudence Etchingham and I meet weekly to discuss our artistic and academic pursuits. Perhaps you would find time to paint if you were to become part of our little circle?"

Madeleine spoke impulsively, believing the invitation would be well received, but her voice faltered at the end. Ellie had the same frozen, frigid look that Madeleine had seen the night Ferguson had taken her to Ellie's house — like she had been confronted with something she wanted desperately to forget. "I am sorry," Madeleine said quickly. "I didn't mean to presume."

The ice in Ellie's eyes melted slightly. "No apology is necessary. I don't have the heart to paint at present. Drawing this costume was an interesting exercise, but I do not think I would be a productive addition to your society."

Ellie folded the drawing into neat fourths and tucked it into her reticule. The crisp way she folded the paper had a sound of finality to it — like a door closing in a blizzard, with Madeleine shut outside. The thought made her stubborn. Ellie had done so much for her, and she wanted to return the favor. "Do think about it, please. Even if you do not wish to paint for us, you might enjoy our discussions. We meet here every Friday at two o'clock."

That wasn't entirely true. Madeleine had missed every meeting since Amelia's betrayal. But if Ellie would attend, Madeleine would go despite her cousin.

"I will consider it," Ellie said. Then she stood, smoothing out her skirts before gathering up her reticule with a gloved hand. As usual, Madeleine felt utterly plain beside her; the dress she had changed into after Ferguson left, a pale yellow muslin, could not withstand the intensity of Ellie's ensemble.

Still, there was a brittle quality to the woman's beauty that bothered Madeleine. With her flame-colored hair and creamy skin, she looked warm and fiery — but like a fire about to sputter out into ashes, rather than one that could be sustained.

"Thank you for everything you have done," Madeleine said,

rising to kiss Ellie's cheek. She owed Ellie more than she could repay, and would do what she could to help cure whatever mysterious unhappiness lingered beneath her supposedly carefree demeanor. "I would have been lost without you. I cannot say enough how very much I appreciate your assistance."

"You saved yourself. But I could hardly ignore you — you did not seem eager to live the life of a ruined lady. Not everyone is suited for such a lifestyle."

"Do you think you are suited for it?" Madeleine asked. "Surely you are not ruined."

"No, not entirely. I doubt I would receive a voucher to Almack's, but as I've no desire to ever attend again, it doesn't signify. My level of disreputability was just enough for my father to disown me, as he did Ferguson, which was what I wanted. Still, I'm glad for you that your ruse worked. It is possible to live a happy life without the full approbation of the ton, but it's not a course I would recommend."

"Then you would choose differently if you were able to live again?"

"Widowhood has its uses," Ellie said, smiling mirthlessly. "Although if I had defied my father from the start and married the man I wished to, I would have become the marchioness of Folkestone as soon as the man my father forced me to marry died. Ironic, no?"

Ironic was not the word Madeleine would have chosen; heartbreaking, or cruel, but ironic wasn't strong enough. Ellie changed the subject, though, saying, "What's done is done, and there is no going back. I must be off to instruct my modiste. I will send your Lizzie back to the house on Dover Street tomorrow with all the necessary accoutrements for the masquerade, and the modiste will do the last bit of fitting when you go to the house to be dressed."

She strode to the door before Madeleine could say goodbye again, but she paused with her hand on the handle. "Do enjoy yourself tomorrow night, Madeleine. I have other plans with Norbury, but I cannot wait to hear how you take the ton by storm."

Ellie left then, seeming eager to go, as though she felt she had shared too much. Madeleine looked at the timepiece on the mantel. It was only two o'clock. Ellie had come unfashionably early to settle the costume design in time for the modiste, and it would be hours yet before she had to dress for dinner. Aunt Augusta was not receiving callers today, since they would all be sniffing about Madeleine to validate the rumors about Ferguson's madness. She couldn't risk going to the shops, either, for fear that the gossip mongers would accost her there. She could write letters, she supposed, or she could embroider, or read a novel — any of the proper pursuits for a not-so-young lady of leisure.

None of it appealed. Afternoons like these, which stretched out in front of her toward a dreary old age, had driven her to the theatre in the first place. Perhaps it would be different if she had a house of her own to manage. As a duchess, she wouldn't lack for staff to oversee, or callers to entertain — or more pleasurable activities to pursue with her husband.

She smiled. Daydreaming about her marriage was preferable to embroidering, and so she indulged for a few minutes, thinking of all they could do together if their reputations survived this scandal. She had been so opposed to marriage before — but she thought she might not mind sitting quietly and reading a book if Ferguson was nearby, if she thought that at any moment he might interrupt her and steal a kiss.

She was so deep in the dream that when the door opened, she

thought Ferguson had indeed come for her. She looked up, the smile on her lips ready for him to devour it.

It was Amelia. Her dream collapsed. She wouldn't just embroider or write letters to escape Amelia — she would willingly submit to a toothpulling, or accompany Lady Harcastle on a tour of the Peninsula battlefields and cemeteries, if it meant she could delay this confrontation.

But Amelia shut the door, standing with her back pressed against it. "Maddie, please..." she said, her voice trembling on the words before she took a deep breath and started again. "It's been weeks since that night, and we haven't spoken in private a single time since then. Won't you give me a chance to apologize?"

Amelia looked like she hadn't slept since her betrayal. There were dark circles under her eyes, and her normally bright hair was lank and limp in its chignon. Madeleine had found it easy to avoid her — Amelia had taken most meals in her room, and only sat for dinner with the family or attended events at Augusta's express order. The fingers of her right hand were stained black with inky patterns; Amelia often got too caught up in the throes of writing to notice if a leaky pen was wreaking havoc on her skin.

Madeleine felt a twinge of sympathy. She willed herself to ignore it. "Does it matter whether you apologize?"

"It matters to me. I think it matters to you, too, even if you don't wish to admit it."

"That is precisely why it doesn't matter," Madeleine said, the heat of her earlier daydream turning effortlessly into anger. "That statement is just like you have always been — believing you are right above all others. It's why you betrayed my secret to Alex, is it not? Because you told me to stop and I didn't listen to your wisdom?"

Amelia flinched under the withering sarcasm in Madeleine's voice. But she was too entrenched to retreat. "That isn't why, Maddie. I didn't want to be right — I was trying to protect you!"

"As it turns out, I did not need your protection. The play is over. No one found me out. In fact, if you had not told Alex and Aunt Augusta, even they wouldn't have known."

"It wasn't merely the theatre I was trying to protect you from — I supported you when you went to Madame Legrand. But I had no reason to believe Ferguson's intentions toward you were honest."

"Because he did not attempt to court you like every other man in the ton?"

Amelia abandoned her post by the door to take the chair Ellie had recently vacated. "I don't give a farthing for my admirers. I would consign them all to the devil if it meant you could go to a ball without being jealous of me. If Ferguson removes your bitterness, I would thank him."

The knife struck home. "Bitter? Why would you think I am bitter?"

"How often have you teased me about my suitors?" Amelia countered. "You know I do not want their attentions, and yet you fling them in my face as though I have something to be ashamed of because of them. If that isn't bitterness..."

She shut her mouth abruptly. Madeleine gasped, the words slicing deep into one of her most sensitive, still-healing wounds. "Do you think I am jealous of you?"

Amelia sighed. "I do not understand why you would be. But I cannot help thinking that you are."

For all that Madeleine watched enviously whenever Amelia stood up to dance her fifth set in a row, and for all that she wished she had a mother and father instead of living a shadowed life with her cousins, it was never something they discussed. How could she have ever told Amelia that she sometimes wished their positions were reversed?

That she wished Amelia was the orphan, not her?

"Do you really not understand what it has been to grow up with you?" Madeleine asked, guilt and jealousy combining to wrap around the ball of acid in her stomach. "With your perfect English beauty, and your family who loves you, and your brothers who would die for you, when my parents were more concerned about their estate than me? Even your talent was easier for you — you can write every day, but the only hobby that brings me joy is something I cannot ever do again. So yes, I am jealous. But what would you have me do? Be grateful to sit in your shadow?"

She started crying as she spoke, scarcely noticing the tears until they started to drip onto her bosom. Amelia's face drained of color as she listened, her blue eyes large and stark, the dark circles under them even more pronounced. Madeleine opened a drawer in the table beside her and retrieved a handkerchief, avoiding eye contact, dabbing at the tears on her skin even though they had not yet stopped flowing.

Amelia opened and closed her mouth several times before speaking. Finally, she said, "I think of you as my sister, not my cousin. It would hurt me just as much to lose you as it would to lose Alex or Sebastian — more, even, since I've not spent more than a week without you since you arrived from France. Perhaps that's why I was so concerned about Ferguson — it was all so sudden. One week, I thought we would be spinsters together forever, and the next..."

She paused, taking a deep breath. "You're going to be a duchess, and I cannot imagine what it will be like here without you. But if you have never been happy in this house, then it is for the best, and I can only wish that you'll find all the happiness in your marriage that was missing for you here."

It wasn't the kind of speech Madeleine had ever heard from her before — a surrender rather than a rebuttal. Madeleine took another handkerchief from her table and handed it to her; Amelia's eyes were just as full of tears as Madeleine's. "It's not that I was unhappy here," Madeleine said slowly, uncomfortable saying the words after keeping them buried for so long, but knowing she needed to be honest — with both of them — if there was any hope of salvaging what they had. "It's that my life in France... it became a dream, something I could imagine as I sat alone on the side of a ballroom, something I could focus on when the desire to run away from an at-home and join a theatre troupe was too strong. Even the theatre was a dream. I just had to believe there was more for me than shopping and needlework."

Amelia quirked a smile at that even through her tears. Both she and Prudence had described that feeling before. But for Madeleine, it wasn't just the tedium of everyday life. "I had to believe that if my parents had lived, I would have had a more exciting life. This circle isn't for me, any more than it is for you. But at least I could tell myself there was a different life that was stolen from me, rather than thinking this is the way I would always have been."

"Well, you will have a different life as Ferguson's duchess," Amelia said. "I just never imagined you were still dreaming of France. I still miss Father, of course, but then it's not the same — losing him didn't cost me an entire way of life as your parents' loss did for you."

Madeleine stared at the tear-stained cloth in her hands. "I don't even want to go back to France now. There is nothing for me there. As much as I may wish it otherwise, my family is here now, and my parents are not coming back."

Then she looked up, meeting Amelia's eyes fully for the first time since she had entered the room. "And I consider you my sister, even if I did not behave like it these past few weeks."

It was true. As much as she had been angered by Amelia's decision to tell Alex and Aunt Augusta about her acting, Madeleine had not forgotten everything else they had shared. It was Amelia who made her feel at home in the nursery during her first few months with the Stauntons, Amelia who first encouraged her to put on plays in their schoolroom — Amelia who made the endless years of spinsterhood bearable.

"Then will you forgive me?" Amelia asked. "I really am sorry I told Alex and Mother, and that I was too selfish to accept that you could marry Ferguson and still see me occasionally."

She sounded so forlorn that Madeleine actually laughed. "See you occasionally? I will insist that you spend whole weeks at a time with us. I am glad for what I've found with Ferguson, but I never intended to cut all ties with you — unless you are foolish enough to believe I would."

"I hoped you wouldn't cut me," Amelia said. But her smile quickly faded. "You may have to, though."

"Whyever would I have to cut you?"

Amelia hesitated. "I just finished a new book. It's already at the printer's, and he will have it in shops by the end of the week."

"That's wonderful news," Madeleine said, genuinely happy for her. "I cannot wait to see it rivet the ton like your last book, even if it was hard for me and Prudence to listen to Lady Harcastle's praises of it and not tell her you wrote it."

"This one is a bit of a departure from my previous novels."

"Not too much, I hope? I know you thought you might be tiring of Gothic romances, but you have such a way with them."

"It is more of a satire," Amelia said. "I trust the ton will be fascinated when word starts to spread."

Madeleine frowned. "What sort of satire?"

"One that will have all of London trying to guess the author. If I am right, between this book and Marguerite's appearance at the masquerade, by the end of the week no one will even remember that they thought Ferguson was a murderer — they will all be too busy reading."

"But you've always been so careful with your books before," Madeleine said. "How could you risk everything now?"

"Atonement," Amelia said, her eyes still stark. "If I can draw attention away from your secret life, I will feel less guilty about the role I played in it. Besides, I've no intention of getting caught."

"This could be more damaging than my acting," Madeleine warned. "Setting foot onstage was a disgrace, but if you mocked the highest members of the ton — there will be no saving you."

Amelia rose, tossing her handkerchief onto the table with a negligent gesture. "I don't much wish to be saved. I've no need to stay in London, and Mother can exile me if she wishes — I've been asking her to do it for ages anyway. Besides, I'm not trying to land a duke like you are."

She said the last bit teasingly, but her tone was warm. Even though Madeleine felt wrung out by their conversation, exhausted by all that had happened in the last eighteen hours, she somehow felt free, too — as though the jealous beast within her had gone away for good. She stood, hugging Amelia as though they were little girls again, unconstrained by propriety. "I hope you aren't caught, but thank you. For everything."

Amelia squeezed her back. "I hope you aren't caught either. You must tell me everything about the masquerade — Prudence and I will be so jealous."

"Prudence especially, I would wager," Madeleine said.

They both laughed. Their easy camaraderie wasn't quite restored yet — and it might be some time before either of them could forget what they had said to each other. But the path was clear before them. And as much as Madeleine had avoided Amelia, she was glad they had finally spoken. If they had gone many more weeks without resolving their tension, they might never have found the words.

After Amelia left, Madeleine contemplated the next few days. She was annoyed that she would have to wait twenty-four hours for their scheme to unfold — but tomorrow, she would dress for the masquerade and Ferguson would escort her there. Ellie had not said anything about what Madeleine would see at the ball, other than that she would be the toast of the evening, but she suspected she would see an element of the ton that she would never have the opportunity to see again.

But she would do it, would do anything at all, if it meant she and Ferguson could marry without suspicion. In two days, she would know whether they had been successful or not — and she could begin planning a life that was really hers, and not just a dream.

CHAPTER THIRTY-THREE

"I still don't like it," Ferguson muttered as their coach waited in the line of equipages slowly approaching Westbrook's mansion.

Madeleine drew her cloak more firmly around her shoulders, soaking in the last few moments of warmth before she would have to surrender the garment at the door. Her costume was designed for admiration, not comfort. "Would you rather be branded a murderer?"

"I may commit murder if anyone ogles you — and they will, I assure you. I would worship that dress if I could have you to myself in it."

"Don't say a hardened rake like you has never seen such a display," Madeleine retorted, her cheeks flushing at the thought of what was to come.

"I haven't," he said flatly. "Seeing you in the foyer when I retrieved you from our house was enough to make me want to drag you upstairs and strip you out of that dress. In the atmosphere of Westbrook's ball... I must warn you that I'm not sure how long I will be able to keep my hands off you."

His eyes were as heated as his words, and she felt a small throb of pleasure deep in her belly. They had said little to each other on the drive out from London to Westbrook's Richmond estate, but that was probably for the best — if he could arouse her just with a few words, they might not have ever reached the masquerade.

The carriage rolled to its final stop and a footman opened the door. Ferguson stepped smoothly to the pavement before reaching up to assist her. Rather than taking her hand, he grasped her around the waist, lifting her out of the coach and into his arms. He released her slowly, so close to him that she slid down his body, feeling every muscle — and his growing erection — through the single filmy layer of her gown. She gasped as she landed, pressed fully against him, wishing just as much as he did that they could abandon the party and go back to their secret house.

"I may not last long either," she whispered, looking up into his eyes and seeing him fight the desire to toss her back into the carriage.

He ran his hands down her arms, grazed against her bottom, and then set her firmly on her feet. "If we see enough people in the first hour, we can escape early and have some time alone."

Alex supported the plan, true to his word despite the impropriety, but he would be watching the clock for her return — which meant the less time they spent at the masquerade, the more time they would have to themselves. "Oui, monsieur le duc," she said, slipping into Marguerite's French accent.

He took her arm and escorted her up the stairs to the grand entrance. A footman took her cloak and Ferguson's greatcoat and she heard rustling whispers rise up around them. If they already drew this much notice, they might not need even an hour to cement Marguerite's return.

"How do I look, monsieur?" she asked, twirling in a slow circle in front of him. It was a vixen's move, one she would never make anywhere else — but here, in this dress, it felt right. She guessed how she must look — the fabric clinging to her breasts and hips, almost translucent in the light, her nipples hardened points as they strained against the gown. Her hair was powdered to disguise its true color and Lizzie had threaded a chain of garnets through her tresses, mimicking the blood-red pomegranate seeds Persephone was known for. She had abandoned the sheaf of wheat as impractical, but a cluster of poppies wrapped around her wrist, and high-heeled Grecian sandals added the inches that Marguerite always displayed on stage. The lace of her drawers peeked out at the hem of the dress. She had never worn them before, and they might shock others more than if she had worn nothing at all — but it was the one concession she demanded for her modesty, so that at least one extra layer concealed her sex under her scandalous gown.

She turned back to Ferguson just in time to see him swallow hard. He looked like someone had bashed him in the head. Finally, he said, "You are the most beautiful woman I have ever seen."

There was none of the polite flattery she was used to from the ton — he sounded absolutely serious, as though he faced a guillotine and wanted those to be his last words. She knew he desired her, but she never tired of hearing it.

She curtsied low for him, feeling wicked as the bodice slid dangerously across her breasts. "And you are the most perfect consort for the evening, monsieur."

"Just the evening?" he asked, arching a brow.

She brushed up against him to whisper in his ear, "Perhaps longer, if fate and mon Dieu agree."

He laughed, low and sinful, and tilted her chin up. "Careful, love. You'll have me taking you home before we've even danced."

She fluttered her lashes at him, a smile playing on her lips. He smiled in return, looking hungry, but utterly in command with the heavy gold circlet on his head and his dark cloak swirled around him. She had thought their masquerade would require acting, but this wasn't an act — this was dark, sensuous joy, giving in to the scandalous behavior his wicked eyes encouraged. In the ton, she could never be so brazen.

But tonight, even though it was an effort to clear his name, belonged to them.

When she looked beyond him, she saw their plan was already working. People whispered behind their fans as they glanced furtively at Madeleine and Ferguson. "Shall we dance?" she asked, pretending the scrutiny did not matter at all. "Unless you do wish to retire..."

Ferguson took her arm again. "Dancing it is, but only so no one thinks I'm a monster for denying you."

This he said more loudly, and it drew titters from the clusters around them. She pretended not to notice. They had agreed that she would feign ignorance of the rumors about Marguerite's disappearance. As much as she loved engaging in behavior that she would never be able to repeat in real life, they were there to salvage his reputation, not destroy hers. She would play the role she needed to play, but she would have to be careful — it would be all too easy to lose herself in the desire that already threatened to overwhelm her.

"Onward, monsieur le duc," she said.

*   *   *

An hour later, Ferguson wasn't sure how much longer he could survive their ruse. The advantage of a salacious event such as

Westbrook's masquerade was that the normal rules did not apply — he could dance with Madeleine as many times as he pleased.

The disadvantage was that he couldn't hold her in his arms, brushing against him with every step, without wanting to find the nearest bed. Not that anyone would raise an eyebrow, of course. The ballroom was looking distinctly thin as the evening wore on, and Ferguson suspected that the extensive pathways and grottoes of Westbrook's garden were being put to good use for any number of liaisons. The house, in the serene beauty of Richmond, seemed purpose-built for these entertainments — which was probably true, since Westbrook's father and grandfather had been notorious rakes themselves.

Still, they were there to prove to everyone that Marguerite was still alive — not to make love in the nearest dark corner. And he would stay true to their plan, as much as it killed him to stay in the ballroom.

Madeleine had never looked lovelier, which was part of his problem. Her gown should have been a disgrace, would have been her immediate downfall if she were there as a chaperone, but it was designed to tempt a man's desires. He had never adored the overblown courtesans who littered the demimonde, but even though the dress was revealing, Madeleine was perfect in it — all the grace of a lady, with the finest pair of breasts just barely swathed in muslin and practically begging for his touch.

He dragged his eyes back to her face. She was smiling mischievously — she may have been a spinster, but she wasn't a fool. "I suggest we retire, monsieur, so that you may examine my... bodice more properly."

Her desire for him struck him like a spur. He hadn't thought he could be any harder for her, but the teasing lilt in her voice proved him wrong. She would never see him as a duty she had to suffer — she wanted him, all of him, just as he was, and as often as possible.

The rest of his life might be an endless series of duties — but with her, it would all be pleasure.

"I do think we've been here long enough," he said, hearing the gravel in his voice. Madeleine had been seen by everyone in attendance, greeted by Westbrook — who made no reference to the night at the theatre, but did not appear to doubt her identity — and exchanged pleasantries with those who were able to reach her in the pauses between dances. Caro skirted the edges of the ballroom, and he had watched warily as she danced with Westbrook, but she had not accosted them tonight. If they could make it to their carriage, Madeleine would be safe and his reputation would be secure.

He pulled her out of the dancers, narrowly avoiding a collision with one of the liveried footmen who passed champagne to the people sitting out the current dance. Ferguson almost regretted that he and Madeleine would never attend another of these parties as husband and wife. There were always masquerades to attend, but they could not behave as blatantly as they had here — brushing against each other, flirting outrageously, as if there was no one in the world but them.

Still, he was glad to be done with it. With his reputation restored, he and Madeleine could marry, the twins could debut, and life might return to some semblance of normal.

But before they reached the staircase, a woman stepped in front of them, interrupting their progress. "How charming," Caro said, her eyes narrowing as she looked them both up and down. "The king of the underworld suits you, Ferguson."

He almost didn't recognize her at first, so sure that they had escaped unscathed, until he heard the bitter note in her otherwise lovely voice. She wore a dress similar to Madeleine's, the cool white linen of the Greeks, but she wore a brilliant diamond tiara and had a dagger strapped to her waist in an allusion that he couldn't interpret.

"Lady Greville," he said coolly.

"We should have consulted each other before the event," Caro said, staring up at him and ignoring Madeleine. "If you were the Aeneas to my Dido, think what a stir we could have caused."

Dido — the Carthaginian queen who stabbed herself in the heart after being abandoned by her Trojan lover. "You look very well, of course, but I have chosen a different consort."

Caro cast a flickering glance at Madeleine, just enough to make it clear that the actress was socially beneath her. "I have little love for Salford's ward, but it does seem callous of you to parade this actress chit in front of the ton when you'd have everyone believe that your engagement to Lady Madeleine is a love match."

"You know how these things play," he said, trying to sound bored. "Lady Madeleine could never attend an event such as this, and I've no intention of giving up all my entertainments."

"Just the same as always, aren't you?" Caro said. "You hold all the power, and it's all directed to your own ends. If I thought you were capable of change, I could forgive you — but you are just as selfish as you were ten years ago."

He didn't respond. Any true defense risked betraying Madeleine's secret. And he could see how his situation looked — most people would politely ignore that he had both a mistress and a fiancée, but not all of them would think highly of him for it.

"I truly am sorry for the manner in which I left England," he said, settling for an apology over an attack. "But I cannot change what I did, nor can I change the consequences for either of us. Now if you would be so good as to excuse us, I must take Madame Guerrier home."

Madeleine had stood silent beside him, maintaining the distant air of a courtesan who knows she is not welcome in the conversation but is too proud to look abashed. He snuck a glance at her profile, wondering what she thought, and was surprised to see some combination of pity and impatience. She didn't think Ferguson was the villain Caro portrayed him as — but she also vaguely sympathized with the other woman, despite the difficulties Caro had caused them.

Caro glanced fleetingly in Madeleine's direction again — then looked harder as she interpreted the emotions on Madeleine's face. "Don't you dare think to pity me, you little trollop," Caro hissed. "He'll turn you out onto the streets soon enough, and you'll be spreading your legs for the closest protector you can find before the week is out."

"Is that what you did when he left you, my lady?" Madeleine said. Her French accent suddenly became a lash. As Madeleine, she would never say such a thing — but here, Ferguson knew she would say whatever she pleased.

Ferguson cursed as Caro's face turned red. "Ladies, this is neither the time nor the place for this discussion." The ballroom was barely half full, but enough people still lingered to notice their argument. The last thing he wanted was for anyone's attention to be drawn to Madeleine long enough to see beyond her costume.

"Since I've no intention of ever talking to your whore again, I should tell her now that she's in for a disappointment if she thinks she's going to stay in your affections."

Madeleine tossed her head in a very Gallic gesture of annoyance. "Can we leave now, monsieur? The company is very dull tonight."

Westbrook strode up to them, and his grey eyes were grim as he looked at Caro. "My dear, would you like for the duke to leave now? I thought he had more sense than to approach you."

She looked uncomfortable, and some of her militant anger deflated. "It was the other way around, I'm afraid."

"You swore to me you would not seek him out," Westbrook said, his measured voice an odd contrast to the sudden look of fury on his face.

She shrugged, a small, helpless gesture that uncovered the vulnerability lurking beneath her hardened shell. "I'm sorry, Westbrook. But he cannot just walk through his charmed life as though he was entirely unscathed, when I almost lost everything! And to see him now, seducing not just one, but two French girls..."

She trailed off, looking at Madeleine again. Ferguson saw what she was thinking an instant before she realized it herself, and his arm was already reaching for Madeleine, pulling her into his embrace as though he could shelter her. "Oh, my God," Caro breathed, really looking at Madeleine for the first time that evening. "You can't possibly be..."

Her brown eyes were filled with shock. Ferguson felt the floor sink out from under him. Caro hated him and would not care to protect Madeleine — she was the very last person he would have chosen to uncover their secret. Madeleine went very still under his arm. She could see their doom too, and she froze beneath Caro's gaze like a mouse before a hawk.

Ferguson thought briefly, instinctively, of escape, wondering if they could reach their carriage before the rumors spread outside and engulfed them. But he had promised Madeleine that they would do everything possible to stay in England. He didn't see how they could, unless Caro could be bought off — but she was rich enough on her own, and too bitter to let such a secret go untold.

"Whatever you are thinking, you're mistaken," Ferguson said to Caro, hoping to draw her attention away from Madeleine before she fully determined what she was seeing.

Caro's shock had turned to confusion, and then amazement. She turned to Westbrook as though seeking an ally. "Doesn't the chit look remarkably like Lady M...?"

"Shh," Westbrook hissed, grabbing Caro in a protective gesture of his own. "Do not say another word."

They couldn't leave, not without making a last attempt to salvage the situation. Ferguson checked his protective instincts, knowing he had to take Madeleine into the lion's den.

"Shall we adjourn to your study, Westbrook?" Ferguson suggested, his voice as calm as if he was inviting them to a picnic.

The earl nodded, pulling Caro with him as he turned to lead the way. Ferguson felt Madeleine tremble under this arm, and he bent to whisper in her ear. "We aren't running, Mad."

He had to keep his promise — and the only way for them to stay in London was to settle the score with Caro once and for all.

CHAPTER THIRTY-FOUR

Ferguson's grip on her arm was uncompromising as he escorted her down the hall toward Westbrook's study. On another night, Madeleine would have found him overprotective — but when that awful realization dawned in Caro's eyes, Madeleine had been grateful for the support. She was still grateful, even though Caro no longer looked at them. The woman walked stiffly in front of them, and Westbrook bent down to whisper in her ear as he dragged her toward their meeting. She couldn't hear the words, but the sibilants sounded harsh — Westbrook was not pleased.

Until their encounter with Caro, the ball had been a dream. She had reveled in it, flirting shamelessly with the man who would be her husband in a way that she could never do in public again — even though she fully intended to behave like that with him in private. But now, with Caro's malice and Westbrook's unclear loyalties, Madeleine felt the dream becoming a nightmare, one she couldn't escape from even though she screamed at herself to wake up.

She may have been daring, may have even given Caro an uncharacteristically cruel retort, but this was not her kind of game. So she said softly to Ferguson, "However you wish to play this, I will follow your lead. Even if we must flee the ton."

His hand closed tighter. There would be a bruise on her forearm in the morning if his tension didn't leave him soon. "That's not what you want, and so that's not what we'll do," he said flatly. Then he looked down at her, loosening his hold as though awakening from a nightmare of his own. "But I am sorry, Mad. If I had known what the reputation I built ten years ago would cost me... I would have endured another decade with my father without complaint if I had known you waited for me at the end of it."

Tears pricked at the corners of her eyes. She knew how much he had hated his father — knew how much it would have cost him to stay. She whispered back, "And if I had known about you, I could have survived any number of seasons as a spinster."

It was true. It wasn't that she regretted the theatre — but it was a substitute for all that her life had been missing, and the hole she had tried to fill was no longer there. As long as Ferguson was in her life, she didn't need the applause of an audience to make her feel cherished.

Ferguson's love was enough. And it finally made her believe that her life could be something special despite all the rules and constraints that society enforced.

Still, she was nervous as they reached Westbrook's study. She had a moment outside the door to collect herself. Westbrook first had to oust a flustered shepherdess and a man dressed as King Henry VIII. The king claimed they were merely talking, even though the woman's skirts had climbed to her waist and her rouge stained the man's white ruff. They didn't seem upset to be caught, though. The woman giggled as they swept past, and Madeleine heard them shut themselves into another room just down the hall. A year ago, she would have been shocked — but now, it just made her wish she and Ferguson could make a similar escape.

They entered the study and Westbrook sighed as he closed the door behind them. "These masquerades are a pain in the arse, but they do lead to some interesting gossip. I'd avoid the settee in the corner, though. My upholsterer is usually as happy about my parties afterward as my guests are in the moment."

Madeleine wanted to laugh, but she kept quiet. As a courtesan, she might have said something ribald. As a lady, she would have frozen Westbrook for such frank talk. But at the moment, she was in a strange twilight realm where she was neither one nor the other. She was sure Caro knew who she was, equally sure no one else had recognized her, and so settled on silence as the easiest course.

Ferguson did not take the same tack. "Caro, this must end now," he said firmly, firing his opening salvo before Madeleine finished settling herself into one of Westbrook's comfortable, masculine chairs. "I was a wretch and I treated you abominably, but you know we never would have suited. There is no cause for you to ruin Madame Guerrier's life in retaliation. Come after me if you must, but leave her alone."

Caro sat across from Madeleine, at the other end of Westbrook's desk; with Ferguson standing on one side of Westbrook's desk and the earl seated behind the other, the four formed an uneasy quadrangle. Caro hadn't looked at Ferguson during his speech. Her eyes were firmly fixed on Madeleine, roving up and down over her costume, hair, and face, as though everything she needed to know was there.

"How on earth you convinced Lady Madeleine to pretend to be your dead mistress is beyond me," Caro said, turning her dark eyes toward Ferguson. "But if you would have her risk her entire reputation just to clear your name, you've changed not at all."

Madeleine was too shocked to say anything. Caro thought she was pretending to be the actress? She had never thought that people would assume she was trying to protect Ferguson, although it made sense — it was much easier to believe she would take this risk, rather than guess that a well-born, properly behaved lady such as herself would have been playing the actress from the beginning.

Ferguson leaned against the closed door, looking menacing in his crown and cloak. "I would not risk Madeleine for my own ends, regardless of what you think of me."

Caro laughed. "How can you say that, when she's sitting right here? She'll be ruined when people hear of it, whether you marry her or not. Unwed ladies cannot attend parties such as this, particularly behaving as wantonly as she did."

Ferguson slammed his palms against the wood behind him. "No one will hear unless you tell them. And I will see you in hell before I let you spread tales about her."

Westbrook stood behind his desk, his urbane humor replaced with something more sinister. "Duke or not, you will not threaten Lady Greville in my house."

"And you will not abet her attempts to ruin my fiancée," Ferguson snapped. Madeleine realized they would both use force if necessary — they were ranged against each other like opposing generals exchanging taunts before the battle commenced.

She clenched her fists in her lap. She had intended to stay quiet and let Ferguson defuse the situation — but he had just struck a match. "If we can all just speak calmly, surely we can come to an agreeable solution for everyone."

All three of them glared at her, although Ferguson at least had the grace to seem contrite as soon as he realized what he had done.

Caro, however, was already incandescent with anger. "I tried to warn you, Lady Madeleine. But if you are willing to marry a man who murdered his last mistress, and would go so far as to attend a party like this just to keep him safe from the executioner, then you're as hopeless as he is. Of course, if I had been a dried-up spinster like you with a duke finally within my grasp, I would be just as desperate to keep him."

Madeleine gasped, feeling that killing rage herself — she pitied the woman, but at the moment she wanted to slap her bitter mouth before it could spew any more insults. Ferguson took a step forward, but Westbrook reached Caro before the duke could. Placing a quelling hand on her shoulder, he said, "Ferguson isn't a murderer, despite his other sins. I saw Madame Guerrier in her dressing room some weeks ago, and I would vow that she sits before us now. There must be more to Lady Madeleine than you are willing to credit, Caro."

It was Caro's turn to gasp. Madeleine thought Caro would finally realize the truth, but she wrested herself from Westbrook's grip. "What were you doing in her dressing room?" she asked, turning in her chair to stare at Westbrook.

He smoothed his cuffs, a nonchalant gesture that failed to draw attention away from the tension in his voice. "If you recall, that night you told me I was free to seek pleasure elsewhere, since you had no intention of remaining faithful to me. I merely followed your suggestion after you abandoned me at the theatre."

Caro turned a shocking shade of red. "Don't tell me you slept with her!"

"And if I did? You would have every right to tell me not to if you accepted my proposal, but until then..."

Ferguson caught Madeleine's eye. She choked back a laugh as he rolled his eyes at the lovers' spat unfolding in front of them. The situation was awful, but at least she could still find humor as long as he was with her.

Caro heard Madeleine's smothered giggle. "If you slept with Westbrook, I swear I will ruin you before the night is out," she said, her color still high.

"I am confused," Madeleine said, some of her daring returning to her, as though she were still Marguerite instead of Madeleine. "Are we here because you hate Ferguson, or because you want to keep Westbrook to yourself? It appears Ferguson may not be the only one who has struggled with love and honor."

That brought the woman up short, and she gaped at Madeleine like she couldn't believe anyone would talk to her like that. Either Madeleine was a proper lady, or she was a trollop of an actress, but either way, Caro's understanding of her could not accept Madeleine's frank assessment.

Ferguson stepped in then, placing a hand on Madeleine's shoulder in a gesture that unconsciously mirrored Westbrook's earlier attempt to soothe Caro. But Madeleine didn't pull away from him — she leaned into him, taking solace in his touch. He shifted his hand to the other shoulder, making the gesture more of an embrace, and she sighed. Caro followed the movement with her eyes, and her lips tightened.

"You have every right to hate me, Caro," he said. "I was determined to anger my father beyond repair ten years ago, and I shouldn't have taken advantage of your desire to experience something better than the lout you had married. You never said your husband would be so unaccommodating if we were caught, and I didn't realize that my departure would affect you so much. I paid for my desperation to leave, though. I never thought I could come back. I gave up hope of having friends in the ton, or finding a wife who might suit me..."

He broke off, and Madeleine reached up to caress his hand with hers. Steadying himself, he continued, "But I have a second chance now, and I refuse to run away from it. Madeleine is the only woman I have ever loved, the only woman I will ever love, and I'm not going to subject her to a lifetime in exile just because of who I used to be."

His hand slid away from her shoulders, and Madeleine made a small sound of distress. But his next move shocked her to the core.

He dropped to one knee beside her, holding her left hand like a knight about to pledge fealty. "Caro, I want your forgiveness, but most of all, I need your promise not to hurt Madeleine for my mistakes. But if that's not possible," and Madeleine felt him squeeze her fingers, "then Mad, I'm begging you — let me go so that you are not ruined in the bargain."

His movement caught her so unawares, and the emotion threaded through his voice surprised her so much, that Madeleine felt her eyes fill with tears. "I can't let you go, Ferguson," she whispered, and it felt like the conversation was just for them, that their worst enemy wasn't watching. "I would rather leave everything I know than watch you leave London without me."

He bowed to kiss her hand. "And I would rather spend every godforsaken night alone than see you cut by your family and friends."

He turned his head to meet her gaze, and she saw he meant every word of it. "You can't leave me. I won't allow it."

Ferguson grinned, amused despite their predicament. "And

now who's the autocrat, my love?"

She wanted to kiss him then, if only so he would stop talking about leaving her, but they still had an audience. She turned toward Caro, who watched in amazement, and gave the woman her best glare. "What say you, Lady Greville? Will you give us time to flee the country first, or do you intend to sound the alarm as soon as you leave this room?"

Caro's face was no longer the angry red of a woman scorned. Pallor replaced her high color, and she was rigidly still as she watched them. She looked like she had just witnessed her own death, and the knowledge of it did not make her happy.

Finally, she said, "Perhaps you are right that people can change, Ferguson. I never thought I would ever see you beg, or sacrifice yourself for someone else."

Ferguson inclined his head. "Escape from the past is possible, Caro. Particularly if you find the person who will love you in spite of it."

That stark look was back on her face. "That may be true, at least for you. Knowing that your intentions have changed..." She broke off for a moment, twisting a ring on her gloved finger. "If you are no longer the devil I knew, you've nothing to fear from me any longer. I'm sure I wish you very happy."

Madeleine wanted to shriek with delight, but the other woman was too devastatingly solemn for such celebration. She looked at Madeleine, and her expression softened just slightly. "If only we all had your daring, Lady Madeleine. Imagine what we might do if there were roles beyond wives and widows to aspire to."

Ferguson rose to his feet, pulling Madeleine up with the hand he still held. "I wish you happy as well, Caro. I never intended for anything that happened between us to affect you for even a day, let alone how long you've lived with this burden. But if you can lay aside the past, the present may contain happiness you haven't even dreamt of."

Madeleine felt like he was talking to her again, but Caro heard the words and nodded. "Westbrook, may I have a word with you, if you please?"

"I do please," he said, striding over to the door as though he could not wait to escort Ferguson and Madeleine out of his domain. But just before he turned the handle, he said, "You've nothing to worry about from me, either. This was never my fight, and I don't care what Lady Madeleine has been getting up to with her spare time these days. I would rather see her onstage than having the future duchess of Rothwell dunning me for the latest ladies' aid subscription."

There was a twinkle in his eyes as he said this, and Madeleine felt the last bit of tension draining out of her. "I shan't step foot on the stage again, but I will be sure to bring the army with me if I need your charity."

He bowed to her, then nodded at Ferguson. "We should dine at White's now that you are returned permanently, Rothwell. Perhaps after the honeymoon?"

He glanced at Caro as he said this, and Madeleine wondered whose honeymoon he contemplated. Ferguson didn't comment on the glance, merely accepted the invitation with much better humor than she had seen him use with others who invited him to dine.

After they said their goodbyes, he pulled her out of the room. The speed of his exit was matched by the slamming of Westbrook's study door. Ferguson didn't take her to the carriage, though — he gathered her up in his arms and kissed her. Pressed against him, in that bit of fabric Ellie called a dress, she could feel every muscle, every ridge and plane, every beat of his heart.

And even though he would be hers forever, without fear, she was too impatient to wait.

So when he gave her his wickedest grin and whispered a dream about a garden — she placed her hand in his and followed him out into the darkness.

CHAPTER THIRTY-FIVE

A week later, Madeleine sat on the edge of Rothwell House's grand ballroom, watching the growing crush. It had been nearly half a decade since the house had been opened on this scale. Everyone who received a coveted invitation would attend — it vied to be the premier event of the month, if not the season.

The ballroom had been kept in perfect condition despite its disuse, and its beauty was unparalleled tonight. The reds and golds of the Rothwell coat of arms glowed in the light of thousands of candles, and the gilded edges of trim around the room were like little lines of fire. The orchestra hid in its own balcony overlooking the dancers, cleverly screened off so that the music seemed to float out over the crowd from a mystical source.

The ball was fit for a princess — or two princesses. Kate and Maria had delayed their debuts, but their added maturity suited them. Rather than attempting to look different from each other, they chose to highlight their striking similarities. Their blonde hair was piled high, matching diamond drops hung from their ears, and elegantly spangled white ball gowns grazed their delicate slippers. The sashes wrapped around their waists were the only way to tell them apart; Kate's sash was a dramatic dark blue, while Maria wore a more romantic rose. The sashes accentuated their figures, and the men enjoyed the effect — the girls hadn't lacked for partners since standing up with Ferguson and Alex for the first dance.

"Shouldn't you be dancing?" Prudence asked as they both watched the crowd.

They sat together, as usual. Madeleine had danced the second dance with Ferguson, and several more dances with a variety of partners, but she was thankful for the lull in her dance card. "Do you know, I used to ache to dance? And yet I've no desire to be out there anymore."

"You would if Ferguson were partnering you," Prudence teased.

That was true. She was saving her supper dance for him, but they had separated for the past hour so he could play the gracious host. A few mamas had thrown their daughters at him, no doubt hoping he would realize his terrible mistake in becoming affianced to Madeleine, and for once he was too genial to refuse the blatant attempts to solicit his dances.

"The duke does seem less dangerous, though, don't you think?" her friend continued, watching him lead a particularly foolish ninnyhammer through the steps of a cotillion. "If he had been partnered with that poor girl two months ago, he would have teased her into such a state of distress that she would have been in the retiring room the rest of the night."

"You aren't saying I've tamed him, are you?"

"Tame a man like the duke of Rothwell?" Prudence said, laughing. "Never. If anything, he's tamed you, now that you aren't longing to do something scandalous."

She whispered the last bit — not that anyone around them would have believed Madeleine capable of bad behavior anyway. To the other chaperones and matrons, Madeleine was still a paragon of virtue, even if she had snagged the most illustrious catch of the season without even seeming to try.

Still, Madeleine pretended to take offense. "As though I could ever be as scandalous as the duke. What kind of lady do you take me for?"

Prudence grinned, but her smile turned sad as she watched the next pair of dancers move down the line. "I will miss you, you know, whether you're scandalous or not."

"I'm not leaving London for the ends of the earth," Madeleine said. "If anything, Rothwell House is closer to your mother's than Salford House is. And I will be desolate if you and Amelia abandon me. Imagine if my only recourse is to form one of those dreary ladies' circles a duchess is supposed to create."

"You're right, of course," Prudence said brightly, but Madeleine saw a shadow in her eyes. "But I may not be in London next year. Mother says we may not come to town next season, since 'it's clear Prudence will not be making a match, so no sense in wasting the money.'"

Prudence's impression of her mother's bluntly harsh tone usually made Madeleine laugh, but there was nothing funny in what she quoted. Before Madeleine could speak, though, Prudence rushed on. "Still, you will be in England, which is a comfort. I'll still have Amelia, too, if she doesn't do anything too foolish. And if she is too foolish — well, there is always the marchioness of Folkestone. I quite liked her when she came to our club's meeting last week."

Madeleine was glad Ellie had attended, even though she walked through the door like one who had made an impulsive decision and already regretted it. She had not brought any paintings and was reluctant to talk about her work, but she did warm up by the end of the meeting and readily agreed to attend the next one. And the fast crowd she ran with gave her better gossip than any of the rest of them ever heard, which made for one of the most entertaining meetings they had had in months.

But Amelia was another matter. The cotillion ended, and Amelia wove her way toward them, abandoning her escort somewhere in the crush. Her face was flushed, and the stain of pink on her cheeks only heightened her loveliness. She usually looked bored at these functions, even though she danced every time she was asked.

Tonight, though, her blue eyes sparkled with barely-suppressed joy and her mouth quivered on the edge of a smile. If Madeleine didn't know better, she would have thought that Amelia had finally fallen in love.

Madeleine did know better, though. She was worried, not pleased, when Amelia dropped dramatically into the chair on her other side and said, "Isn't this the most wonderful ball ever?"

"I prefer Lady Spencer's ballroom myself, although the supper here could tip the balance in Rothwell's favor," Prudence said solemnly, pretending not to notice that Amelia was nearly mad with happiness.

Amelia laughed. "But the conversation here is delightful."

"Weren't you just dancing with Sir Percival Pickett?" Madeleine asked dubiously. Sir Percival was one of Amelia's least favorite suitors, but the man had never quite taken the hint and Amelia was too conscientious of propriety to reject an offer to dance.

"Yes, and he still has pretensions to literary grandeur — claims he's writing a poem for me that will set the whole ton on its ear," she said with a grimace. "If it sets anyone on their ears, it will be in an attempt to drown out his awful rhymes. But he had the most wonderful things to say about a new book he found in a shop on Bond Street. He said it was the most daring satire of the ton that he's ever read, and predicts it will take everyone by storm."

"Sir Percival's opinions on literature surely don't sway you," Madeleine said, hoping that her guess about the provenance of the book would prove incorrect.

"He actually does have reasonably good taste in what others write — it's his own talent that is lacking," Amelia said. "But we really must find a copy of The Unconquered Heiress. We wouldn't want to be the last souls to have read it, after all."

Madeleine felt her stomach drop. Prudence frowned as she leaned in to close the circle between them. "Don't say it's already popular?"

Amelia grinned, and Madeleine knew why she was in such high humor. It was the same effervescent wonder Madeleine had felt during those first few weeks on the stage — like she had accomplished something no one else had ever done, conquered a fortress others had thought impregnable. Keeping the secret of her success had only added to her joy at first, but as the secret became more dangerous, the accomplishment lost just a bit of its luster.

But it would be worse for Amelia. While Madeleine had wanted to act for her own sake, and was ready to give up the acclaim that went with it, Amelia wanted her work to be recognized. When her first books were published, she was pleased to sell them, but she still chafed under the requirement of publishing with a pseudonym.

If this book became a sensation, would she be able to watch the success without saying anything? Or would she ruin herself to gain the fame she wanted?

For now, at least, Amelia took the safe course. She bit back her smile and said, "It could come to nothing, of course. Only two of my other partners have mentioned it, and neither of them are arbiters of taste."

Madeleine almost demanded to know what she was thinking, but they could not talk openly here. And anyway, the conversation could wait. Not enough people had read it to make it an utter success, and no one would find her out unless Amelia wanted them to.

Besides, Ferguson was striding toward them through the crowd — and unlike their first ball, Madeleine knew which of them he sought.

She hadn't thought it possible, but he looked even more handsome than he did during their first meeting. His dress was similar, with a perfectly cut midnight blue jacket accentuating his muscled shoulders and his tight breeches showing no need for the padding other men used to round out their calves. It wasn't his clothes or his well-toned body that entranced her, though.

It was his eyes, the love and humor in them, and the genuine smile on his lips. The cold arrogance — and the wounded boy who hid behind it — were gone, at least with her.

"You are the luckiest woman in England," Prudence muttered beside her.

"You never know — he may still be mad," Amelia mused, staring up at him as he came to a stop in front of them.

"If it is insanity to take Madeleine when I know this circle comes with her, then I am guilty," Ferguson retorted. Amelia laughed in response, the high pleasure of the dance still threading through her smile. Madeleine forced herself to stop worrying about her cousin, at least for tonight. She was just glad Ferguson and Amelia had reached some sort of unspoken truce, even if they did not yet know each other well enough for affection.

"You could order me to abandon them — you might murder me if I refuse, after all," Madeleine teased. It was safe to make the joke now; "Marguerite's" appearance at Westbrook's masquerade was all anyone had discussed for days, and talk of putting Ferguson on trial for her disappearance had ended entirely.

Ferguson gave her his most menacing glare. "I will certainly consider such drastic measures if you do not dance with me now, Lady Mad."

She placed her hand in his, felt the strength of his fingers around hers, and wondered if she would ever tire of his touch. Looking at the mischievous gleam in his eyes, she doubted it.

He pulled her into the circle forming for the supper dance. "I should have known you would pick a waltz for this, your grace," she said.

"I cannot waste my opportunities with you," he said, his tone serious. "How I am to last another three weeks until the wedding, I have no idea."

"I wish we didn't have to wait either," Madeleine said, shivering slightly as his hand came to rest on the curve of her hip.

"We could always run off to Gretna Green like Westbrook and Caro," Ferguson said. He sounded amused, but Madeleine suspected he would toss her in the nearest carriage and drive north immediately if she gave him any hint that she was willing.

"It's easy enough for them — the ton expects scandals from both of them, and may look fondly on their sudden love match. But if I married you so hastily, without the kind of grand affair they all expect..."

Ferguson smiled down at her. "We'll give them the grand affair. And then, my love, it will just be us."

"And your sisters. And your aunt Sophronia," Madeleine reminded him.

He grimaced. "That reminds me — Ellie said she would be happy to move back into Rothwell House to look after the twins while we are on our honeymoon. She didn't say why, and I thought she would never want to leave Folkestone's townhouse. But I wonder if the marquess is finally returning to England to claim his title."

Madeleine looked across the room and saw Ellie deep in conversation with Lord Norbury, her usual companion at these types of affairs. The woman's eyes were stark in her pale face, made even paler by the glorious fire of her hair. If anything, the strain somehow made her more beautiful. Madeleine hoped Ferguson was wrong — or, if he was right, that Folkestone's return would not cause Ellie any more grief.

"Ellie is welcome, of course. It would be nice to have a sympathetic audience while I try to learn how to be a duchess."

"You already know everything you need to be a duchess," Ferguson said.

"Really? I hardly think..."

Ferguson cut her off. "You know how to dress — and how to undress," he said, his voice dropping low so that only she could hear him. "You know how to converse, and you know more pleasurable things to do with those lips. You know how to arrange flowers — and if I recall from our interlude in a certain garden, you know how to leave them disarrayed."

Madeleine was blushing furiously at this point, but she was laughing too. After they had left Westbrook's study the previous week, Ferguson led her into the garden — and she finally, fully understood the "dangers" waiting for a young woman in a moonlit grotto. "I do not think your aunt Sophronia would approve of my method of flower arrangement."

"The old bird probably did the same thing herself when she was young. The garden of Eden must have had flowers, after all."

She laughed again at his deadpan tone. Then, she looked out over the sea of dancers. Ferguson, with his calm self-assurance and utter confidence, seemed so foreign compared to the dilettantes of the ton — but it had taken her years to find those same qualities within herself. It wasn't until that night in Westbrook's study that she realized she wasn't merely leaning on Ferguson's strength — they were strong together, like two pieces of an ancient rock that had been broken in two and finally pieced back together.

She turned her gaze back to him, and he smiled down at her as though he could look at her for decades and never tire of the view. They may have been strong together, but that didn't mean her heart couldn't melt when she saw him smile. "Well, if that's what I have to look forward to as a duchess, perhaps it won't be so bad."

"I rather think it will be wonderful," he said.

THE END

Books by Sara Ramsey

A Note From The Author:

I am neither an actress nor a French orphan, and I am certainly not a duchess (despite my fervent wishes otherwise – Prince Harry, call me). While I have always loved the fantasy of Regency romances, I didn't need to employ the subterfuge used by the Muses of Mayfair to write my books. For that, I feel supremely thankful.

I must thank everyone who believed that my writing was a worthwhile endeavor. Their support started long before I sold a single copy, when it was all mad dreams and the occasional scribbled sentence. My parents always let me choose my own path, even when it took me to different continents and strange professions. My brother and sister have also supported me through everything, while always reminding me of my roots. Those roots now extend from my childhood home in Iowa to my adulthood home in California, and my friends mean more to me than I can express without sounding maudlin. I am grateful beyond words that my family and friends have treated my writing as a serious endeavor instead of a pleasurable hobby, and I hope to live up to that support.

On the business side, thank you to my agent, Jennifer Schober of Spencerhill Associates, for working her derriere off to help get my stories out into the world. I am also grateful to the Romance Writers of America® for connecting me with some amazingly savvy authors, including my fellow 2009 and 2011 Golden Heart® finalists and all the wonderful members of the San Francisco RWA chapter.

Finally, I want to thank you for reading *Heiress Without A Cause*. I'm thrilled that you chose to spend your time with my book. Whether you loved or loathed it, I do hope you'll leave a review at your favorite online book site. And you are always welcome to write me directly at dearsara@sararamsey.com.

Thank you again! Amelia's story is up next, and I hope you'll join me for it.

Sara Ramsey
San Francisco, California
January 2012

Photo by Misti Layne

Sara Ramsey writes fun, feisty Regency historical romances. She won the prestigious 2009 Romance Writers of America Golden Heart award with her first book, *Scotsmen Prefer Blondes* (formerly titled *An Inconvenient Marriage*). The prequel, *Heiress Without A Cause* (formerly titled *One Night to Scandal*), was a 2011 Golden Heart finalist.

Sara grew up in a small town in Iowa, and her obsession with fashion, shoes, and all things British is clearly a rebellion against her hopelessly uncool youth. She graduated from Stanford University in 2003 with a degree in Symbolic Systems (also known as cognitive science) and a minor in history. Sara subsequently worked at Google for seven years in a variety of sales, management, and communications roles. She left Google in 2010 to pursue her writing career full time. Read all about her Regency obsessions and upcoming works at www.SaraRamsey.com.

Made in the USA
Lexington, KY
07 March 2012